Red Audrey and the Roping

Jill Malone

Ann Arbor
2008

Bywater Books, Inc.
PO Box 3671
Ann Arbor MI 48106-3671
www.bywaterbooks.com

Printed in the United States of America on acid-free paper.

Bywater Books First Edition: May 2008

Cover designer: Bonnie Liss (Phoenix Graphics)

ISBN 978-1-932859-54-6

This novel is a work of fiction. All persons, places, and events were created by the imagination of the author.

For Brooke and Gavin

Acknowledgments

For reading, for thoughtful advice, and for their encouragement, thanks to Gailyn Taylor, Almeda Glenn Miller, Nance Van Winckel, Craig Pratt, Joan Opyr, Kelly Smith and Caroline Curtis. Thanks to my family and everyone at Auntie's Bookstore for lifetimes of love and support. To the ladies of the book club, I owe you.

Sessions with Dr. Mya: Day 1

Somehow the Montana dykes are to blame for everything. That much is clear, that much is certain. I have to explain about that. If she asks, I'll explain.

I dreamt of Audrey again: Audrey in her red jeep. This time I knew it was a dream. My mother sat in the passenger's seat with her bare feet propped on the dash, and her hair tidal. Audrey drove and I sat in the back. My mother reached out, put her hand on Audrey's neck, and smiled over her shoulder at me. I said, "But you're dead," and then I was in the street watching the jeep careen down the road as though no one were driving.

I hate this fucking hospital. Six birds of paradise bob from an orange bucket in the corner of the room like brilliant animals. Yellow pikake leis drape the phone, the end table, the entire world, with the delightful smell of cat piss. The pug-faced nurse is changing my IV site and will soon begin to draw my blood. The Montana dykes are to blame for everything.

Another nurse—the glum, hairy one—has just reminded me that I'm going to see Dr. Mya shortly. It's possible that this makes the fourth time I've been reminded just this morning, or the fifth. Anyway, it'll be my first time in a wheelchair since I woke in hospital. Usually they move me by bed.

I have to explain. If my mind would sort properly, I could explain. This is a different room I'm in now. The last had fewer windows. I don't know which floor this is, but it's high: I can see the corner of a high rise with blue-tinted glass and several condominiums huddled across the skyline. Someone on an upper floor revels in potted geraniums.

I miss Audrey's jeep: the wild, unholy brawl of it; rumble and clang too distracting to enjoy a CD; the seats as rigid and knobby as elbows; the road never smooth beneath its tires. Still I dream its red and rumble. I dream its girl.

"I don't think this vein is any good."

The pug-faced nurse isn't apologetic as she removes the needle, so much as cowed. Ever since the nurses had to yank all the floating Get Well balloons from my room because I couldn't stop screaming, they've been apprehensive about upsetting me. It takes so little to upset me now.

"Is there a nurse on this ward who knows what the fuck she's doing?" I call into the hallway.

Beside me the pug hesitates, as if she's waiting for another nurse as well, then she takes my arm as confidently as possible and tries a vein at my wrist. Beyond the window, the harshest days of summer pass without the benefit of nurses, CAT scans, and air-conditioned suites.

I remember a day just on the cusp of summer when I'd spent the morning surfing and returned to Audrey's after a late breakfast, expecting to have the flat to myself to work on my lesson plans. When I carried my bike in, I found Audrey sitting in the living room wearing slacks and a sleeveless button-down white shirt rather than her paint-flecked smock. Her hair still wet and dark around her impish face, she smiled at me.

"Thought maybe you'd like to catch a movie this afternoon."

"You aren't working?" I asked her.

"Too distracted today. I feel so restless. There were kids tossing a baseball on the street corner by the studio. I could hear them inside even with the windows closed. Let's go to

Restaurant Row. I have no idea what's playing. We'll just see if anything appeals to us."

"Have you eaten?"

She shook her head and I remembered that I hadn't kissed her, though I wanted to then. Audrey had this way of bouncing when she was excited as if her body couldn't quite stabilize itself, and she hopped off the couch and toward me in a single bounding motion, a tackling rush.

As I caught her, my bike toppled to the floor behind me. Her legs cinched around my waist as though we were teenagers and I held onto her with a sense that this girl was fleeing suddenly from this flat, this embrace.

The pug has taped the new IV site, gathered up her paraphernalia, and now slips away as Nurse Crumb saunters in with a plate of chocolate chip cookies. It must be Monday.

"Well, Jane, have a cookie for your grievances."

She places two cookies on my untouched breakfast tray and smiles down at me.

"You'll need your strength for your session with Dr. Mya this morning."

Dr. Mya? What kind of doctor allows herself to be called Dr. Mya? I suppose that's the giveaway—the obvious indicator that she's a psychiatrist—the stilted formality of dropping the surname that one encounters with old southern women or preschool teachers. I push my breakfast tray toward Nurse Crumb.

"I can't eat this shit."

"Just eat the cookies, then. I added coconut and cinnamon for you."

Nurse Crumb, an obscenely fat woman who stands 6 feet tall, applies her makeup flawlessly to accentuate her dark blue eyes, and styles her blond hair as if she might fly off to a red carpet event at any moment. Her eyes often disappear into her face and her bright white teeth gleam in the jolliest smile I've ever seen. She serves as charge nurse on the ward and can be as menacing with her chocolate chip cookies as some men are with crowbars.

"What time's my appointment?" I ask between bites.

"11:00 a.m."

She beams at me encouragingly. I almost don't get the cookie down.

"Can I have some morphine?"

"Now, Jane, you know you have to discuss that with your neurologist. I'm sure you'll see Dr. Bocek this morning on his rounds."

Crumb and I have developed a routine in the weeks I've been bound in Kapiolani Women's Hospital. She hassles me about my emergency contacts, or more specifically, my absence of viable emergency contacts, and I harass her about being denied morphine for the plague of bee swarms and chisels that inhabits my head.

Weeks ago, after the saturated oblivion of morphine, Crumb appeared in my room like Jesus, and spent several sessions trying to coax an emergency contact from me along with some rational account of the accident. The hospital will tell me what has happened to me medically, but they refuse to reveal what happened to me physically. Apparently it's not just a game, but also a significant part of the recovery process to be able to describe the events that led to your coma.

Crumb kept asking what I was thinking during the accident.

"You remember something; you must. Have you a visual picture of the event?"

That's a visual picture as opposed to an auditory picture.

"I don't remember."

"You aren't trying."

"If you can read my fucking mind, then why bother asking questions?"

"Ms. Elliot, if you don't take this seriously, you will prolong your recovery."

Prolong my recovery, as if that recovery had already begun and I was, spitefully, just dragging it out to be difficult. We've evolved since those early sessions; now she calls me Jane. And today I've realized that the Montana dykes are to blame for everything. They even ruined that day with Audrey, that day on the cusp of summer.

At Restaurant Row, Audrey and I caught *Run Lola Run*, amping to the energy of the film, the actors, the metaphysical time vortex and existential conceit of the plot, wondering aloud as we left the theater how many do-overs each of us actually got. Then we drove to Aliamanu for meat jhun from Soon's Korean Barbeque for me and vegetables with rice from the Chinese restaurant around the corner for Audrey. We ate in her jeep, parked under a sprawling oak tree, the kim chee acidic and startling to the palate. Cars tore down the boulevard just beyond the parking lot; hot and bright, the afternoon swelled around us as urgently as the passing cars. Strangely, the traffic sounded like waves breaking.

"The girl in that movie was hot," Audrey said.

"Who knew German chicks could look like that? *Fraulein:* it's sort of a damning word."

"I spoke to one of my friends from grad school this morning."

"Oh yeah?"

"An ex-girlfriend actually. She's coming to Oahu in a few weeks for a visit with a couple of mutual friends. They'd planned to stay at another woman's house in Kailua, but that fell through so she wanted to know if they could stay with me."

I knew she'd told them yes. Of course she'd said yes. Maybe kids playing ball on the street corner hadn't made Audrey giddy after all. I wanted summer to have inspired the same restlessness in her it had in me. That morning I'd thought of my father and Therese in the orchard with the trees blossoming, the fragrance attracting bees and wasps to flit and drone; the skin of my father's face becoming thinner, more delicate. My mother would never be old, or whole, or mine. I dreamt of leaving Oahu. I wanted different choices, another do-over.

"How will you make room for them?"

"They'll bring sleeping bags and camp in the living room. They're here for fourteen days. You'll like them."

I'll like them. It didn't seem to matter whether I'd like them or not since they were her friends. Audrey scooped a mushroom carefully with her chopsticks. At the Soon's counter behind us a steady line had formed, customers crowded the aisles awaiting their soda or lunch plate. All the narrow outdoor tables were occupied.

"If you could change any day of your life," I asked Audrey, "which day would you change?"

"I made a mistake in grad school," she said eventually. "I slept with a girl I didn't like because I was afraid to hurt her. For weeks after I felt nauseous."

"So if you had a do-over you would hurt her instead of sleep with her?"

"If I had a do-over I wouldn't have gone to the bar that night. I'd have stayed home and worked or gone for a long walk or to see a movie or anything else. I'd have skipped the whole scenario."

She drank her fruit punch, the straw honking against the plastic lid.

"If you had a do-over?" she asked.

I'd been pondering that question for years. I couldn't save my mother. But the dentist, wouldn't I have left her differently? Even with Emily I could think of whole months I would have changed.

"There was a day, at Bubbies Ice Cream Parlor, a hot fucking day. I almost broke up with Nick. I had a speech ready and everything. Before anything evil happened."

6

"So you wouldn't change the fact that you'd dated him at all?"

"No."

I tried to imagine never having dated Nick. No Venice, no brawl with Emily (or at least not the same brawl with Emily), no scars on my back and wrists, no trouble with the faculty at U.H., no drug test. At the office I had a picture he'd taken of me one day at Sea World. Too much sun behind my head made the photo seem unbalanced, but my face looked so happy, so weightless, as though my image had been tampered with.

"That doesn't make sense to me," Audrey said.

How could it make sense? She hadn't loved Nick. I wasn't sure I had loved Nick, but I didn't hate him, not even from this distance.

"You think I'd be happy now if I hadn't dated Nick?"

"Happy?" she said the word as though it were new to her. "I don't think that's the point."

I didn't want to know the point. The topic of conversation depressed me almost as much as the idea of three strangers camping in Audrey's living room for two weeks. I tossed the last of my plate lunch into the garbage. On the drive back to Audrey's, I thought about the moment the bike dropped behind me in her flat, the feel of the handle bars dragging against my calf, the heft of her legs around my waist, her shirt collar rubbing against my earrings.

Audrey reached across and massaged my neck, her fingers pressing deeply into the knots and muscles. She let go to shift and then massaged again. I groaned, closed my eyes, imagined the jeep gliding along the surface of a wave.

"I'm reading this book," she said, her voice cast above the squeal and rumble of the jeep, "by Djuna Barnes. Have you read her?"

"No."

"It's about obsession."

Her hand released to shift again, then returned to my neck. Through our opened windows the heavy, grating sounds of traffic clanged. The business district of Dillingham Boulevard always seemed dirty and obscure. I kept my eyes closed, exhaled the word "Obsession."

"Yes. Her sentences make you feel claustrophobic and aroused like these dark tortured characters with their psycho-sexual impulses feel claustrophobic and aroused. It's about a woman no one can hold."

"Claustrophobic and aroused could be the definition of obsession."

"I worry sometimes you might be that woman."

"Which woman?"

"The one no one can hold."

She dropped her hand to downshift; the engine idled at the light.

"I don't know what that means," I said.

"They used to have these people, professional mourners. They were paid to attend funerals so it seemed like a good crowd had turned up to pay tribute to the deceased. The mourners cried and wore somber clothes and seemed as if they really were bereaved. Sometimes I think you're so into grief that you deliberately destroy things, people, just so you can mourn them."

I watched a seagull loop above the water in the distance. We passed Aloha Tower Marketplace, large blustery women waddling toward the parking lot with unwieldy white and blue shopping bags. Strollers littered the sidewalk.

"That's an awful thing to say."

"I'm afraid of it sometimes: the cost of loving you."

"There's a cost to loving anyone," I said stupidly, not wanting to think in specifics, or assign values, or argue.

"Yes, but the cost is always different depending on what you wager, what you're willing to lose."

In the condominiums high above us lights shone and

people moved about preparing dinner, watching television, recovering from another Sunday. Clouds obscured the setting sun and I rolled up the window, turned on the CD player. Tori Amos singing: *I believe in peace, bitch.*

Bill, a sallow-faced orderly with a frizzy mullet, navigates us onto the elevator and illuminates Floor 8. I've been in Kapiolani Women's Hospital for four weeks—comatose for the first seventeen days—and this is my first trip by wheelchair. My first trip to the Psych ward to meet Dr. Mya Perez, the purported guru of my recovery; the woman assigned to determine the precise nature of my injuries. I'm twenty-nine years old and completely fucked.

Bill knocks at the threshold of Dr. Mya's office and wheels me through the opened door to the fore of her desk where he promptly leaves me without a word. The room smells of spice, cinnamon or nutmeg. Behind her desk, the petite doctor stands and takes off her brown-rimmed spectacles. Her black hair is pulled tightly back and pinned at the nape of her neck. She looks to be thirty-five, fit, and probably Filipino; her skin a light brown, remarkably fine against the burgundy of her skirt and blazer.

"Good morning, Jane. I'm Dr. Mya."

"Morning."

After grabbing a pad and pen from her desk, she moves to a leather chair across from me and sits, adjusting her legs demurely, before sliding her spectacles back on.

"How do you feel this morning?"

Sarcastic? Exhausted? Embittered? Blissful? Sore? From the walls of the doctor's office, several Dali prints hang: a grotesquely stretched pair of elephants trundling across a red and orange sky; a giraffe on fire; Narcissus perched at the pool beside his strange twin; a white ship walked along the surface of the water by an elongated woman grown

9

from the masthead; a view of a woman's back with the sea sprawled beyond her opened window.

"I feel swell today. Don't I look swell?"

I gesture with my good hand from the cast on my right arm to the frightening metal contraption securing the pins in my right leg to the cast on my left ankle, mindful of my IV stand to avoid flinging it at the serious woman across from me. Maybe the room smells of vanilla, or almonds.

"My head hurts," I whisper. "They're not giving me morphine anymore."

"They are, but the dose has been lowered."

"Too low."

"Jane, what's the last thing you remember before the hospital?"

There was a girl. There was an accident. Maybe those two sentences—those two concepts—are interdependent: there was a girl, an accident.

"I must have been dreaming."

"What did you dream?"

The doctor leans forward now, her pen clutched in the hand that lies casually in her lap. Something very antiseptic emanates from this doctor, something prim and hard that makes me wary of her. She belongs in the hospital—*to* this hospital—like the gowns and the screens and the bizarre sonar equipment they hook me to.

The tarmac slick with rain: I kept slipping, my clothes and boots soaked through and my gloves heavy and useless. A fog had settled over the airport.

"I fell, I think. I have this sensation of falling. And then a jar of peanut butter in a kitchen cupboard, I have a visual of the jar sitting on the shelf."

There was an accident and a girl. I think about Emily in her garden that summer I came home, her hair light with surf, her arms cut, the danger of everything she meant crossing to me in her tied paisley sarong.

"In your kitchen?"

"No. This kitchen seems more rustic, almost like a cabin, and I had to search to find the peanut butter. I came upon it accidentally, actually. I remember being surprised that it was on a shelf by itself."

I can still feel myself falling, the jolt and panic of my rabid heart.

"What else do you remember about the kitchen?"

"I was alone in the kitchen in the early morning. Light sort of spilled into the window above the sink, the rest of the house still dark. I crept around, trying to be quiet."

"You were afraid to disturb someone?"

"Yeah. Yeah, I guess someone else must have been in the house."

A flash of red on the pavement like a flag.

"What else do you remember?"

"I took the peanut butter with me, grabbed it on my way out the door. A screen door that didn't actually fit in the doorframe, I pushed it open and left."

I don't tell her my leg hurts every time I think of that door: the dense wire of the screen against my fingertips; the heavy, thwack of the spring; the smooth wooden frame.

"And then?" she prods.

"I remember looking back at the house: a dark, box-shaped house with overgrown hibiscus shrouding the windows in the front yard, a desolate corner."

"The house doesn't look familiar to you now?"

"No, I don't think I'd seen it before."

"Where do you go after leaving the house?"

"I don't remember. There's the peanut butter, and the door, and then I'm looking back at the house and that's all I remember."

Dr. Mya leans back in her chair; her body had tensed and relaxed perceptibly. I realize, randomly, that my jaw clenched while I listened to her questions.

"What is your job, Jane?"

"I'm a teacher."

"What do you teach?"

"Latin."

Myths, I want to add; Greek and Latin myths with their inevitable violence: murder, curses, and rape. Fragments of poetry and epics and history, scenes of tragedy in a dead language translated by bright, scrubbed twenty-somethings in a classroom like a greenhouse.

"Where do you teach?"

"At U.H."

"You teach at the Manoa campus?"

"That's right."

"Full time?"

"No, I'm an adjunct professor: afternoons, part-time. In the mornings, I work for UPS."

"Leaving that house is your last memory before the hospital?"

My last memory? No, I have shards of memory from some later point: Emily on the hammock leaning over me. That slow motion lean like Grace Kelly illumined red, sinking into a kiss with Jimmy Stewart in *Rear Window*. I remember Nick coming into the bedroom, walking toward the armoire, a girl on the bed laughing. I remember Audrey in a yellow summer dress, standing in front of an easel with a hand on her hip. Something has already happened. Something about the way she is standing, how she's struggling against the painting suggests I've already damaged her.

I'm sick of this hospital. It's like Audrey's jeep in its noisy, reckless frenzy. I don't understand how I got here. There was an accident, a girl. And I'm trying to create a whole memory of the accident, a whole memory of the girl. I can't start with Audrey, though. I have to work up to her. She isn't clear yet. Not like the Montana dykes; them I get. Their visit fucked me up. Their visit gave Audrey perspective, a context in which to view me. I can't start with Audrey, but I'll get there. Trust me. First there were fruit trees and a woman. Her name is Emily and I found her on my way home.

I.

Not the house with its pillared Colonial stylings—white three-story with green shuttered windows, the requisite columns supporting the triangular overhang, the trellises of flowering clematis—not the ornate wrought-iron fence with its memory of city zoos, not even the girl, astonishingly long-legged in a tied paisley sarong, not my own exhaustion, the fifth rental of that Saturday in May—the other four squalid, airless rooms too close to freeway on-ramps or children's playgrounds—no, I stood on Akahi Street that evening in the rain, with my bike resting against my hip because of the trees: a copse of guava trees in one corner of the sprawling yard, and mango in the other, breadfruit and chinaberry trees, jacaranda with its lavender bell-shaped blossoms. I had not seen such well-tended trees since I'd left the orchard, not in all my long years in the pastures of Ireland. The slender, brown-haired surfer chick stared at me through the iron bars, pruning shears balanced casually on her shoulder.

"Casing the place?"

"I've come about the rental."

She smiled, or it seemed like a smile and nodded, her hair slipped across her bikini top as she opened the gate for me. Barefoot, she wore her sarong like a primitive—high on her thigh, low on her waist—her silver bellyring glared at me as she crossed the sidewalk to shake hands.

"Emily," she said. Her fingers thin as spider's legs.

14

"Jane."

She headed through the gate and turned half-back toward me for a single, appraising look. Wide and muscular, her shoulders were tanned and lightly freckled; her arms seemed unnaturally long as she gestured for me to catch up. It took two long strides to even step with her as we walked along the stone pathway through the mango grove past a koi pond with fat speckled fish.

"This is the first week I've advertised," she said. "It's odd for me. A girl came to see the studio this morning—completely bizarre—she smelled of mold. I hope she works in a laboratory somewhere."

I fell behind, distracted by the sprawling garden. At the lowest tier of the backyard (there were three tiers adjoined by steps), brambles hid the ground and colossal banyan trees crowded out the sky. Within this jungle sat a wood-frame studio, its windows facing the backside of the main house, the garden paths, and a thin, grassy alleyway.

I hurried after her into the vines—dense and prehistoric—with a certain anxiety about centipedes. Upon entering the bright orange front door, the ceiling of the studio arched high above our heads, muting the drum of rain. The large room—hardwood floors, window-box seat, kitchen nook, French doors—had two bay windows that lent the room a light-streaked quality despite the trees as if we were still in the early hours of the morning.

"No one's ever lived here," she said. "I used to store my surfboards in here. It was a garage once."

The furnished room had an inviting pulse: the small round table and two farm chairs huddled across from the cyan-tiled kitchen; the stainless-steel refrigerator and stove; and an oval woven rug cast before a large futon sofa. The strange, comfortable furniture appealed to me, like suddenly assuming someone else's life. In the long, narrow bathroom, the tub stood on claws. And I knew, the moment I noted the claws, that I would settle in this place.

While I wandered around, she leaned against the front door watching me, her thigh muscles flexing.

"I love it," I said finally.

She nodded and led me to the side porch where two Adirondack chairs looked out at a laurel hedge and a couple of banana trees.

"There's a hammock too, on the far side of the studio."

"You stored your boards here?"

"Seems terribly selfish doesn't it? God, you're really fucking white. You don't look like a tourist, but you must be, yeah?"

I felt myself flush, which, I knew, just made the rest of me look paler.

"I've been living in Ireland. Not much chance of tanning there."

"What were you doing in Ireland?"

"I worked at the Linguistics Institute in Dublin."

"And now?"

"I've going to teach at U.H., the Classics Department—a Latin instructor."

"So is that a promotion?"

A promotion? No, more like a getaway. I thought of the Belfast dentist in her kitchen discovering the note I'd left for her, the cupboards emptied of my clothes, the sneaking lowness of my vanishing act.

"It's hard to say. At the Linguistics Institute I was a researcher. I haven't taught since I was at University."

For something like the hundredth time I thought of the ridiculous position I'd assumed: leaving the challenging, interesting work for which I had trained seven years to return to Hawaii and the unknown of a job which might not give me the slightest pleasure. And leaving the girl—I'd

16

commuted by train to Dublin five days a week to share her flat, her life—after three years, ever since I'd met her at a pub, that night she'd kissed me on a bridge walking back to her flat. Grasped my collar in her fists, our lips numb with cold, our faces burned and wind-whipped. She'd tasted of malt. I'd put my hands under her coat against her belly to keep from shivering.

"You're an Island girl, though."

"Maui. Left after high school; this is my first time back in nine years."

"Will you be comfortable here tonight?"

I looked up at her; a thin white scar at the corner of her right eye dimpled when she smiled.

"So I can have the place?"

"Of course. I'd invite you in for a drink, but I have to be at work in twenty minutes. Come up to the house tomorrow morning and I'll make you breakfast. Not too early."

I watched as she hurried toward the main house through several rows of meticulously haphazard and disparate flowers. Moments later, a light on the second floor appeared as dusk sifted over the garden. So I would live here, then. Lightly the rain continued to fall. Leaving the dentist, her wild, crow-colored hair, the job, the meticulous contacts I'd developed, I would live here. Overhead the banyan trees groaned wearily as I turned from Emily's window, remembering the one-road town in west Ireland where the dentist and I had watched daylight fade across the surface of a creek. A heron had crossed into the reed thicket. Below us water slapped against a wobbly wooden boat. Futility slipped beneath my clothes with her hands then and I knew that the shape we shared was spliced and hopeless as industry in that valley of sheep pastures, heather, the memory of famine.

I had returned to Hawaii to teach Latin at University. Now I would live for ambition and ambition alone. Even as I biked back to the hotel to secure a shuttle for my duffels, I found myself wondering: quarter to seven on a Saturday night, where the hell did this Emily chick work?

In the afternoons for much of that spring and summer, I biked around Waikiki, weaving through the poor suckers stalled by red lights, accidents, the endemic traffic, to watch tourists shop for their sickly pink and green outfits along the blistered shop fronts, or head downtown to Magic Island where Filipino boys caught their low-rider trucks on yellow speed bumps in the parking lot. Sometimes I'd join in a volleyball game, or stare at the thin line of horizon resting at waist height across the cobalt stretch of the Pacific, before winding my way home to the studio through the sleepy streets of Manoa, usually in the rain. I found during those rides that I came to know the city as intimately as I'd known Dublin though Honolulu was by no means as friendly. Most of the people I met were tourists, students on summer break, or retired ancients burning their days running the length of Ala Moana beach, each of whom had her own agenda, her own vision. It was not a city of like-minded and familiar people who wanted to drink in a carousing pub, or venture to plays, or discuss the weather the way old generals discuss strategic military campaigns. Oahu was disjointed and alien, more foreign country than state, and I felt isolated in a way that I had not expected.

But that first morning in the studio, I woke with her name in my mouth: Emily, and something like hopefulness. A long balcony stretched along the backside of the house, with three tiered stairs dropping through shocks of color from the flowering trees to the shadow of the banyans. Later, after I knew Hiromi, the old Japanese caretaker with bald spots who could kneel all day weeding with her wide-brimmed peasant hat and blue-rubber clogs, I'd understand the cultivated wildness of the garden: Hiromi subdued the greedy plants as ably as she encouraged the shy species. But my impression that first morning was that the place had been overrun: the flamelike flower of the heliconia draped beside the yellow ginger; poinsettia flailing alongside the stone pathway to distract you from the spider lily growing quietly near the fuchsia plumes of the bougainvillea. Added to the mix were dozens of rare and exotic flowers like Philippine orchids and orange trumpet vine. Somehow the dappled colors and styles lent a lush random beauty to the place.

I'd slept as dreamlessly as the dead, shrouded in my sleeping bag on the futon, and woke late. Nearly ten o'clock before I sprinted up the last short staircase, through the French doors into a solarium. Inside, the rooms of the main house were painted in Seussian primary colors; the rooms had high-ceilings, wooden floors, and flawless French-provincial furniture.

I tried to smooth my wild hair and rumpled clothes. With a growing sense of unease, I crossed the long narrow hallway to the kitchen, which was easily twice the size of the entire studio, bright and cool with a row of white fans churning silently overhead. In the middle of the room stood a marble island with rows of copper pots suspended above it, and behind the island, a six-burner gas stove with a built-in grill. Cabinets lined the walls on either side of the stove; two dishwashers, a walk-in, and a double stainless-steel monster fridge/freezer combo did not even begin to crowd the room. The walls were painted in two shades of bold yellow like a banana shake.

"Jesus Christ," I shuddered.

"Good morning."

Like an apparition she appeared from a little alcove that must have been the pantry, smiling at me hospitably. She wore a green sarong this morning and a hooded U.H. sweat-shirt. Her hair wrapped tightly in a bun and secured to the top of her head with chopsticks, she looked the part of the local girl perfectly. Her eyes puffy, her face still glowed from sleep.

"Yes. Good morning."

"Thought I'd make omelets."

"Brilliant."

She handed me a cup of coffee, motioning for me to sit on one of the stools at the bar. Straining my ears for other human sounds from the house, I continued to stare at the splendor of the kitchen, incapable of calculating the price tag for a place like this, miserable that I had skipped a bath in my hurry.

"Cream?"

"Yes, please."

I stirred the cream into my coffee watching her slice mushrooms, yellow bell peppers, ham, black olives, cheese, and jalapenos. Relieved beyond expression when she took only two plates down from the cupboard, I began to enjoy the rich flavor of the coffee, the aroma of the ham.

"This kitchen's a dream. Are you a chef?"

"No," she laughed, "my brother. He's in San Fran now, unhappy again. Do you know any chefs?"

I shook my head. She had a great laugh; it softened her whole body as if she'd become a child instantaneously.

"They're never happy. My mother lives in Paris so she tried to get my brother to live there with her and intern at any number of these amazing restaurants. He lasted about seven months. That's how it is. And then the next restaurant is the one he has always dreamed about and he's going to have so much more artistic freedom and he really respects the owner, blah fucking blah until his next phone call when he explains why he's already quit that one and at another place since the owner of the last place was such an asshole and Charlie had no creative license there."

She smiled and added, "But the new one is always different."

"How long has your mom lived in Paris?"

"Oh, god, maybe ten years? She's married a publisher there and I doubt she'll come back. My mother is so into melodrama; Paris is the perfect city for her, you know? All that angst. She was a jazz club singer in Japan and then later here. She's retired now that she's got a little gut, but she loves to live in a city that still respects jazz."

She tossed eggs into one of the copper skillets and added a dash of milk.

"So your accent is Irish?" she asked.

"An amalgam I guess."

"How long were you there?"

"Nine years. I went to Trinity College in Dublin through my doctorate and then worked at the Linguistics Institute for the last few years; traveled around too."

"Why Ireland?"

The ham sizzled when she added it to the veggies in the skillet. She turned on the filter fan above the stove.

I always dreaded the "Why Ireland" question, changing my answer every time depending on the person asking. Why Ireland? One of my mother's favorite films was *The Quiet Man*; fishermen's sweaters seemed so rugged; my Australian father had once told me that Ireland was a country like no other; I went to find god.

"I don't know. It just seemed unnatural not to live on an island and I wanted easy access to Europe without being on the Continent. Ireland was the spot."

"Never made it to Ireland. I spent several weekends in London, passing back and forth to Paris. Not enough time to catch much besides a couple of plays and the Tate Gallery."

She plated the omelets with toast, and brought me a

glass of guava juice. We ate with impossibly large silver forks. Her skin was fair and delicate beneath the tan and the middle of her nose slightly pink. Later I understood that Emily had been exceptionally nervous that first morning—talking too quickly and telling too many personal details to a girl she had known less than half a day—but at the time I just read her as quirky. Wildly animated, her eyes seemed to punctuate whatever she said:

"God, I love Maui. I biked up Hana last time I was there and nearly died. It was scorching."

"Yeah," I said, "I had a nasty wreck on Hana when I was a kid. My dad took me biking there and I thought I saw this boar tearing around in the underbrush down from the road. I freaked and slammed right into a boulder. My dad, convinced I'd had a seizure, started screaming and shaking me. I thought he'd give me whiplash."

"Seriously? Were you all right?"

"I had to have stitches," I showed her the scars; "both elbows and my left knee. There was a lot of blood."

She fought the urge to laugh at me, her scar crinkling at the corner of her eye as she got her grin under control.

"I've stayed in Paris for months at a time, but I couldn't handle living abroad for years. Have you ever heard of the Casket Girls?"

"Are they a band?" I asked.

"No," Emily laughed. "They were immigrants to New Orleans from France in the early eighteenth century. 1718, I think. Anyway, each girl brought a coffin with her for a dowry. I have this visual of them standing beside the docked ship with their French fashion and their coffins and welcome to the new world, you know? That must have been surreal."

"Well, that's a cheerful little story."

"I suppose more than anything then you had to be pragmatic."

Behind Emily, another pair of French doors opened to a small patio with several overstuffed chairs. I wanted suddenly to be outside, to watch the garden, to stare at anything besides the curve of her neck, the drastic cut of her biceps, that patch of freckles on the bridge of her nose.

She looked over her shoulder and back at me.

"Do you want to sit outside? It's warm in here."

I don't remember talking much as morning melded into afternoon; rather I listened to Emily's stories while the sheath-edged heliconia nodded along with us against the rail of the patio.

"What do you do, for work, I mean? What's the job you ran off to last night?"

"I own and manage the Blue Spark at Restaurant Row."

"Is that a restaurant?"

"God, I keep forgetting you've been living abroad. No, the Spark is a dance club—an extremely profitable and time consuming dance club, unfortunately."

"Success isn't a good thing?"

"Honestly, I wanted to sell it, but my mother insisted we keep the club as long as money kept pouring in. And it has—more, in fact, than before I took over."

It turned out that Emily's mother had not been just some obscure jazz club singer (as if the house weren't indication enough); she was Michiko Nomura, the Japanese piano prodigy who'd immigrated to Hawaii with her parents when she was sixteen and revolutionized the local music scene with her bizarre throaty voice and wild stage antics— *She's insane but in an endearing way.* Eventually, Michiko married Texas cattle baron Owen Taylor (father of Emily and her chef brother, Charlie); invested in the nightclub scene at Restaurant Row and made money, barrel upon barrel.

Owen Taylor died of heart failure when Emily was in

grade school, although she said he was away from home on business so often that they'd never been close. Emily was two years older than I—she'd turned twenty-nine in January—and had graduated from U.H. with a degree in sociology. ("A necessary degree," she laughed, "if you're going to run a bar.")

"My mother," Emily said, "speaks English randomly—you know, transforming slang for the effect—*Good Jesus, Baby*, is one of her favorites, or *we're just talking about wiggle*— she has a million of these ridiculous sayings. And they've become so much worse as she's grown older."

She handed me another beer. It seemed less trouble-some to look at Emily when she was talking, her forehead creased whenever she concentrated, or her eyebrows arched in a mock of surprise.

"On my sixteenth birthday, right, I invite my friends over for a slumber party: pizza, movies, boy gossip—the whole bit. So we're at the table and somehow we end up talking about our fathers. Mine died when I was eight so I was always curious about girls who had dads, I guess. Anyway, halfway through the conversation my mother suddenly exclaims, *I wish I had had bondage with my father!* in this incredibly loud forlorn voice."

I felt my face color and Emily started laughing:

"Exactly. I went bright red. I was just looking at her like you've got to be kidding. Of course she meant 'bonding' with her father. But you know, she was always proclaiming horrible shit like that. Jesus, it was a travesty."

Eventually her mother bought a flat in Paris and moved there permanently after she'd married her third husband. ("The second guy was in fashion," Emily said. "It got really ugly before it ended.")

"So I maintain the house and investments here, and man-age the Spark. I can stay because she left."

I thought of my father in the orchards, walking the rutted

24

paths carefully as if he did not have each step memorized. How his women had chosen for themselves. How he had not been a factor.

I didn't know if my father waited for me to come back from Ireland and live on the orchard, or if he had no expectations at all. We had never discussed what would happen. We had never discussed anything beyond the orchard. Our whole lives were there in the trees and the beams of the house. In the fence line and the rutted paths, the pitched bark of the high-strung shepherd, Toby. There was no family outside that orchard, and I could leave because he stayed.

"The investments pay for the house here and my mother's life in France, and my job at the Spark pays for the documentaries."

"Documentaries?"

"I'm a partner in a production company, *Tantalus Films*. We try to grab promising directors from festivals. That's my partner's job; he's the scout. I'm the money. It's been really exciting. We're in our fourth production right now and they seem to run more smoothly each time, which is promising."

"What kind of documentaries?"

"This current one is about this kid who's a mathematical prodigy in Oregon. They're, you know, watching him interact with people and problems and documenting the results. So far we haven't shot anything locally but that's my goal. I'd love to see a documentary on the Pali Lookout, or some aspect of the North Shore ... the collapse of the sugar cane fields, that would be really interesting, yeah?"

Her eyebrows arched as she looked at me, smiling self-consciously as if embarrassed by her own ardor. I grinned.

"Yeah, I'd pay to see it, especially about the Pali. It freaked me out when my dad took me up there when I was a kid: the thought of all those soldiers pushed over the cliff, and the freaky pork story, too. I mean have you ever heard of another horror story that involved pork?"

We were drinking Cape Cods now and I held the vodka in my mouth a moment for the burn. Emily had this endearing habit of grabbing my thigh whenever she wanted to emphasize her point. It was like being branded, the sudden pressure of her fingers on my skin.

II.

In April 1985, my mother drove her vintage orange Camaro seventeen miles from our house and slammed into a cement retaining wall. The impact didn't kill her, not immediately. When a local boy biking home from school found her that afternoon, her body was still warm.

Being fifteen, I'd slept late that morning, woken to the smell of gingersnap cookies in the kitchen, and assumed— as had Therese, our young Filipino housekeeper—that my mother had left for her habitual stroll through the orchard.

In his report, the medical examiner noted that my mother bled to death over a period of not less than two, nor more than four hours while I sat on the kitchen floor with ginger- snap cookies, Sex Wax, and my surfboard. Therese said later that I never cried for my mother that day. She said I was a brave girl. I thought it strange to call such coldness brave.

My mother never wore shoes and never laughed. I don't know how she'd found the keys to the Camaro; my father had hidden them, and forbidden her to drive years earlier. She had taught school on Guam, and later, after she married my father, on Maui, until she'd collapsed, suffered a spell, had an episode … and was relegated to the orchards with me, the summer I was five.

In the morning, after the men left for the orchards, my mother walked slowly around the house, staring out each of the windows. A tall, tense coffee-colored woman, with long, frizzy hair that roped down the length of her back, high-strung as a cat, incapable of coming to rest, she paced the house, manically bare-footed, her toenails chipped and grouted with mud, the soles of her feet thick and calloused. She told stories among the mango trees whenever I followed her to the orchard. While conjuring characters and plots, she'd swing her feet slowly like heavy pendulums from her perch atop the thickest branch of her favorite mango tree. On my back, in the tamped down section of the rutted path, I listened with my eyes closed to lore and myth spooled into gleaming threads she wove over both of us like a net. I was her disciple then, that sweet summer of my mother's decline.

Once there was a young man whose sister disappeared. Every day he walked to the river to weep and pray. One morning, as the light slanted through the birch trees, the river took the shape of a woman, her hair flowed over trembling shoulders, her face blurred and shimmering. The water god's body shuddered like the surface of the current.

"Why do you wake me with your wailing?" she asked, her voice draping over him like a dream. "I have slept a thousand years and would sleep a thousand more."

The young man prostrated himself before the river god:

"Oh, but I beg you, most kind guardian of the river, to tell me what has become of my sister. She has vanished in the night and I am sick with loss."

The river god groaned and felt the squander of being awakened.

"Your sister has left this place with her lover. She is happy. Grieve no more; she desires not your mourning."

The young man looked at the river god, but did not believe. A clever plan appeared to him.

"If she has run with her lover, I will leave you in peace. Mighty god of the river, would you but grant me a vision of my sister to sate my grief?"

She cast herself high into the air, spreading her foam

edges the width of the banks: "You would ask a vision, then an embrace. You would ask an embrace, then a visitation. You would ask a visitation, then an arrest. Schemer, how your sister will mourn you!"

Extending her fluid arm toward him, she pitched forward: a dizzying torrent of rage and froth like a wolf pack devoured him. In a moment the water receded from the banks, revealing a bowed orange flower just at the water's edge. The river god smiled and sank beneath the surface. Water lapped at the bank like tongues.

Beware what you mourn.

My mother asked me if I thought myself the child who escapes or the child who flowers. I had no heart to tell her I am the river.

III.

It was a Crayola box kind of evening: the whiskey blitzed our skulls like a locomotive and some guitar-driven post-punk caterwaul hummed around us as if despair spilled from the walls. I thought we'd be drowned: this room full of beautiful people with their stylish comments on celebrity, fashion, and travel all banded together to discuss the most essential and lasting elements of pop culture.

I was hungry for Ireland then, for the wind-burned desolation of an island with winter and European notions to influence its development. After wandering the Seussian rooms with my green beer bottle in search of some rational discourse, I finally settled on the patio at the back of Emily's house, overlooking the banyan trees. The night was close and warm. Behind me in the house, I heard laughter and the rumbled bass mechanisms as if through the filter of a telephone. Outside in the dark were frogs.

My head was swirling so I sat down on the back steps to steady myself. Outside the cottage—my studio—the garden lamp was on, casting an eerie glow over the plumeria. I didn't notice him until he spoke:

"Don't you like parties?"

He was grinning, white Cheshire teeth, a perfectly applied tan, large brown eyes beneath a fro of brown curls like some Hippie Gap Model. I grinned back.

"Too much bass guitar and whiskey."

He nodded and sat down on the step below mine.

30

"You're the Latin teacher."

I examined him more closely: he wore Levis with a button-down shirt, slippers, and a Shark watch. Surfer boy.

"Not yet, I start fall term."

"I took Latin from Dr. Adams at U.H. my junior year. She's really hot for an older chick—imagine Barbara Stanwyck running declensions. I had this recurring dream about poking her in the language library."

"That's a lovely visual. I hope I can keep it out of my head when I meet her."

"You're too cute to teach Latin. No seriously, a Latin teacher should be like a nun, you know, grave and otherworldly—aside from Dr. Adams, I mean. You laugh, but I'm serious. Now my wife would be an excellent Latin teacher. She's exactly like a nun."

I kept laughing, but not quite as effortlessly.

"How long have you been married?"

"Decades and decades. Don't ever get married. You aren't married are you?"

"No."

"No. You're too cute to be married. I'm too cute to be married. It's all become terribly confused."

He kept smiling as if he were talking in a perfectly normal way giving a strange girl professional and marital advice while calling his wife a nun. I spray-painted *WIFE* across my mind to keep everything else out of my head.

"What does your wife do?"

"She's an attorney—well, she was an attorney. Now she works for Senator Yoshi as one of his deputies. Politically she's absolutely rabid."

"Do you always discuss your wife at parties?"

"Oh, god no. You're just really lucky. Whiskey?"

He handed me a bottle of Jameson and grinned in a goofy, harmless way. His shoulders were surprisingly wide, and I tried to visualize him running declensions, marrying a

31

lawyer, fucking Barbara Stanwyck. I took a swig of Jameson straight from the bottle and gave up trying to sort the deck. Wasn't I cloistered as well?

"So you've been riding my proto boards?" he asked.

Proto boards? My mind tried to sort out the diction as well as the context of the question.

"You're Ryan Grey," I said at last with something akin to reverence.

He blushed. I had pictured him as some has-been in his forties who still talked with a California lilt. Hippie Gap Models are not hardcore surfers; they're too busy eating egg whites with yogurt or throwing tantrums to do anything as potentially scarring as surf.

"You're fucking Ryan Grey. Man, your Mako Surf Company boards are unreal—I've ridden the Kali and the Ika—keep in mind I haven't surfed in nine years—and these boards just glide, man. They're so smooth and natural. Emily just smokes on them. I'm still awkward out there but these boards are a great disguise."

The blush spread to his ears and down his neck; I imagined it crawling across his chest like a rash.

"I don't—you know I don't actually make the boards. I just test protos same as Emily. My dad is the board maker. He named a line after me in a Christopher Robin gesture because I was born on his fiftieth birthday and he thought that was a fantasy trip. So you're into longboards, yeah? The Kali is my favorite ride."

"Yeah, it's a beautiful board. We've surfed nearly every day since I moved in."

"Emily's been telling me to use you in the ad campaign. She said you look like an Island girl and talk like some mutant international model so you'll appeal to all markets."

"Why don't you use her?"

"Emily? We did. When we were in high school both of us worked the campaign. It was completely absurd; the two of us posing on the beach with the boards and riding these sad little waves so the photographer could get clear shots without being in the water past his waist. We bailed on the whole thing and have drafted friends ever since."

Sure, an ad campaign. I'd always wanted to be in an ad campaign, maybe wearing my hair up in a pink bow with one of those pudgy bathing suits from the fifties with the flared skirt attached. I could dance hula while surfing two-foot waves. We'd been exchanging the bottle of Jameson like war buddies, throating the smooth shots in elegant hits; the din of the party throbbed in the rooms behind us like primitive memory. It was extremely likely that I would be sick.

"Why haven't you been surfing with us?" I asked him.

"Shit, I've been in California the last two weeks. But I'm psyched to go out with you two. We have to go super early, though, by 4:00 a.m., so I can get back for work."

"What are you, a milkman?"

He giggled. Truly, like a little girl.

"Yeah, I'm your milkman, baby, call me and I'll come on by. No, I'm a ramp manager at UPS: I start work at 6:00 a.m."

"Ramp manager?"

"I know, it sounds like skateboarding, but it's a legitimate job: we unload the plane and transport all the packages to the sorting center."

"6:00 a.m. must be hard on your social life."

"Not me, never. I'm with a nun, man. Surfing is practically my entire social life ... and the odd house party of course."

The arms of the banyan tree groped toward me through the dark. I had Van Halen rattling around my head, and this sweet goofy boy next to me like a relic from the sixties. This was pure grief. This was suffering. I wanted to dance up and down the steps like a character in a musical. I wanted that insulated life where boys like this weren't married and

I had never crashed into a dentist determined to love me. I wanted to kiss him and I did, falling against his mouth as my last comrade in this mad garden.

"Hello kids, keeping warm?"

I looked up and caught the glare of a halo of light around the face of a tall girl standing over us.

"Is that your wife?" I asked.

Ryan Grey looked up and shook his head, "My wife wears serious clothes. That is not my wife."

The girl was laughing now and I understood that it was Emily. I climbed up and shook her hand, "This was a marvelous party. I've really enjoyed myself."

"I have no doubt. Obviously I've missed all the fun."

She picked up the Jameson bottle that we'd spilled and took a swig. I stood as straight as possible and walked down the steps toward my studio. The garden was underwater; there were bats flitting on the surface like gulls. I'd kissed a hippie and shaken hands with an heiress. Oh, how we unravel and gleam.

IV.

The light filtered through the trees with a smoky gleam like gold dust. My meeting with Dr. Grace Adams was scheduled for nine o'clock, so we put off surfing and I stayed up all night worrying about whether or not I would fulfill this woman's expectations and my own ambition. When I biked to campus the morning of the meeting, there were only a few people milling about the grass courtyard. Sprinklers droned by the language building and I darted between their cycles and up the wide stone steps.

Inside the chilled building, the sound of my footsteps winged through the hallway with a lonely hollow thump. Dr. Adams' office—a large triple-windowed room with old-fashioned dark leather furniture and four walls of bookcases—was on the second floor. When I arrived, she wasn't in her office, so I waited in the doorway, surveying the books I could see for anything I might recognize. A coffee cup on the table had steam rising from it and her computer monitor's screensaver flashed alphabet shapes bouncing like raquetballs.

"You must be Dr. Elliot?"

I turned to face her and discovered a petite tanned white woman with puffed brown hair and very red lipstick, who did, in fact, resemble Barbara Stanwyck. She wore jeans and a sleeveless blouse, which I took to be a good sign. Her earrings were violently blue, dangling in a haphazard shiver.

"Jane Elliot," I said stupidly.

"Come in, Dr. Elliot. Do you want tea?"

She held a cup out to me, which I accepted, hoping that I wouldn't spill it in a bout of self-consciousness. I followed her into the office and sat in the large leather chair directly across from her desk—swallowed instantly in the palm of the slick cushion. The tea was orange, extremely acidic, even though she'd added honey. I twirled the cup in my hand and tried to remain calm. I was a child in the chair, scrunched and dwarfish, stretching my neck to see her over the expanse of her cluttered desk.

"Dr. Elliot, you have impeccable qualifications and I'm pleased to have you join us. I worked with James Montgomery on several different exchange programs and his Latin instruction is superb. I had no reservations about offering you the instructor position."

I wished I had a cigar, to go with the chair, or a snifter of brandy.

"Dr. Montgomery," she went on, "gave a glowing review and your transcript made the decision obvious. I'd like you to teach second-year Latin. The students are disciplined and the coursework interesting. I think you'll enjoy these classes, and they'll be an excellent way to prepare you for the more rigorous graduate-level courses."

She went on to describe the small, handpicked staff and the various teaching schedules—I would teach three classes in the afternoon, five days a week. This first year, I thought, watching her earrings flutter, would be a respite— a relief—while I learned my craft.

"Yes, Latin is very popular at U.H.," Dr. Adams was saying. "It's the only language that doesn't require a lab. All Latin classes meet five days a week for an hour a day and every student must have two full years of a language in order to graduate, so the department stays busy—especially now."

36

I nodded. The pungent orange tea had dazed my senses; I chugged the rest of the tea and tried not to swoon.

"Our undergraduate classes are always full, so we cap them at twenty-four students."

"A friend of mine," I said, "took Latin as an undergraduate, and he told me the homework is reviewed each day during class and there's a test every other Friday."

"What's your friend's name?"

"Ryan Grey."

"Oh, Ryan. He was quite a student. He took Latin for two years. I was trying to get him to take the third year, but I think he panicked about the research paper."

I smiled. It sounded just like him.

"Our classes do function as you mentioned. Latin, as you know, is essentially about memorization, so the students must review constantly and be tested often. You'll teach the second-year courses for fall and spring term and next year we'll discuss adding some graduate courses to the mix—based on the review of your students' progress, of course. Do you have questions, Dr. Elliot?"

"Which hours will I teach?"

She took a sip of tea and flipped through a ledger on her desk.

"Your first class begins at one-fifteen and you'll have classes throughout the afternoon with fifteen-minute breaks in between. I work in the afternoons as well, as does Dr. Greer; Drs. Myers and Delvo work in the morning and the TAs are split with four handling morning classes and four working in the afternoon down the hall from you. I've brought you the course books for our graduate as well as undergraduate classes, but don't worry about reviewing any except your own course book right away; take your time to adjust to our pace here: you have a whole year to familiarize yourself with these."

She pointed to my right and I followed her gesture to

one of the many piles of books on the floor, noting she'd marked a particular stack with a pink Post-it note and my name in a loopy grade-school script. Standing, she eased her way around the desk, relieved me of my cup, and paused a moment, her earrings rocking hypnotically.

"Oh, Dr. Elliot, you're required to have one hour of office time every day, just in case a student needs you, but most of the time you'll find that you can use that hour as prep time. Most of the students do very well in our program and rarely require tutorials."

I nodded. The class structure was so well planned, so meticulously designed that I could focus all my attention on the language—the reinvigorating pursuit of Latin—the interactive exchange with the students, and the stimulating environment of a classroom. This ideal of the classroom as a forum appealed to me after years in the more clinical, dispassionate post of a researcher.

"Would you like to see your classroom and office?"

She walked briskly for a small woman, her puffed hair moving in rhythm with her footfalls. The Classics Department, Greek and Latin, was contained in Moore Hall: the classrooms on the first floor and the offices on the second. Down the hall from Dr. Adams' office, was a narrow room with one bare metal desk, three swivel chairs, and a second desk swathed by precariously stacked binders, workbooks, frayed hardbacks, and piles of rubber bands. A long thin window in the center of the room viewed the grass courtyard where considerably more students now lounged, books cast open beside them. I set my own stack of books on the bare desk. Outside the door, the office was tagged Dr. Jane Elliot and Dr. Samara Delvo.

Dr. Adams led me down two flights of stairs to the classrooms I had hurried past that morning. Mine was the last room on the left just at the corner of the building. The two exterior walls were constructed entirely of windows so that the room seemed like a high-ceilinged greenhouse. One wall had a dry eraser board and there were four long tables gathered around an overhead projector perched upon a podium in the center of the room.

"Your teaching method is your own as long as your students perform well on their exams. Of course, my office is open to you for anything you might require. I expect that you will perform very well here, Dr. Elliot. I try to give my teachers a lot of latitude, in the hope that reducing their stress levels will in turn reduce the stress on their students."

After Dr. Adams left me, I stood beside the podium and stared about me. The ceiling was at least seventeen feet high and coupled with the two walls of windows the room took on the haloed quality of a cathedral. In two months' time I would be conducting a choir in the basic chant of language, urging them to see the significance of each intonation, the clues for translation disguised in each part of speech. And somehow all I could think of was my mother's story about language.

The gods made cats in the shape of letters and told them to work together to form words. But the cats stretched their shapes out of proportion when they woke from their daylong naps, and bickered so mercilessly when they were together that the words were distorted and illegible. Finally, the gods made each cat a complete alphabet so that words must be pieced together over a lifetime. With all this pressure, the cats slept even more often, and spelled very short words.

V.

One scorching morning in July, Emily suggested we try a
new beach and leave our boards at home.

"Ever been to Cockroach Cove?"

I shook my head.

"It's the beach they used in *From Here to Eternity*—Burt
Lancaster and Deborah Kerr rolling around like juveniles.
Good place for sea turtles."

We packed her Miata with poké, juice, and towels,
slathering each other with sunscreen for the two-lane drive
out to Koko Head. In the parking lot a group of young men
flew Chinese kites high above the cliff face, the wind rattling through their colors nervously.

On the far side of the lot, a thin trail plunged down
through the cliffs to the cove below. As we snaked down I
watched the waves break in brilliant plumes of white—the
ocean a stark, accusing blue—and thought of the Cliffs of
Moher on Ireland's west coast. The Belfast dentist—her
crow-colored hair whipped to a spectacular frenzy by the
breeze—and I had hiked up late in the afternoon with a
couple of backpackers from Australia and eaten tomato and
cheese sandwiches while the sea raged 200 meters below.
"There be dragons," she had said, capturing the mythical
quality of the view and the hike and the future.

Above Emily and me, the sun crouched. We spread our
towels on the dark sand and ate some raw ahi, grateful to
stretch our long legs. Behind us, the mouth of a cave gaped

and giant scalable boulders reared up as if to challenge the looming cliffs. Just above and to the right of the surf, a rock shelf stretched along the cove floor like a sidewalk.

"Let's sit up there, yeah?" I pointed at the shelf.

Sitting at the edge, we held our feet above the water as the waves cradled into the cove, occasionally spattering us in a salt-spray after an especially furious break.

"Should have brought some beer," Emily said.

I looked at my watch; it was not yet 10:00 a.m. She saw me and waved her hand absently at the horizon.

"OK, OK."

"This beach is amazing," I said. "Have you actually seen turtles here?"

"Yeah. There are always divers down here too. I think they hold training sessions in the cove. Masked people will suddenly pop up, making this gasping noise—extremely disconcerting. This used to be my favorite beach when I was in school. I'd come down here a couple of times a week. In fact, I came down here the day after the whiskey party. It's kind of my what-the-fuck-were-you-thinking beach."

"How's that?"

"Haven't I told you about the whiskey party?"

"No."

"The week we graduated from U.H. we had mad parties. We were practically drunk the entire time. So the night of graduation, I have a whiskey party at my place. Only whiskey—no chaser, no dilution—and Jesus, I have never seen so many wretched, groping, vomiting, bleary-faced drunks in my life. It was sick. Of course, I was as drunk as the rest of them. I slept with this guy who was dating one of my friends at the time, Laura Dragan; she was also at the party and ended up sleeping with Erica. We found them the next morning, naked, in the king-sized bed in my mother's room. Erica, who was bi, just looked kind of embarrassed, but Laura freaked out. She kept screaming: 'I'm not bi, I'm drunk.'"

"Jesus."

"Yeah, it was priceless. We repeated that line for years. Last I heard, Laura was teaching in a public school in New York City. She was never stable."

Emily and I sat side by side, the ocean at our feet so blue it might have been white. Beneath us, the rock shelf felt smooth and warm. I watched chicken skin creep up her arm.

"How is that a what-the-fuck-were-you-thinking story?"

"I woke next to Laura's boyfriend just hating myself. The night of the whiskey party, I'd been hanging with Erica and there was this vibe between us that I'd never felt before. We were smoking pot on the balcony and she leaned her face really close to mine and whispered something into my ear. I have no idea what she said, but I panicked and bolted. That's the only time I've ever done that."

I speculated which *that* she meant: flirted with a girl, slept with a friend's boyfriend, panicked and bolted, hated herself. Emily wore a white bandana low on her forehead and her hair furled out behind her like one of those Chinese kites. The sea yawned to the edge of the world. I wanted to touch the scar beside her eye. I wanted to name things without language. I wanted to tell her about my mother.

By the time I was a senior in high school, being the suicide kid had lost all of its novelty. Some of my classmates had forgotten and would slip occasionally, asking if my folks were going to the Class Day Parents' Potluck, or if my mom could volunteer to chaperone the next field trip. Slips like these were a relief to me; I wanted so much to have parents like everybody else. But each one hurt as well, reinforcing my otherness.

I took Graphic Arts all four years of high school as my cruise class: we had a couple of official projects every term; otherwise our time was our own. Higashi, our instructor, drank whiskey from a thermos and spent his free time harassing us about crushes and rumors of crushes. He decided that I needed a pal and would call me into his office to chat about all kinds of bullshit, from surfing in Australia (which I revered) to fishing for swordfish (which I abhorred).

Higashi always wanted me to confide in him about my feelings. Was I overwhelmed with high school, because it was OK to be overwhelmed with high school. Did I miss my mom, because it was OK to miss my mom. If I ever needed to talk to anyone about um, women's issues, he'd had four daughters and three wives and was an expert on, um, women's issues. Higashi was a huge Japanese man with pockmarked cheeks and giant calluses on his thumbs.

"From my lawnmower," he'd say. "All year in this place: the relentless green."

He was the teacher you could swear around, the guy who let you bitch to him about whatever angst you'd stored up since the last time you'd bitched to him. I couldn't ever tell him anything important, but I loved to sit in his tiny office with the Macintosh on the metal desk like an altar and listen to his raspy grunt of a voice. Higashi was the only person who talked about my mother's death casually— unreservedly—as if there were no reason, neither shame, nor sadness, not to discuss it.

After the police came to report my mother's suicide, my father kind of stopped speaking. He became more gesture than person: a knife brushed against a plate at the table, boots scuffing the floor in the morning, shoe indentations in the long orchard grass, a palm rested lightly on my head. We moved around each other comfortably like dogs, often walking through the orchard at night until I was so exhausted that I could barely climb the stairs to bed.

Sometimes I felt that we were two old men, waiting in the house where our lover had left us. The house and the orchard a relief of ourselves: hollowed and austere. At night

I would dream of sitting on his shoulders, the scary thrill of being taller than everyone else, my legs hugged against his chest like a newborn. I dreamt once that I was in the car with my mother, that I was driving, and my father was the one who found us. He sat on the hood of the car and looked at us through the windshield.

"Why?" he asked finally.

I waited for my mother to answer him, but when I looked over she was already dead, her glass eyes staring. My father waited.

"She was so tired," I said. "She was just so tired."

My first semester in Dublin, I was wild with grief. Somehow the city reminded me of my mother—my isolation made her keen again—and I couldn't shake the sense that somewhere in the streets or shops I would meet her and have to introduce myself because I'd changed through the years though she hadn't. Eventually, I gathered some mates and settled into the restlessness of school, but I never lost the sensation that she might pop around any corner: her dark face a blot among the impossibly white Irish.

My father and I wrote letters; I held more words from him than he'd spoken for years. I couldn't tell him about hunting my mother. Instead I'd describe the battering music, my classes, the sea's drum, all the ruins scattered about the countryside, and the grandparent-like couple who'd claimed me as their own.

During my undergrad, as in high school, there was a succession of boys: boys who wrote poetry and boys who read poetry, painters, a sculptor, several actors, and two teachers. I never told any of them about my mother. Over Christmas, my last year of graduate school, I took a train to Belfast and stayed at my friend's flat while he went to Greece. The city was not derelict or frightening in the way I'd been led to expect, the brick buildings were beautiful and Victorian, all the neighborhoods tucked behind green

44

hedgerows. And I met this dentist in a pub and wandered away with her. What if I had panicked and bolted then instead of later? What if my mother had been braver? What was Emily trying to tell me?

She stood, tall and exquisite in the glaring morning, peeled the bandana from her head, and sprang from the shelf into the sea, her toes pointed back at me before they too vanished. In the fall, I would discipline my energies to focus exclusively on teaching Latin to undergraduates.

"Come in," she called. "The water's fine."

Oh the relentless green, I thought. All year in this place.

VI.

Above me in the tangled branches of the banyan trees, bats flung themselves in the pitch of dark as I lay on my futon beside the opened French doors, waiting on sleep the way a soldier might wait for reinforcements. Maybe I was already having visions of her moving through the hollowed house, barefoot and a little drunk: her fingers sweeping along the walls, a streetlight grazing her brown hair like a bullet. Maybe I already felt desire tugging at me in the early summer while I tried to remember Ireland, to hold it against me in the smother of close dark.

Some nights I would walk through the narrow, silent streets of Manoa alight with my solitude. Cycling through town those wicked hot afternoons didn't bring sleep any sooner, so most days that summer Emily and I would surf the pre-dawn swells with Ryan Grey, catch an early breakfast at this little hippie café, and sleep away the morning. Surfing was a rush, a kinetic high that overwhelmed my deep exhaustion and lent those days a sense of genuine accomplishment. We had surfed. We had seized all the vigor within ourselves and wrestled our potential like Jacob.

Grey threatened to keep me company on my night rambling, adamantly refusing to see insomnia as anything other than a party he hadn't been invited to. After our first meeting, I'd entertained the notion of a crush with the heir to a surfboard legacy, but it quickly passed into a filial impulse that surprised me. This goofy mellow guy being married to a ferocious political insider seemed tragic, and I found myself, in spite of everything, wanting to protect him.

"His wife is incredibly ambitious," Emily explained the morning after that first party. "They married during college and she just has no place for him now. She's one of those brilliant chicks who can convince you of anything. It's only later when you think about the conversation that you realize you didn't agree with anything she said, but somehow at the time, you'd just stood there nodding. She spends most of the year on the Mainland, working for the Senator in D.C. Poor Ryan, he's always had no luck with women. He'd never ask for a divorce, though. Talk about clinging to scraps."

I'm not sure why I regarded him as off limits. Perhaps my determination to focus on teaching, perhaps I knew we'd make better chums than lovers, perhaps I sensed a more serious crush would ambush me. But Grey and I fell into friendship effortlessly; both of us letting go of the notion that something else might thrive under our skin.

Grey, as it turned out, had dated Emily during high school, though, he qualified, they had never been *really serious.*

"She was always a little fast for me. Too confident, you know, too wild. I was always a little afraid of her."

Late in the summer, after an evening at the Blue Spark, Emily drove me out to Black Point Beach. We hopped the iron fencing and skirted along the rough white stones of the beach until we came to a small cove braced against a rock wall.

Emily's face had edges as if it had been torn from a larger sheet of paper. As I shielded the match from the wind, she lit the pocket of twigs and newspaper at the center of the stones we'd gathered well back from the shoreline. I was naked, chilled after swimming over the fat round rocks just below the surface of the water. For a moment the newspaper held the thin yellow flame. Emily's face went dark again. Black Point Beach barreled in loud swells just beyond our bare feet. The thick rope swing, suspended from the palm tree at the water's edge, seemed to move across the surface of the moon.

"Here," she said, tossing me the matches. "You light it."

While I held a match against the newspaper Emily leaned into it and blew. I watched the flames glare against her pale skin and blacken her eyes. Behind us three houses sat in dark hulks like hillsides. She squatted next to me, our shoulders touching, and massaged my hands.

A child told her story to stand up and walk. She watched her story hobble away through the cornflower field. In a moment it was too late to recall.

The fire flickered without much warmth or enthusiasm. Emily rubbed her hands against the outside of my legs like a trainer. Her hands burned the surface of my skin. I shivered into a towel, her body bright and warm against mine as if I still shielded the match in my palms. I name that moment, I name that place, as the one that moved beyond what I could handle. As the one that moved.

VII.

It rained all that weekend before my classes began. A torrent that Hiromi, the caretaker, fought bitterly in her rubber boots and peasant straw hat; piling bricks around the garden and digging moats to hold the water back. I stayed indoors, fingering through my books in a distracted, juvenile way as the rain drummed.

In an effort to reduce the musty smell in the studio, I kept the French doors opened and stood outside with my cup of coffee, letting the rain splatter against my bare feet. A vision of my mother crept into the garden, and I saw her among the mango grove with her disheveled hair and sad baggy clothes. Trying to remember one of her stories, I thought instead of the autumn my father had taken us to Europe. I remembered little of the trip—shards of memory, really—but I knew my mother did not want to go, had balked for weeks, even to the moment of our departure from the airport terminal.

Of the five countries we visited, Germany held my most vivid recollections. Cater-corner to our hotel we discovered a bakery where they made chocolate with toys inside each piece. I had a train engine in one of the pieces I ate. I remembered large stretchy gummi bears that you could buy from vending machines, and pubs with growling men whose dogs lay at their feet as they ate tremendous white sausages and fatty pork.

During the last week of our trip, my father insisted we

visit Dachau Concentration Camp; arguing that one must see even the brutal historical sites firsthand for context. I can still see that twisted metal at the entry gates and the brown hard-packed earth in and around the grounds. Bitterly cold, the air had the fermented scent of a barn, and we moved among several other tourist groups with a muted trudge. At the ovens, my mother wept. I remember the look on her face, how it was more a hole than an expression.

"Do you have more coffee?"

I felt Emily's hand on my shoulder even as I heard her voice and, overwhelmed with the rain and nervousness and my heavy dead mother, I turned into her and was lost. My face pressed into her collarbone as if I could push inside her and hide my body beneath her ribs. Lodge against her spine and become another self, more solid, calmer. Was it possible to gather into each other?

"What is it?"

Her hand came around my head and I thought of Ireland and the dentist, the danger I'd inhabited by remaining in this garden with this girl, the absence of tenderness and the failure of stories.

"What is it? What is it?"

Her hair smelled of green apples; she held onto me with something like despair. We were mirrors, clinging images. I wished that I knew more languages so I might have a word for everything.

Had I sought Emily to fill a void in myself or a void in her? It seemed to me that we would never understand one another, and the alien in her felt like a failure in me. Her hair slipped through my fingertips, thick and soft, her body braced against my body as solidly as core. I thought of the scar at her right eye, its luminescent whiteness. I wanted to ask her: Who suffers more, the living or the dead? *Ut lingua deficio*?

50

VIII.

To my relief, classes began that August without cries for revolution or disgruntled students marching the halls demanding my resignation. My second-year students were quiet and studious, prepared each day and willing to participate. Most of the students were Japanese—only a handful seniors—and all of them looked grateful when I said pronunciation was not vital to their grade since Latin survived essentially as a written language.

Dr. Adams had written a single, thick textbook to be used for the first two course years. Monday through Thursday each week, we studied a lesson: vocabulary words, grammatical usage, verb conjugation, and a translation exercise using any lesson from the previous weeks. One Friday we'd review the week's work and the next Friday we'd test cumulatively. The classes required very little improvisation on my part (barring startling questions from my brilliant and gifted darlings) although the prescriptive nature of the instruction required me to work harder to keep the students interested and challenged so that no one would be underwhelmed by the routine.

During class time we would do a group grading session of the previous evening's translation exercise, review the previous day's usage, and then go over the new vocabulary words and usage lessons so that the students could complete their next translation exercise. Instead of the monotonous and dismal translations we'd hammered against when I was in high school, Adams had used Greek and Roman myths for each translation exercise, interspersing poems, and challenging the students by randomly repeating previous lessons' vocabulary words and grammar usage.

In fact, the only time of the day my students' zeal subdued—dashing my deluded notion that they'd taken Latin simply because they loved the sound of it in their mouths—occurred when we ran declensions. By their very nature, declensions can be monotonous—sometimes one has to spice things up by declining verbs to the rhythm of *La Cucaracha* while doing a little Latin dance—but running declensions was my favorite activity. In our greenhouse, with the light filtering onto my students' heads like vague halos, I felt holy, as if the lot of us formed a chanting chorus of heaven. The rounded, dead words in their mouths rattled the windows, moved the tables and chairs, until even the overhead projector vibrated with the crescendo. It was glorious, thrilling, and triumphant! I expected trumpets to usher princes on elephants through campus to the very throne of my golden black-haired angels. I would have dressed them in purple capes and shiny knee-length boots; a mantra to transcend all time:

traxerim	ceperim	monuerim	iactaverim
traxeris	ceperis	monuerimis	iactaveris
traxerit	ceperit	monuerit	iactaverit
traxerimus	ceperimus	monuerimus	iactaverimus
traxeritis	ceperitis	monueritis	iactaveritis
traxerint	ceperint	monuerint	iactaverint

Having a room full of twenty-somethings seated on wooden chairs around rather short-legged tables seemed absurdly suggestive of grade school, but I'd found all of my students to be dedicated and focused on the work assigned them. At the end of the second week, they took their first exam and all scored better than eighty-four percent. I had an assortment of majors in my classes: a great many pre-med students; Liberal Arts and Humanities students; and a surprising number of business majors. Apparently, compulsory language labs for every other foreign language class had made Latin very popular indeed.

Joy was what I most wanted to impart to them; my passion for oral declensions—the calming, repetitive song like an incantation spoken between us privately, devoutly—seemed the ideal tool to convince them that Latin is beautiful: the very shape of the words in one's mouth, the translations, the transformation of nouns, verbs, and adjectives. Most of the time, however, my primary function seemed to involve keeping the students from stroking out with self-inflicted pressure.

When I called on Angie, a tall, stork-legged Korean girl, to read the entire translation after we'd gone line by line, she flushed and blurted: "Oh, mine's a disaster. I didn't realize they were sisters and I translated the genitive incorrectly."

She looked mortified and I could see red marks all over her translation where she'd attempted to correct her initial mistake. Beside her on the table, her textbook—its spine meticulously duct taped—her laminated flashcards, her homework all but annotated and I felt my task keenly: these kids needed some fucking perspective.

IX.

During midterms, we had four bomb threats at U.H. The Manoa campus has a long history of bomb threats coinciding inevitably with midterms, finals, and term papers, so during our first staff meeting with Dr. Adams, the professors were instructed to tell our Latin students that in the event of a bomb threat, we would take our test outdoors in the grass—rain or shine. More than once on my way to class, I saw the yellow police tape and a couple of officers with their dogs stalking through the eerily deserted quarantine. A certain amount of space around the particular building had to be secured as well, so occasionally two halls would be closed for inspection and sometimes the classes would be huddled around in the grass nearby carrying on with their lectures. It was surreal each time I came upon such a scene—the calm pedestrian response to a frighteningly maniacal threat which was exerted with no further objective than to have an extra day to study—and after living in Ireland where bomb threats and bombings shade everyday experience, I felt S.W.A.T. teams and felony charges a more suitable response. Still, we struggle in our own ways, and our way did insure that Moore Hall did not receive any bomb threats.

I developed the habit, that first semester, of splitting my required office hours before and after my class time so that I wouldn't go mad at the end of the day, and also to foster relations with my bizarre office mate, Dr. Samara Delvo. Delvo taught in the morning, and kept office hours through lunch until about one-thirty each day. In the back half of our cement office her desk shouldered piles of workbooks, Latin texts, and various volumes of the Oxford English Dictionary, which loomed unsteadily above any student daft enough to sit in the impossibly short-legged wooden chair at the end of the desk. Delvo kept four rubber band balls in the otherwise empty desk drawers to fling absently against the cement walls (or me) as she talked on the phone. She did not keep a computer at her desk—*Security is too easily compromised, Elliot; never give students the opportunity to plant porn on your hard drive*—but carried her laptop around in her black shoulder bag to classes, the office, and home again.

A tall robust woman in her early forties, Delvo was a little thicker than usually considered attractive, but the extra weight sat proportionally on her body and her bold confidence (nearly a conceit) gave her a strangely sexy demeanor. In tight stretch tops and blue jeans, she wore her thick black hair pulled away from her face into various styles of braids. Her nose was wide and slightly flattened; she had cat's eyes with elegant, perfectly curled eyelashes and a laugh like a gunshot.

When I came into the office one morning in October, she looked up at me and nodded.

"So a student this morning—a third year mired in some cosmic crisis—demands to know the point—the point, he says—what is the point of learning a dead language?"

It upset her simply to repeat the incident. Her face had assumed the stern teacher's mask of rebuke. I contained my grin and widened my eyes to simulate astonishment.

"What did you say?"

"I told the class it was a good question and they could each write a thousand-word essay exploring the answer. You should have seen the daggered rage his classmates cast at the little bastard."

I laughed until she joined me, and the sternness slipped from her expression. For Delvo, Latin was not the enlightening discovery I had experienced, rather a rigorous science to be etched on the body methodically and with full awareness. To her, Latin was a law; and to question the law, heresy.

"It's really not funny, Elliot."

"Come on. They're under a lot of pressure; half of our students are pre-med."

"Pressure? What the devil do these insulated spoon-fed hatchlings know about pressure? We're talking about Latin, Elliot. We're talking about the very foundation of modern language: the scaffold for communication."

"You're writing a thousand-word essay too?"

She flung her rubber band ball at me.

"Oh laugh, laugh. You would have been infuriated by such a question as well, and you know it. Elliot, you were educated by the Irish—a people who have struggled—passionately struggled—to maintain their own language for hundreds of years despite savage oppression. No doubt you observed this passion firsthand and felt a kinship with it."

"Every one of my professors carried around an etymology dictionary."

"I well believe it: another world entirely."

I leaned back in my chair, considering the mass of texts on her desk.

"Yes," I said, "but there is a level of devotion that tumbles into fanaticism."

"How so?"

Now she had adopted her empirical expression and scooted her chair around the corner of her desk so that we might have a clear line of sight. She wore a French braid today with a silver clasp.

"I took a poetry class my second year from an amazing poet, Paula Monahan."

"Yes. I'm familiar with her work."

"Of course you are; you really do read everything. Anyway, we wrote original poems for her class and she bickered with my use of 'inhaling' in one of my poems."

"Why?"

"My line described the consuming nature of love, how my narrator was 'inhaling with both hands.' Monahan thought the usage improper."

"Certainly it was."

"It was a poem."

"Yes, Elliot, but words have limitations—even in poems. Gertrude Stein said overuse of a word renders it meaningless. 'Love' for instance."

"She also said a rose is a rose is a rose."

I kicked my feet on top of my desk and chucked the rubber band ball back at her, adding, "Language must stretch to grow."

"You can't mean it," she said. "You can't seriously think that diction has no boundary, that words are flexible. What would be the point of proper definitions if anyone could come along and fling words about as though they were darts?"

"Take your argument to its logical conclusion and we'd still be speaking like Chaucer."

"Chaucer would never have spoken like Chaucer since we're on a slippery slope. Social growth is different, often an intolerable and destructive influence—now children learn to talk from television—but there are still rules governing usage and grammar and they are necessary rules, just as it is necessary to have a universal standard of spelling."

"I'm not advocating improper usage, but I think pressure can be put on words without breaking them. 'Inhaling with both hands' became a visual metaphor for my narrator evoking the way lovers test each other through intense sensory pressure until the senses meld together. My use of the word 'inhaling' was a natural evolution of this process of oral and sensory exploration. Not to mention the denotation of gathering greedily."

"This is now a conversation about sex rather than language."

"For me they are often the same thing, Delvo."

"Yes. No doubt you inhale with both hands like your narrator. I wonder that Monahan did not object to the possible drug implications of that statement. They've only just occurred to me."

She laughed in a great boom, her chest heaving with reverb.

"You're a cynic," I accused her.

"As you say."

"The Irish fostered a devotion to language that already existed in me, but their efforts to save Gaelic from extinction are a proof for my argument. Language evolves: Latin exists today in the root structure of Spanish, Italian and French, but we no longer speak it as the Romans did. The Irish can educate their children in Gaelic, but the language can't be expected to survive outside Ireland. And will their children's children speak Gaelic? Despite their best efforts, the French cannot insulate their language from corruption by foreigners, or by natives. Pidgin will exist in Hawaii for all time, but not necessarily as it was spoken in the 1960s— lazy talk transforms in slow motion along with standard English. Language will stretch, it will corrupt, it will die out; dinosaurs exist now as crocodiles."

"Not nearly as impressive, crocodiles."

"I'd hate to be in the water with one."

"You have an admirable argument and if you were a poet, I might concede to your right to exert pressure, but as a teacher of language, isn't your obligation to protect and enforce the accepted grammatical and etymological rules that govern proper usage?"

"Language as articulate communication? Can't we strive for more than a text of proper usage? As a teacher, I must challenge them. That's my role."

"A role for which you are well suited, Elliot, though I would have had a mutiny on my hands if I had rebutted my student this morning with your arguments. Imagine if I'd told the class that my colleague suggests it is the natural course of language to evolve or die. Survival of the fittest words, is that it? I shall go home and have a bath, and hope that you are wrong."

Sessions with Dr. Mya: Day 2

Nurse Crumb of the many bellies decides to drop round and bully me.

"Jane, you really are exasperating. I've never had such an ungrateful patient. Can you imagine, for one moment, what it must be like to nurse a girl who has not the least interest in recovery? Must you hang from your bed as if awaiting the rest of the chimpanzees?"

"I have to get rid of these pukaki leis. They're making my head ache."

Wielding the garbage can, she carefully dumps the pile of leis into the garbage, scrapes the remaining petals from the bedside table, and ties the plastic bag into a tight knot, which she passes to someone in the hall for disposal.

"Swell. Now can we fumigate?"

"Ever the jester," Crumb replies. "Now, why don't you use your dynamic mind to conjure up a phone number for anyone who might care that you're alive in the world?"

"My head aches. How about some morphine?"

"You're being weaned."

"A character-building convalescence?"

"Quite. I hope it sticks."

"Am I seeing Dr. Mya today?"

"You know you are: second session at 10:00 a.m."

"How about a shower?"

"I don't shower with patients."

I laugh in spite of myself.

"Who's the jester now?"

"I'll have Lucy give you a sponge bath, if you like."

"Which one is she?"

"She is the one who will give you a sponge bath."

"Well, that's clear enough."

Crumb looms bedside for a moment to jot something vital in my chart, then disappears without another glance in my direction. Twenty minutes later, the pug-faced nurse rolls a supply cart into the room. Lucy's identity clarifies; she looks as pleased as I.

"Well, thank god it's you," I say.

She shows me her most potent and withering glare, then scuttles into the bathroom to fill her basin. Can I really allow this midget to bathe me?

"No one else available, then?"

"Just me, I'm afraid."

"I'm afraid as well."

"Don't talk, please," she says. "This will be over quickly."

"It's comforting to know thoroughness is a motto here."

Stingy with the tepid water, she dampens my skin the way a gardener might mist flowers in her greenhouse.

"I appreciate your conservationist's spirit, but I don't want fifteen of these a day, so would you mind being a bit more liberal with the water?"

She soaks me, then seems to regret it as she hurriedly towels the excess water away from my arm cast. After applying dry shampoo, the pug rubs a towel hard around my head as if trying to grind off my ears.

"Take it easy, I've got a fucking head injury!"

She stops instantly, throws the towel back onto the cart, and looks at me anxiously. Probably the nearest thing I'd get to an apology. My gown set right, the basin emptied, Lucy toddles from the room.

In this nearly greaseless condition, I'm delivered to Dr. Mya's office, where she ushers me in ceremoniously.

"Good morning, Jane. Isn't it lovely today?"

I glance at the window behind her and note the rain has stopped.

"The view from your window is better than the view from mine."

"Has your neurologist told you that sarcasm and edginess are typical after a head injury and particularly in the case of a coma?"

"He's told me a lot of thi—"

I stare at her a moment, refusing to swallow or gape openly. In fact, my neurologist has urged me to be patient with the confusion, headaches, temper tantrums, and lack of motor control, but the patience of others is tested more often. Without appearing to notice my chagrin, she continues:

"Nurse Crumb tells me you're being ornery about your treatment"

"Did she actually use the word 'ornery'?"

"Yes."

"Amazing. Which part of my treatment, specifically?"

She dips her gorgeous head to consult her notes. Today she wears a blue pantsuit with the same brown-framed spectacles. Maybe the blue gives the effect of youth, or warmth, because she looks less rigid and exacting, though, of course, our morning session has only just begun.

"She didn't specify except to state that beyond your resentment about the doctor taking you off the morphine drip, you didn't much care what happened to you."

"There's an astute caregiver entombed inside that body of hers."

"Is it your impression that Nurse Crumb doesn't care about your recovery?"

"I haven't really thought about it."

"Do you daydream, would you say, in your hospital room?"

"Of course."

"About what?"

"A life entirely apart from this."

Maybe I daydreamed of the last best moments, the times when I might have chosen differently. If I'd chosen. One night Grey picked me up at the studio for a house party on the North Shore; an ex-girlfriend he'd bumped into recently had called and invited him. Cookout and free drinks, man, he'd told me. How much more perfect could it be? He wore khaki shorts with a coffee-colored Mako Surf Company shirt, T & C slippers, and just a touch of cologne.

"How'zit?" He greeted me with a kiss.

It felt like months since I'd seen him and I started laughing the moment he kissed me. The B52s' "Love Shack" blasted on the car stereo as we cruised through traffic that balmy summer evening.

"So I wanted to invite your girl to come along, too," Grey said, "but I figured you'd be weird about it."

"Oh yeah?"

"Would you have been weird about it?"

"Probably."

"You should relax, Janie, seriously. She's a nice girl, I'm a nice guy—we'll all be fine."

Dusk draped cobalt blue over the island and I thought of Audrey at home reading *The New Yorker* in her recliner, a cup of peppermint tea balanced on her thighs. It had never occurred to me to invite her to the party.

"You're right," I said. "I should have brought her."

Grey tossed me his cell phone: "Call her up. Tell her to meet us."

"She'd planned on a quiet evening at home, you know?"

"Call her."

I dialed Audrey's number, waited three rings before she picked up.

"Babe, it's me. How would you like to meet us at this party?"

"Where is it?"

"Haleiwa. Hold on, Grey's just handed me directions to the house. Will you come?"

"Sure."

I gave her the directions—Grey's nearly illegible scrawl requiring extra time to decipher. She said she'd shower and leave the house in twenty minutes. We'd already passed the narrow bridge leading toward Waimea Bay and were driving through the intricate, fern-shrouded neighborhoods looking for Number 588.

Long before we saw the house number, we heard rave music pouring into the street, and the loud, haphazard voices of revelers. From the alley where Grey parked the car, we watched a girl pitch high into the air from the backyard nearest us, her mouth opened in surprise or delirium as the beer in her hand splashed over her head in a self-baptism. The hibiscus shrubs hid the trampoline from sight until we walked through the gate and saw the girl on her third bounce, a slick of beer rolling along the surface of the trampoline, and dripping from the deflated blond frizz of her hair.

"Jesus, Grey, what time did this party start?"

"Hours ago, apparently."

Plastic runners circumnavigated the house, guarding every walkway from the throng of partiers. A girl with a squirt bottle doused a couple who'd wandered into the banana trees to make out. "Stay off the grass, you fucks! Walk on the plastic! Yes, that's right, w-a-l-k on the p-l-a-s-t-i-c. Jesus Christ."

"She's one of Jenelle's roommates," Grey whispered as we walked toward the house on the plastic runner. "She's extremely anal."

"Yeah, this and other late-breaking news."

"You'll dig Jenelle, though. She short boards North Shore—hard-core chick."

Inside the house the white carpets, white furniture, white paint, and white curtains nearly counteracted the myriad luau shirts these drunken white boys wore like flags —reds, blues, parrot-green, and yellow. Obviously the party had been going for hours. On the dining room table a co-ed group of ten played quarters, sloshing Jagermeister onto the table and carpet in their hysteria. In the living room a guy wearing headphones had propped his turntables on cement blocks, a loop of dance funk roaring from his speakers.

"It's like we've wandered into a frat party," I said.

"No shit. Where the fuck's Jenelle?"

We toured the house, stopped in the kitchen where six guys were shooting tequila at the sink to grab a couple of beers, then ventured onto the front deck. On the far side of the deck, a tanned chick with orange-tinted hair lounged in an Adirondack chair, smoking a joint, oblivious to the chaos on the other side of the door.

"Jenelle?"

"Ryan, you came! I'm so glad. Sit, sit. You must be Jane. Yeah, just pull that chair over. Jesus, is this a nightmare? I don't even know any of these assholes."

"Isn't this your party?" Grey asked.

"No, Kara, our roommate invited these people. Just a little cookout, she said, a few people. These fuckers have been drinking since 10:00 a.m. I wanted to leave but figured they'd try to torch the house."

"Kara's not the chick with the water bottle?" I asked.

"No, that's Hannah, and my god is she pissed. It's just a matter of time before she calls the cops. Last time I saw Kara, she was headed for the trampoline."

"Oh. We saw her on our way in."

In the front yard, spider lilies swayed sociably in the only section of the yard devoid of sculpted bonsai trees. I sensed the house belonged to water bottle-toting Hannah—she of the white furniture and the desperately manicured lawn. No doubt, cops were imminent.

"I've smuggled a cooler of beer out here," Jenelle said. "And of course I've got pot, so it's not like we have to mingle with those fucking whack jobs. I hope you guys ate dinner."

Neither Grey nor I had, but we'd chomped dried cuttle-fish and iso peanuts during the ride out, so it wasn't like we were famished. I worried, suddenly, that I'd invited Audrey to this travesty, making it impossible for us to vanish for at least an hour. Apparently, Grey had been sharing my thought.

"I'd say we should ditch this party," he said, "but we called Jane's girlfriend from the road and invited her. It'd probably be callous to leave without her—unless you think she'd be into the trampoline, Janie."

I felt my face redden as Jenelle took in the girlfriend angle. As lightly as possible I said, "You never know what might happen if she meets those tequila guys on her way in."

Jenelle passed the joint around, and opened herself another beer. We talked about surfing big swells while the house vibrated behind us. Jenelle routinely attacked fifteen-foot swells—ten feet was the most I'd ever managed successfully. I thought most big wave surfers were demented; particularly the ones that used jet-ski tows instead of paddling out themselves—like the rich bastards who bragged about climbing Everest when underpaid Sherpas had lugged their gear, set up their camp, cooked the meals, and guided—the jet-ski phenomenon seemed like cheating to me. Still, I'd come out many times during the winter to watch surfers in wetsuits grapple with the monster Waimea swells—no tricks, no cushions—just those wild, fearless bastards determined not to be swallowed in the break. Jenelle's knees and shoulder were scarred from a smash into coral reef two summers previously—an incident which had cost her a board. She hang-glided as well; obviously, this chick junked on adrenaline.

Over the front wooden fence peeked a few sleepy houses, a sagging volleyball net, and the pointed nose of a surfboard. Aside from the revelers, it seemed like a quiet neighborhood. Mostly surfers and fishermen settled in Haleiwa, willing to bear the commute for a chance to live near some of the most fantastic surf and fishing on the planet. Held together with duct tape, many of the North Shore station wagons, trucks, and vans—pocked with rust-holes and cardboard patch jobs—illustrated the commitment of North Shore residents.

"So what kind of work do you do?" I asked Jenelle.

"I'm a paramedic."

Shocking.

"Actually there was an insane accident a couple weeks ago. One of the meat wagons—sirens gunning, lights lighting up the sky—shoots through a red at an intersection downtown and this fucking ancient, this old fucking man poking along, completely deaf, slams into the ambulance, flips the fucking thing over, kills the paramedic in back with the patient— who also dies—and the paramedic driving is in fucking traction right now. Word is, he won't walk again."

"Jesus," Grey said in a shocked voice that may have been a response to the awestruck way she'd told the story as much as to the story itself.

What was this chick like when she hadn't been smoking pot? Beyond the deck, the wooden gate knocked closed and Audrey in white knee socks and a short sage dress smiled at us. Frazzled from the drive, her curls made her look vaguely hyper, or maybe it was the way her approach seemed timed to the throbbing ache of the music spun by the scrawny punk inside. She moved like a dancer or a cop: cocksure, dangerous. I realized then how much I'd looked forward to her arrival.

Grey stood and introduced her to Jenelle, who passed Audrey the pot and broke open a beer for her. I made space on my recliner, and Audrey leaned against my legs, reaching her hand back to mine instinctively.

"The party's inside?" she asked.

"We've exiled ourselves," Grey said. "Those people are seriously unwell."

He explained about the house's inhabitants, and the agent with the water bottle guarding the perimeter. Audrey took a long swig of beer, her hand sliding along my forearm as she adjusted on the chair.

"I need a light," she said, gesturing with the burned-out joint in her right hand.

Jenelle tossed her lighter to Grey, who lit Audrey, leaning into her to shield the flame—both of their curled heads glowing suddenly in the darkness. Above us, the cold stars arced. Audrey blew smoke into the air, and announced that she had news.

"The commissioner approved my proposal."

Grey and Jenelle looked at me. I looked at Audrey. What fucking commissioner?

"What proposal?" Grey asked.

"Our graffiti-art project."

"OK, but from the beginning—pretend Jenelle and I have no idea what you're talking about."

"I teach art-project classes to third graders in Aliamanu, and we've been talking about doing a community project. The kids wanted something meaningful—you know, something more challenging than decorating for a bank promotional. Anyway, we brainstormed and formulated a plan to white-wash all the graffiti around the freeway on-ramp by Moanalua Gardens, and the kids drew a proposal for the artwork they would paint there instead. We submitted the proposal and I got a call this afternoon that the commissioner approved. We'll have our permit and funding within the month."

"Funding?" I said. "You mean the commission's going to pay for the supplies as well?"

Audrey nodded, a grin swallowing her sprite's face. "And the proposal is really exciting. The kids are going to paint a mural of native birds and plants that have become endangered by introduced species; they've just learned about evolution."

Grey and Jenelle clinked beer bottles with Audrey, obviously pleased for cause to celebrate anything.

"That's very cool," Grey said. "We should drink to the project … maybe something sexier than beer?"

He looked at Jenelle, his eyes suggesting a daring venture. Luckily, he'd found a girl game for anything.

"Absolutely," she said. "Let's raid the house."

When they opened the front door to slip inside, an overwhelming thrum blasted out, suggesting orgies, blood sacrifice, all manner of pagan rituals in the impossibly white room ten feet from the recliner where Audrey had turned, kneeling, to push my legs apart, and drag slowly up my body until her mouth met mine in a kiss of beer and pot and strange desire as if we had new bodies, as if we were new lovers. And I should have lit up like kerosene.

I should have been pleased at the commissioner's approval, at Audrey's well-earned excitement, at the tired, lush neighborhood and her skin. But this mad party, this stupid irritating paramedic—the obvious, extreme-chick fanaticism—had already bummed me out, so now the astonishing news of Audrey's best-intentions project, the commission's endowment for her innovative class and her clever students, her manifest goodness and merit felt like an accusation. Why hadn't she told me about the commission or the proposal? Why hadn't she shared her enthusiasm with me? Was she trying to protect me—with my cheerless, staid teaching job—from her own good fortune? Her hips shifted as she slid her hand under my shirt. My mouth tasted like iron.

"You know, you're an introduced species," I told her.

She'd felt me stiffen and her hand stopped against my left breast. Leaning back on her knees now, she regarded me: "So are you, Jane. Your father's Australian and your mother Chamorran."

"Yeah, so you can whitewash all of us."

Her face then .... Her face lost everything beautiful: crumpled before me all at once like the dying. A flare of red shot through the night, over the fence, and I turned from her as a second flare swirled behind the first.

"Fuck, we have to get out of here."

Hoping to outrun the cops and my temper and her expression, I grabbed her hand and pulled her from the deck, through the pristine lawn, over the fence, into a neighbor's yard, through a hedgerow, and into the red jeep at the end of the dirt road. She sat in the driver's seat and stared straight ahead.

"What about Ryan?"

"He drove, remember?"

"They looked like they wanted to be alone anyway."

For a moment, I didn't understand her. They, who? The jeep's engine had just turned over when we saw a third red light flashing from the alleyway behind the house. Audrey maneuvered a U-turn and we darted away, neither of us speaking on the drive home, my mind consumed with her face. When I'd released Audrey's hand outside the jeep I'd felt hypothermic: a sudden, terrible absence of warmth.

We drove through the pineapple fields for centuries, Radiohead crooning from the stereo in a futuristic swell as the jeep growled down the single-lane road. Had Grey and Jenelle wanted to be alone? I hadn't noticed, although he had blushed whenever she'd directed a question at him. The sky swathed Audrey's red jeep, the eerie sheathlike fronds of the pineapple, the dull stretch of road.

Maybe I dreamt then of barreled tsunamis, a rocketing ambulance, the unfathomable mouth of a red-haired girl because suddenly the engine cut and Audrey's hand on my shoulder roused me. She'd parked on the dirt road behind my studio.

"You coming in?"

She shook her head, "Not tonight."

"Look, I—"

"*You* invited *me* to that party. If you hadn't wanted me to come, why'd you call and invite me?"

"No, I—"

But there was no explanation for the blood in my mouth, the whitewash accusation, the resentment that had flared and swallowed me whole. Afraid suddenly to see her dress slip from her shoulders, the streetlamp fracture the white of her back into a prism, the angled indigo bones of her shoulder blades, her copper hair, the silver slide of her spine; afraid to tremble against her fingertips, yes, to tremble even after she touched me, even then, I climbed from the jeep and watched her drive away.

"Jane? Jane?"

Dr. Mya kneels beside my wheelchair with her hands at my temple.

"Yes."

"I was only asking about daydreams. I didn't mean for you to have one."

She smiles up at me, obviously relieved my eyes can focus on hers.

"I'm sorry. You just asked me something."

"I asked you to be more specific: you daydream a life apart from what?"

"This hospital, this accident."

"You daydream about your life before the accident?"

71

"Sometimes. I mean sometimes I actually dream things that happened, and other times I dream things I don't remember."

"For example?"

"I have these vivid memories of walking through the streets of the U.H. District in the middle of the night." In Dr. Mya's office I can smell the slick of the rain on the pavement and the stir-fried fish from someone's flat; trees taking shape like old men; the world bled of any color beyond black and the cast of streetlamps. "I have these distinct, sentient visuals, but I don't know if they happened. I can't remember if I really experienced them."

"Confusion like this is normal, Jane. You've had a very serious head injury. What else do you remember?"

"A girl's face in the sunlight watching the windsurfers at Kailua; this mad chick dancing on stage at Anna Banana's; my greenhouse classroom—I have millions of image fragments swirling in my head."

She adjusts her spectacles and fiddles with her pen before asking: "Do you enjoy teaching?"

"Yes. More than I imagined possible."

"But you'd had trouble at the school, hadn't you?"

"It's U.H.; everyone's had trouble."

"You mean the strike?"

"Beyond that. Universities are terribly political in a grade school way—there's a lot of passive-aggressive, bureaucratic bullshit that inhibits a teacher's ability to challenge and a student's ability to become enlightened."

Over her head, the sun glares brilliantly against the windows of the opposing buildings. This office is becoming less comfortable by the moment. The anger of my recovery, of waking to find myself an invalid, is as random, as consuming, and ultimately as bewildering as my anger at Audrey that night in Haleiwa. My throat and head have begun to ache.

"Do you feel that you challenged your students?"

"Not as often as I meant to. I took teaching very seriously."

"On a typical day teaching, give me some highlights."

I tell her that I often arrived before noon, in time to catch my office mate, Samara Delvo. Occasionally Delvo would stay while I wolfed my lunch and we'd argue about linguistics, the thwarted philosophy of higher education, whatever.

"Delvo's a beefy woman with a tenacious, stubborn mind. I'd eat, look over my lesson plan, meet with students by appointment or drop-in, then teach all afternoon. I'd leave around six and bike home."

"What were your students like?"

"Bright. They were really bright and studious."

"And you felt challenged by the work?"

"Challenged? No. I expected to be teaching graduate-level courses after my first year. Instead I taught second-year Latin term after term."

"Why the discrepancy?"

"Lack of money is the official version."

"What did you enjoy most about teaching?"

"Recitation—that chorus of voices running declensions. It was like the sound of God."

"Do you believe in God?"

"Of course not."

She looks at me a long moment before adding a note to her journal. I imagine her penmanship to be old-world and remarkable, the way grandmothers scribe. The light in the room pierces whatever I look at, spotting and blurring objects.

"You applied for the teaching position by phone from Ireland, is that right?"

"Yes."

"That's quite a transition."

"It was time."

"You weren't happy in Ireland?"

"Who can say?"

73

"You can. Your own happiness is subjective, isn't it?"

"Often. Often I felt happy."

"So you left because teaching at U.H. was a better opportunity for you?"

"Better, different … I wanted to come home."

"You grew up on Oahu?"

"I wanted to come home to Hawaii."

"You were more forthcoming during our first meeting."

"The morphine probably helped."

She looks at her pen, then back at me. Do they make cinnamon incense, or cinnamon perfume? What am I talking about? Hadn't they stopped giving me morphine several days ago? No, they'd lowered the dose. Too low. I'd said the dose was too low.

"What happened in Ireland?" she asks.

"The inevitable divorce."

"Your marriage ended?"

"Figuratively."

"So the relationship ended."

"Yes, all of them."

Dr. Mya stares at me. What does she see? Injuries? Does she see beyond the casts and IV to the scars on my back? Would my mother have liked her? Would my mother have liked any of them?

"How many sexual relationships have you had as an adult?"

"I have no idea."

"Think about the question."

I shake my head, not sure how to start the calculation.

"*Relationship* seems out of context."

"Why?"

"Sometimes sex isn't that complicated."

"Do you believe that statement?"

"I want to believe it. Let's say it's the hypothesis I've tried to prove."

"Have you found proof?"

"Not definitive proof. No."

"How many sexual partners have you had?"

"Around forty, probably."

"Would you say that your sexual relationships have been complicated?"

"Yes, but not always for me."

She nods. How have we digressed to this? Does anyone have uncomplicated sexual relationships? Is she trying to confuse me? Who wears powder-blue power suits anyway? She seems very suburban housewife suddenly in this cinnamon-infused pen—very Girl Scout leader—as she sits, ankles crossed, making notes in her immaculate hand.

"Are you currently in a relationship?"

"I don't remember."

"What's the last thing you remember?"

"I'm tired."

The room swims around us and her voice struggles toward me through the water. I can see the disturbance. Then the room isn't flooded, but hollow and girded like a mineshaft. From across these landscapes, I hear her and the panic vanishes.

"What's the last relationship you remember?"

"The surfboard heir."

X.

Emily and I sat on the shaded hill overlooking Kailua beach, eating shave ice with azuki beans and a scoop of ice cream, watching the windsurfers. I'd tried windsurfing once in junior high. Cursed with featherweight arms, I found the whole experience severe water torture—a casual drowning—completely removed from the elegant skirt of the five sailors skimming across the water this afternoon.

We'd spent the morning playing beach volleyball with a group of Marines who kept reciting Beastie Boys' lyrics with a Pentacostal fervor that evoked the disturbing image of SS Troopers as they nailed the ball in short unfocused strokes. They took turns flirting with us: fingering Emily's bellyring, running down any ball I set, supplying iced beer between games. Emily indulged them with more kindness than she usually showed the casual groper: military guys were a staple of the Spark; sailors descended on the place twice a month, cash-fisted, sporting drinks for any local girl who gave them a glance if they couldn't keep time with the polished legs of the owner/manager. Besides, we had to humor them; the net was theirs.

Most Sundays, we drove the lonely sprawl of the Likelike Highway to the unlikely haven of the windward side: water rippled by the constant breeze, palm trees stooped and overburdened; Kailua beach was fairly shallow, often windy, and sometimes reeked of sewage, but the silence of the beach—away from North Shore crowds and Waikiki tourist droves—went far to recommend it. It might have been a beach on a different island, more like Maui than Oahu, cottages tucked into narrow neighborhoods, mango trees behind ramshackle wooden fences, sand on the streets.

Two dogs ran loose along the shoreline below us, charging the water to retrieve the tennis ball their owner tossed into the waves. We wore sweatshirts over our bikini tops, and I was wishing I'd brought socks. Emily kept resting her head against my shoulder. Her skin smelled of calendula.

"I saw a shark once while I was surfing," I told her.

"Seriously?"

"Yeah, I'd skipped school and been out all morning, catching one sweet swell after another. I was paddling out when I saw it: this dark silhouette in the crest of the wave breaking maybe five meters beyond me. This sleek, shimmering shape skimming through the water and I just freaked. I flipped my board and paddled madly for the shore. The next hour I spent running up and down the beach looking for it, but it had vanished."

"Jesus. That's crazy. Were there any attacks that year?"

"No, lucky for me. Since I'd cut school, I couldn't report that I'd seen a fucking tiger shark at the beach. Imagine the guilt if someone had been attacked out there."

"Are you going home for Christmas break?" Emily asked.

I'd been back in Hawaii since May and had yet to visit my father and Therese. Somehow the summer had gotten away from me, and I couldn't decide if I should make the trip for Thanksgiving or Christmas. A hop to Maui wouldn't take an hour and was fairly inexpensive, so time and money weren't the obstacles. I didn't want to think about the obstacles.

"I don't know. I'm still kicking it around. You going to Paris?"

"Nah. I went last year. I thought about visiting Charlie, but he's working Christmas and Christmas Eve—which is utterly lame—so I guess I'll just hang here."

I looked her over. She'd finished her shave ice and crumpled the paper cone in her hands, rolling it between her palms like Play-doh. I'd never considered inviting Emily to spend Christmas in Maui—I wasn't even certain what such an invitation between us would mean. But, as we watched the dogs hurl themselves into the surf after their ball, there was no question that she wanted me to ask her.

I had never told Emily about my mother's car wreck. Shouldn't it have been easier to confide in a girl who knew what it was like to lose a parent when you were still a child? She was so nonchalant about her father's death; no, not nonchalant, but resigned, accepting. I raged against my mother still and the feral core of me fought to hold those things I could remember, to safeguard them in the same silence my father practiced.

One of the dogs, a black lab, swam way out to catch a ball the owner had over-thrown. She pawed the water smoothly, riding over each crest, swimming at a diagonal. My favorite stories of my mother's were dog stories. The protagonist was always the same character, Misha, the Great Pyrenees, who had been a powerful, benevolent king until a treacherous sorcerer transformed him into a dog.

Misha was very lonely as a dog and decided to create a companion. He journeyed for several months to the clay pools and, once there, began to roll the clay into shapes— a circle for the head, long cylinders for the legs, a round-edged rectangle for the torso—until he had created the form of a woman. Every day, he lay on the clay form of the woman, allowing his shaggy body to warm the clay until one morning he was roused from sleep by the sound of a heartbeat deep in the clay chest.

For six more months he lay on the body, as vital organs took shape inside her, the clay lightening into dermis around a core of bones; delicate features formed in the malleable circle as strands of hair began to bloom and creep

78

along the curve of her head like vines. At last, one morning, Misha felt the body stir beneath him and stood quickly as her eyes opened for the first time. She drew her hand over her face, to shield out the sun, and rolled onto her side. When he saw that she shivered, Misha lay beside her until she clutched the fur of his coat tightly against her, straining for warmth. He could hear murmurs; she was singing.

Every day she grew stronger, the skin more defined around her body, the hair longer and more buoyant. Her body was a lighter brown now, both her hair and eyes were brown as well, and she moved slowly as though her body retained the texture of clay. Misha slept beside her each night as a companion, as a guardian; he was content for the first time since the sorcerer had placed the curse upon him.

But the sorcerer was never content. He had often watched Misha, and reveled in the old king's suffering. Whenever possible, the sorcerer would spark a wind storm or a deluge, anything to remind Misha that he was a defenseless dog without subjects or throne. For months, the sorcerer had monitored the clay woman's birth closely, awaiting his opportunity to torment the old king. One night, after shrouding his arrival in thunder, the sorcerer cast a sleeping spell on Misha, and then kidnapped the woman.

Misha awoke many days later and panicked when he found himself alone. The air thick with her scent, Misha ran to the clay pools and up the cliffs and along the pathways through the forest, searching for her. Though he came upon many bones, he found that none belonged to her, and to avoid the confusion of coming upon the same bones over and over, he buried the bones deep in the earth and continued to hunt for his companion. He hunts for her still.

"Where'd you go?"

I felt Emily's hand on my leg and looked over at her. I wasn't crying. The wind had blown sand in my eyes.

79

"It's getting cold. Let's get out of here."

She watched me a second, then we both hurried to the car.

On the drive back to town, I watched her shift gears—her fingers long as spider's legs, thin and practiced in the cupped stroke that propelled her along a swell. Emily reminded me of an anime character: her large brown eyes evoking concern and defiance simultaneously. Somehow, her lean jaguar body managed the contradictory postures of tense stillness so that she never seemed to be at rest.

Emily and I didn't have a comfortable friendship. None of the easiness Grey and I shared existed with Emily. Instead, there was a palpable friction—sexual and tense—a flint between us always, ready to spark.

On Tuesday night, Emily took me to catch a funky band at Anna Banana's. Inside, the club was composed entirely of light-colored wood like a country lodge and seemed coated in a dim yellow light. We entered the heavy double doors to the African beat of drums and footfalls syncopated wildly; half Latin, half Congo and burning through us like fever.

The crowd was twenty-something locals, mostly surfers, and the bartender generous with her shots. On the stage, a twelve-piece band wailed while this fragile, nose-ringed, dreadlocked hippie chick danced just to the right of the main stage. After a long drum solo, she came to the fore and hurled some crazy jazz vocal, stretching her vowels just to the last thread of holding. The crowd held her groove as a tangible surge gripped all of us, our bodies shuddering, bouncing, gleaming on the dance floor like a fresh catch of rainbow trout tossed into the bottom of a boat. We danced until we couldn't breathe—the taste of blood in our throats.

"This chick is mad, yeah?" Emily said.

"Do you know her?"

"Yeah, she was in an art history class I took at U.H. my last year. Her name's Selene."

Emily took a swig of Heineken and grinned. A line of sweat slipped the length of her jaw line and she smothered it absently with the base of her beer bottle.

"What?" I asked.

"I always wanted to fuck her."

I watched the woman on stage more closely then, her mocha skin and china doll eyes. Her chiseled ab muscles flexed when she riffed. Her body petite and agile like a gymnast, a mischievous impulse curling the corner of her mouth as she bit into the microphone, or cast it behind her head to throb with the bass drum. Sex was thick in the sweat-clouded air, in her voice, on the hum of dance floor, and I looked over at Emily to find that she was looking at me. What follows is all potential.

XI.

All of the striped pool balls herded like zebra to the middle of the table, resisting my cockeyed efforts to insert them into any of the pockets, scowling at me with their black-numbered faces. We were keeping time at Grey's on a rainy Saturday night in December while Emily worked at the Spark; Grey shooting pool and me trying to keep the cue ball on the table. We'd been debating dancing at Anna Banana's or checking out some live local music at Duke's, even catching a movie, but our inertia had so overpowered us that I was actually holding a pool stick (crookedly, but still) with intent.

Grey's run of the table didn't help my filthy mood: I'd missed Thanksgiving at the orchard, waited to the last conceivable moment to tell my father I couldn't come, tempered his holiday voice with disappointment. Throughout the fall, I'd rationalized that my classes were sucking all my energy, that I had not a fucking joule to spare and needed the long Thanksgiving weekend strictly for recuperation. My father would understand. We could spend the entire Christmas break together and I wouldn't have to grade papers or worry about student conferences since a new semester wouldn't begin until the second week of January. We'd have the highest quality of time together over Christmas break.

In fact, Dr. Adams had invited me to have Thanksgiving at her home with an intimate group of friends and colleagues.

Flattered and swollen as a puffer fish, I had accepted, convinced I might finally breach the inner academic circle. This was the road to teaching graduate-level courses, to tenure. I attended the event in a conservative black dress, sporting a moist batch of pumpkin brownies and an excellent bottle of Bordeaux. During dinner we discussed the role of myth in art; the corruption of the American psyche through institutionalized religion; the hapless mania of the Goth movement; the notable differences in the European (Irish) notion of education versus the American (Hawaiian) one. I had ached to discuss meaningful, beautiful things with a room full of intellectuals, I had expected the sort of inspired exchange I had with Delvo, amplified to a terrific degree, but something false spoiled the evening. Some reserve or artifice that I couldn't seem to break through in the other guests: there was no brightness to the discussions—the evening had devolved into a rant against bureaucrats and administrators—and I found myself craving the solitude of the trees and the lull of my mother's story voice.

As we gathered before the fireplace, clutching our cognac, Dr. Adams asked me for the second time that evening how I'd settled in. I must have looked blank or even despondent since she soon asked whether or not I was quite well. Later that night as I'd walked home, I felt nothing more purely than my own cowardice. What a rotten bastard of a daughter I'd become.

With a sharp tap, another solid ball fell into the leather net of the pocket.

"This is lame, Grey."

"What do you want to do?"

"Don't start that again."

"Jesus, Janie. What's with you tonight?"

"I'm such an asshole."

"Yeah, but what's with you tonight?"

He grinned at me, his head cocked, brown curls deliber-

83

ately unruly around his tanned face. Too beautiful to be upsetting, that was his great advantage.

"I should have made a trip home for Thanksgiving."

I set my pool cue against the back of the couch, grabbed a beer, and crashed in the leather recliner facing the colossal wall-sized television. Grey's romper room was a teen-aged boy's wet dream: fully stocked bar, Godzilla television and speaker system, laser disc, pool table, table tennis, leather couch and recliners, and Playstation with racing and sports games. A sort of cultural haven.

"So you'll go for Christmas."

He grabbed his beer and sat opposite me in the couch, his bare feet stretched across the coffee table; his toes hairy as a hobbit's. I nodded at him.

"I don't get it, Janie. What's the problem?"

"It's just, you know, I'm thinking I should have gone back for Thanksgiving or even for the summer. I haven't been back in nine years."

"Yeah, so another few weeks won't matter. You'll go back for Christmas instead. Where's the problem?"

"No, it's just—Jesus, I don't know. I don't know."

He took a long swig, watching me as he drank. He set the bottle on the table and crossed to the recliner. Straddling me, he pinned my arms to my side, reclining both of us backwards.

"What if I came with you?"

"To Maui?"

"Yeah, I'll come for the weekend. Hell, if I enjoy Maui, I'll come back the next weekend too."

"You've never been to Maui?"

"I've been up Hana before, but never to the country. It'll be fun. My wife's going to Boston to her sister's place, but I vetoed that fucking idea. Let me come to Maui with you. You don't want to worry about me all alone at Christmas with nothing to do."

I gestured to his television, the Playstation games, laser discs, bookshelves of CDs. Sure, nothing to do.

"What about Emily?"

"Well, we can't fucking leave her; she'll come with, of course. Come on, say yes, say it's the perfect idea."

He massaged my shoulders in his massive hands, pressing into my neck. Why not take both of them to Maui?

"I can't believe I'm considering this. I'm such a coward."

"What's to consider? We'll have a blast, unless your dad's antisocial or something."

Not antisocial. No, but my dread had lessened the moment Grey offered to accompany me. I was afraid to go home. I was afraid of all that I'd left.

"You'd really go? What if you hate it?"

"I hate it and I only have to get through the weekend. No trauma. This is perfect."

His knees rested against my hips. Relaxing his grip on my shoulders, he stretched his hands behind me and rubbed my lower back. Clearly pleased with himself, he grinned— his thin lips stretching across his face ghoulishly, his seal eyes wide with excitement. He was such a boy—such a child in his endless capacity for pleasure.

"This is perfect," he said again.

I leaned forward and pressed the top of my head into the curve of his chest. For a moment, I'd felt an impulse to kiss him, but it had passed. Suddenly I knew exactly what I wanted to do with my evening.

"Eight Fat," I sat up and looked right at him.

Grey's eyes sparked again.

"Karaoke, yes, brilliant. We'll get good and drunk, belt out the disco hits."

I called Emily from Eight Fat Fat Eight, a downtown bar with killer chicken and poké, multiple dartboards, and decades' worth of karaoke music. Grey was singing *Me and Bobby McGee* when I closed the phone booth and dialed the Spark. It was a while before Emily came to the phone. I'd gone back to our table, refilled my glass from our third pitcher, and still made it back before I heard her asking hello.

"We have a plan."

"Yeah?" She sounded impatient.

"Good night at the Spark?"

"It's mad here. What's the plan?"

Definitely impatient; now was not the time to tell her about the trip to Maui.

"Grey wants both of you guys to come to Maui for Christmas—all three of us."

I was yelling into the phone: the plan too thrilling to relate in a normal tone of voice.

"Ryan wants us to come?"

"Yeah. It was his idea. Perfect, yeah?"

Something wasn't right. I wasn't telling this right. There was a long silence on her end; no joyful yelling.

"Emily?"

"I can't talk about this now."

"Why don't you leave the Spark early and meet us at Eight Fat. Grey's doing *Blue Bayou* right now. The crowd's—"

"I'm busy here."

"Yeah. I just wanted to tell you the plan—"

The phone went silent and my vision had become alarmingly blurred. Concentrating on returning the phone to the cradle, I tried to figure out what had happened. She must not have understood the plan. I hadn't explained right.

I went back to the booth to wade out the blur; Grey was singing some fucking John Denver song. Holy Jesus, the guy had lungs. I wanted to call the Spark again and explain. I wanted to lie down on the booth or under the booth even.

86

Lie down on the nice cool floor and listen to Grey belt the commune classics.

Grey made me drink two full glasses of iced water before we left. When he dropped me off at home, I washed the film of tobacco from my hair and skin, sober enough to realize what Emily was pissed about, but not sober enough to come up with a solution. Maybe she wouldn't come to the studio anyway. I pulled the futon out, determined to watch for a light in the main house.

The next morning, I woke with an ax in my forehead.

Halfway through a pot of coffee a couple of hours later, the day looked like it might come off after all. The front door opened and Emily stood on the threshold.

"Coffee?" I asked.

She shook her head.

"Coming in?"

She didn't move.

I stood up and walked toward her. She wasn't looking at me. She wasn't coming inside.

"Look, about last night, I'm sorry. I didn't mean to make it sound like I didn't want you to come. Of course I want you to come. I wanted to ask before. That day at Kailua, I wanted to ask about Christmas, and then … I just didn't know how."

"You didn't know how to ask? What the fuck, honey, you had all night to come up with a better excuse than that."

"It wasn't exactly a productive night."

"Really? But that's when *Grey* dreamed up this *fabulous plan,* right? So the night wasn't completely unfertile."

Her voice had turned nasty. She bared her teeth at me, her muscles tensed, her face contorted with anger. I moved backwards into the studio. Not *High Noon,* for Christ sake; I was in recovery. I sat down at the table and looked up at her. She was finally making eye contact—the full fierce stare.

Weren't we dancing around the obvious? Emily knew exactly why I hadn't invited her myself, and now she was trying to force me into the most pitiful role of all pathetic clichés: the desperately unrequited. Irritation crushed the last of my hangover like a cigarette; I stood up and crossed to her again.

"Let's talk about why you're really upset."

"We *are* talking about why I'm upset."

"Bullshit. You know I want you to come to Maui."

Something in her glare quavered for a moment, but she held. We were really going to do this? I rubbed my forehead with my hand, my final stall tactic. Fine, we could both suffer.

"You know I want you to come to Maui."

"I know Ryan wants me to."

"Oh, for fuck's sake. I didn't know what it would mean to ask you. I don't know what the hell's going on between us. You know exactly what I want, so spare me the fucking stage production. If you want me just say so, and if you don't, quit bitching about not being asked first, like some goddam grade schooler."

I walked into the kitchen to refill my coffee cup. My hands were trembling, temper burning through my head until even my hair hurt. She didn't say anything, though I could feel her body in the room as acutely as one predator senses another in the darkness. Amped up, I'd made the very speech I'd dreaded for months to the very girl I'd tried to protect; the adrenaline left me shaky and sick. I wanted to kick Grey right in the sack. Behind me, the door closed with a sucking sound like quicksand.

I thought I'd run mad if I stayed in the studio, so I biked to Honolulu Zoo. The monkeys were extremely soothing. Monkeys had stress figured out: you're pissed, you scream; you're irate, you smack something/someone; you're happy, you hang upside down from your jungle bars. It was a hazy day and the zoo was packed with hyper kids in various states of stickiness dragging their parents along the pathways from the tiger exhibit to the reptile house. Most of the exhibits hosted invisible animals, but just walking through the zoo seemed to settle me. No one would have to endure awkward silences or embarrassingly unrequited and torturous declarations of feeling. The solution was really that simple: I would move.

That evening, the sky broke and I biked home, pelted with rain. I opened all the windows in the studio to avoid that musty, enclosed smell of mildew. The air was cool, but I slipped sweats on and lay in the hammock, cradled in the overhang. It would be a shame to leave the garden. The hammock rocked in time with the rain.

The hammock quaked as she climbed in, nearly toppling both of us. She smelled of cigarettes and gin. I felt her hair against my face, and reached through the dark to brush it back over her shoulders.

"What time is it?"

"Almost three. Sorry I woke you."

She lay on her side, pressed against me in the casual collapse of the hammock. Remembering the morning, I stiffened involuntarily, dropped my hands to my sides, tried to fathom whether or not she might be an apparition.

The hammock settled with our weight; I felt her breathing against my cheek, her chest expanding into my body almost as quickly as mine expanded into the night. Without speaking, she reached up and smoothed my hair back from my forehead. Her fingers traced my face, softly around my eyes, down my jaw line, lingering on my lips so long that I wanted to open my mouth. And something in me ached.

Her fingers smelled of nicotine. She moved over me and I felt her hair in my face again. This time, I couldn't bring myself to sweep it against her. Would movement shatter the vision? Her fingertips were light and warm. In my head the child's rhyme played: going on a treasure hunt, x marks the spot; spider's crawling up your back; blood rushing down. The air cold against my skin, I stifled the impulse to seize against her in the headlong rush of a wave against reef. In the garden, tree branches groaned.

As her mouth opened against mine, I shuddered the way a child does before sobbing. The taste of gin sudden and sweet; what I felt most deeply was pure hunger and went on kissing her, my fingers slipping the length of her spine, pulling her on top of me. We tumbled from the hammock onto the ground. All that was depraved and weak in me tangled my fist through her hair—this gazelle whose heart fluttered against my chest—pulled her head back, and bit into her throat. I wanted to get beneath the liquor and cigarettes to taste the salt. I wanted sea and blood. Desire slipped into something feral and terrifying that rolled over us until we tore at each other like leopards. Emily cried out and begged me to fuck her.

XII

Since I had seen the house last, my father had completely remodeled, led by an impulse I couldn't even begin to fathom, to update the bathrooms with modern tile; shiny new faucets and knobs in glimmering silver sat inside cream-colored porcelain sinks; the mirrors and modern art (drawings and watercolors) were new; the paint fresh and warm; carpet upstairs in the bedrooms and down the hallways had been removed and the wood floors refinished so that the house seemed young, shiny, and completely alien to my memories. How long can you live in a coffin, my rational self asked. How long can you remain static?

There were skylights in all the upstairs' rooms and the light shone through with importance. My father walked us through the house and motioned to the improvements, watching for my reaction, gauging my response. Is it all right that I've changed the house? Is it all right that we are not as you left us? I wanted to hold onto him in the new rooms, to assure myself that his heartbeat was unaltered, that his smell was still lavender soap and earth. Why had I expected to find him the same? Why hadn't I hoped that he, too, would have grown?

"It's beautiful," Emily said once we'd settled again in the kitchen.

The cabinets and counter tops were new—the colors now oak and sage respectively—and a bay window had been added to look onto the orchards from the kitchen table. Light had changed the feature of the place, and this man, this thinning-haired man whose blue eyes were etched by crow's feet, his cheeks softened by lines and tiny red flecks like urgent freckles. He had lost weight and held himself less like a rod and more like a tree—he looked stronger in his age than the father I remembered.

"It's just amazing," Grey agreed. "I hadn't expected anything so modern. I guess I'd pictured a farm rather than an orchard. I mean, this place goes on for acres."

Toby, the old shepherd, was settled at Grey's feet, his muzzle white, his sanguine temperament now calmed toward comatose. He had licked our hands when we came to the door and returned to his bed in the kitchen while we toured the house. In an extreme and heroic effort, he'd stood, walked four steps, and collapsed against Grey's boots when we resettled in the kitchen. I could hear the short push of his breathing.

I watched my father move around the kitchen, arranging wine glasses on a tray with a plate of cheese and crackers. As far as I remembered, we had rarely entertained. A couple of potluck dinners after harvest, but then the wives of his men had done most of the work, letting me watch over the drinks while they prepared the table and the dishes; cleaning everything afterward while I collected the garbage and put the bottles in recycling.

He wouldn't let me help him now, and cradled a bottle of wine in his arm as he balanced the tray to the table. When he sat down, his eyes never having left me, he uncorked the bottle and remarked, "Still so thin."

Grey and Emily grinned, ready to join the game:

"I told her she'd never have to worry about sharks while we're surfing."

"Ever seen a shark attack a stick?"

(Laughter.)

92

"We had to tie her to one of those kid ropes when we went up to Pali Lookout."

"Yeah and then weight the rope."

(Much laughter.)

"Jane won't ever get locked out of the house."

"She can drop through the mail slot."

"She can slide right under the front door."

It was their standard shtick, and my father was enjoying it as much as they were.

"You know, they wouldn't let her give blood."

"Well, you have to weigh at least ninety-five pounds."

"When she was a child," my father said, "the school nurse would send home sealed letters that Janie was entrusted to deliver. The envelopes each had twenty pieces of folded paper inside. The first sheet always had one question: Are you feeding this child? And the rest were blank. After a couple of months of this, I asked Janie why the nurse was sending her home with nineteen blank sheets of paper."

Here he paused; Emily and Grey fidgeted with anticipation—practically vibrating off their chairs for the punch line. He brought it home:

"So Janie tells me, 'The nurse was worried a breeze would carry me away without the extra weight.'"

(Decades of laughter.)

I smiled with them in an exasperated way so as not to encourage the routine past all forbearance. These were old jokes to a thin girl. I'd had boys pinch my legs all my life, asking how I could hold myself up on those slivers. Stork-girl, bone, heroin-baby, waif, I'd heard every thin joke. When I turned sideways, did I disappear? Was I strong enough to lift a fork to my mouth?

My father's eyes were bright again in the folds of his wrinkles. His brown hair cropped close to his skull and sprinkled with gray like shards of glass suddenly in the sand. He patted my hand good-naturedly and shook his head. I was a good sport, his look said. I had always been a good sport. His accent was ever slighter, so that the Australian lilt curled the ends of his speech and seemed to slip away in the middle of his sentences. He was still handsome, though, beautiful and old.

"You're a good girl, my Jane. And I'm glad to have you home."

I hadn't spoken since we'd arrived. Emily and Grey had introduced themselves as the new house, the new father, overcame me. I rested my hand inside his hand and smiled. I thought if I opened my mouth, I might weep.

"Would you believe Therese is fifty now, Janie?"

On the flight from Oahu, in my best shorthand, I'd told Grey and Emily that Therese had helped raise me.

"Therese," my father explained now to Emily and Grey, "has lived here since before Janie was born. She's become middle-aged while Toby and I have grown old. She's driven into town to buy food for supper. Expect something lavish; the grill's going."

"Jane told us you taught her to surf, Mr. Elliot."

"Please call me Caleb."

"Caleb," Emily tested his name in her mouth and grinned. "You taught Jane to surf?"

"She used to wake me every morning before dawn and we'd drive down to the beach to longboard. You should have seen her, tiny little arms like jackknives shooting her through the water: absolutely fearless. One summer, then she was just a seal out there—sleek and wild."

"And fast," Emily said. "Jesus she's fast. When she first moved to Oahu, she was going on and on about how she'd been away for so long and it would take her months to get back into shape and oh my god, the drama! So we're out there the first day and she's up on the second wave—I can't even keep up with her—she's cutting into the crest, skimming along the barrel, one-legged, throwing shakas, dancing hula up and down the length of the board ..."

They all laughed and this time I joined them, my stomach knots loosening as they all talked me down. Sensing somehow this was too much for me, Emily and Grey had taken the pressure off; they were blocking for me, letting me bide my time, hang back, watch the field.

We talked in the kitchen as the slant of light receded slowly through the length of the room and Toby kept time with the insistence of his sleep. Therese kicked the door open at nearly six o'clock, her arms full of groceries, and more in the truckbed. Emily, Grey, and Dad ran out to grab the rest while Therese pounced on me like a pitbull. She was Filipino, a compact, exceptionally strong woman with cropped hair and deep-set, searching black eyes. She wore a denim skirt, doubtless for company, and a button-down lilac linen shirt with her standard blue T & C slippers. She didn't look anything like fifty.

"Doesn't anybody feed you, girl? My god, you're the same stick as always. Now you've got some crazy hair too. You dyed your hair blue? You're some kind of grudge character?"

"I think you mean grunge."

"Oh, grunge. Grunge is even worse. You're one of those grunge characters with the piercings and the tattoos and the black-sack clothes and hair that's never washed?"

She felt my face as though I might be hiding piercings, brushed at my hair in a hopeless effort to tame it, and smiled up at me.

"You're thinking of Emily, Therese. She's got a bellyring and everything. She's with the cause. She's warring against the man."

Therese had turned her sharp, accusing eyes toward the door as Emily entered. She spotted Emily's bellyring and let go of me. In honor of meeting my father, Emily's croptop fell just below her ribs and her sarong came down nearly to

95

her knees; she was virtually twice clothed. Therese eyed her carefully.

"No, this one's a hippie."

Emily laughed, set the grocery bags on the counter, and shook Therese's proffered hand.

"And what do you think of my little girl?" Therese asked as she wound her arm around my waist.

Emily put her hands over my ears and whispered: "I think she could use a lot of help."

"Did you help dye her hair blue?"

"They're henna highlights; they were supposed to lighten her hair."

"God, you are a hippie. Nuevo hippies, I can't believe it."

"It's not really blue, Therese, it's just a blue glow around my temples. It was supposed to be an auburn highlight."

"Auburn highlight on black hair? There's the first flaw in your logic, girls. When does it come out?"

"Oh, it's almost out now. You should have seen it two weeks ago."

She didn't look convinced. Two weeks previously, the top of my head had been the color of the cookie monster, much to the amusement of my students, who had taken to calling me Post-Punk. Now the black was reclaiming my scalp.

"You have to eat more. Eat more and no more blue hair. Your father will grill steaks and oysters. There's rice in the cooker and you two can help make the fruit salad, yeah?"

Fresh mangoes, starfruit, papaya, grapes, and kiwi were sliced and sprinkled with cinnamon to make salad, the acid burning our fingers as we sucked the mango seed for fruit we couldn't reach with a knife. Ripe orchard fruit tasted bolder and sharper than any other fruit I'd ever known; I was high with the burn in my throat, the tangy flare of each bite, holding the starfruit and mango in my mouth like a child to prolong the delight.

That evening, we sat for hours, drinking wine and gorging ourselves on oysters with sliced jalapenos doused in shoyu and strips of flank steak. My father brought out the whiskey and brandy as night fell into the orchard over the chirp of crickets.

Emily and Grey cleared the plates while I washed the dishes. At the sink Emily sidled behind me and put her arms around my waist, pressing her face into my neck. I flinched. Her hands slid loose and she withdrew.

"We're the only ones here."

I looked behind me to see a vacant kitchen—the chairs pressed neatly under the table—the surfaces all wiped and gleaming; everyone else had gone up to bed. I toweled off my hands and stretched toward her.

"Sorry. It's just weird in my childhood house, you know?"

"Yeah. I'm tired anyway."

Without looking at me, she turned and went upstairs. I hadn't told Emily and Grey about my mother's suicide. I hadn't even explained about Therese. How could I explain? Slowly, Toby stood and stretched before hobbling to the door. I followed him outside into the familiar dark.

XIII.

The five of us walked through the orchard in twilight, my feet quickly readjusted to the paths as if nine years had not passed, and my father told Grey and Emily about harvest—the urgent shift of wooden ladders and wheelbarrows along the pathways and trunks as the men plucked the fruit rapidly in a single delicate pull, and crate upon crate were loaded into trucks to be driven to Kahului for market or transport to Oahu. When I was a child, harvest had seemed painful to me; the trees overburdened with their fruit like monkeys whose young clung to their backs and bellies. As the men worked, the branches and leaves rattled and trembled until I imagined the trees fighting back the only way they knew against these deft looters.

My mother had told me that the trees in the old days were sick with dark; their bark white and shredded, their sores bled sap as their leaves fell in dark piles that covered the ground. The tender of the trees was old and ill as well, but his daughter, Sophia, was slender and green as a sapling. Alone, she roamed among the trees, tending to their wounds even as she knelt by the bed of her father, feeding him soup and mopping his brow with a wet cloth. Each day as her father became weaker so too the trees groaned and shrugged against the dark. Sophia began to despair for the trees and woke her father to ask his advice.

"The trees mimic your illness, Father. Is there no relief for either of you?"

Her father shuddered and raised himself on twiggy elbows to look at his daughter more closely. Like a vine, his white hair fell around his face, as he contemplated her question. He knew but one way.

"I am to die, my girl, but you might live forever and the trees with you."

"How might I, Father?"

"You must become like them."

"In the dark?"

"In light and dark, child. If they heal, then the world will be light and dark again, for the trees color the world."

Never to run or walk again, always to root in a single place with a single view would be hard indeed, but the dark was hard as well, and the sickness.

"I will be a tree, Father. I am not afraid."

He nodded. He had known of this day for many years.

"Help me outside, child, and we shall transform the world."

She gathered her father from the bed, his body thin as a dogwood, and they walked from the cottage into a nearby field. A brook ambled through the field, and her father told her to run along its bank and not to turn back. She hesitated a moment and then fled from his side.

She ran in the dark and let the sound of the water guide her steps beside its bank, she ran as her chest began to tighten and her skin tore apart. Her legs sank into the cold earth even as her head burst with branches, her hair shaping into leaves. Her mouth opened in one single motion of despair, swallowed in the maple trunk that enfolded her heart like a coffin.

From the cottage, her father watched her transformation until his own heart gave out and he fell in the field. Later the sun climbed the sky above the cottage; the trees had healed.

Grey and Emily were each given guest rooms and I was

in my old room, which had been re-painted, a soft Irish orange. Through the skylight, the stars pricked, and I lay on the bed, looking at the sky for hours until finally I got up and walked through the orchard again. The wind was cold enough that I shivered in spite of my jeans and sweatshirt. Though my feet guided me along the paths easily enough, the branches had changed shape and dimension so that these trees were not the trees I had left but some new beast grasping toward the sky. In my absence the orchard, the house, my father had morphed with a spirit that had eluded me. Was that what had happened? I wasn't sure. Never in my life had he talked so openly, particularly among strangers, and he and Therese shared a tenderness now that was new to my observation. Had I missed these signs at eighteen, or hadn't they existed before I went away? The house no longer ached with my mother's absence—that palpable sense of loss that had encased us as if behind glass—a dead woman filling up the world. Had I dreamed that grief? Had I mourned alone these years?

I stopped walking when I came to the mango grove; it was nearly 4:00 a.m., the sky arched above me, and I was a child again, aching to be held. From among the trees, a form emerged.

"Jane?"

"Here I am."

"It's too dark to walk out here."

"You have to keep to the path."

"Follow me, Jane."

I stood up and moved toward her. The distance between us spread. Her shape receded as though she were in danger of vanishing. I ran forward—the impression of her slid into shadow the way stars disappear at sunrise—still the distance between us grew.

"Mother?" I called. "Mother?"

"Where are you, Jane?"

I opened my eyes in a fever, someone pressed against me, in the dark room, the warm bed.

"Quiet, honey," she whispered. "You'll wake the house."

Emily held onto me, covered my eyes with her right palm, and leaned hard against me, as if to keep me rooted to the bed to the room to the planet. I was inside again, or still—I wasn't sure which—only that I was chilled and trembling against Emily's tensed body. She'd braced herself, ready for me to struggle.

I let out a breath and felt my back muscles ease. Something in my throat choked, releasing a sound like a whimper. She held me tightly and leaned hard forward until I fell back against the pillow. Rubbing her hands up and down my arms, she rested her cheek against my cheek until my breathing slowed.

I'd seen someone in the orchard. Had I been in the orchard? I shivered into the sheets, into the warmth of her body, her mouth on my throat.

"What happened?" she asked.

"I dreamt, I dreamt something horrible."

I curled into her and slept heavily, a hibernation. When I woke late the next morning, I was alone in my room and could not separate the real from the imagined in what I knew. On the nightstand, the alarm clock ticked noisily, and I climbed from bed slowly, nursing my body as though I distrusted it.

Rice sat hissing in the cooker, a font of steam rising toward the open window merging with the brilliant sunlight slanting into the room. Therese was alone in the kitchen when I came downstairs. Focused on prepping supper (bul-go-gi from the look of the meat), she started when I came up behind her.

"So you wake, sleepyhead. Thought you might stay in

bed all day like in high school, little princess. They went surfing. Ryan and your father wanted to wake you, but Emily said you'd slept badly."

I pulled a pitcher of juice from the fridge and poured a glass. Her face tight with worry, she reached out and pushed my hair back from my face.

"So you slept badly?"

I nodded. Her fingers were cold, her hand small.

"I still have insomnia. I've just learned to live with it, you know, I don't even mind anymore. But last night—"

"Last night?"

"It was something else. I was awake and asleep, dreaming these bizarre frightening things. I was outside in the orchard but I was inside with this fever. I'm not sure which."

"Nine years is a long time. Was it hard to come back?"

I looked up at her black eyes and tried to smile. Not too serious, please.

"Have I neglected you, Therese? Have I neglected you and Dad?"

"Nine years is a long time."

"The house is another place altogether. And you and Dad—"

Her ears colored and she turned back toward the counter as though to check the meat.

"Are a different couple."

She spun back toward me and met my eyes defiantly, daring me to go on.

"Aren't you?" I said, and reached my hand to her wrist.

A smile played across her face, and her shoulders relaxed.

"It means something that it doesn't bother you."

"It makes sense. I was stupid never to notice."

"There was nothing to notice before. Something happened when you left; I thought your father would never survive your absence. I wasn't sure I would. It was terrible—the emptiness of this house without you—and those first few years I don't know how we managed. You smile, but it was terrible. I'll never forget your father's face, so empty. We'd eat in the kitchen, in the dark, both of us getting old.

"Then, after we came back from your graduation, something had shifted. You'd graduated with honors; your professors loved you; you looked so glamorous with your short hair and European accent—nothing like the little girl who'd left us. We came home and attacked the house. Lifetimes we worked on this house; put everything into perspective."

"A deconstructive evolution?"

"Oh tease if you want. I took care of you—since you were little—it never occurred to me that I might love him. I loved you. That was enough while you were here."

"It seems so obvious now. I'm pleased; don't think I'm not pleased. It's just the shock of finding so much happiness here. I feel like I walked into someone else's life."

"But you allow we deserve it?"

"Of course you deserve it, Therese, both of you. Jesus Christ, am I a heartless bitch that you ask me that?"

"I'm asking your mother's daughter."

I felt crushed suddenly in the kitchen with the woman who had raised me, endured my sullenness, my temper and the bouts of silence I'd inherited from my father; that she would ask such a question for such a reason felt like betrayal. Anger growled from the pit of my belly and my fists clenched. Who was my mother's daughter that such a question could exist between Therese and me?

"Fuck this, Therese."

"I'm asking your mother's daughter."

"She answered already."

"You answered."

"We're the same person."

"No."

"We're the same fucking person, Therese."

"No."

"I am my mother's daughter."

"You're more than that, Jane. I asked you if we deserved to be happy."

"Yes, and I said *Of course.*"

"You said *Of course your father and I did.* Don't you deserve it, too?"

My face felt hot. I was so angry that my jaw ached where I clenched it. A taste in my mouth of gingersnaps, I saw myself waxing my board on the floor as Therese's bare legs moved around my periphery. I hadn't thought she meant me. I wanted to touch her face, ease the intensity of her black eyes, the strain between us that had arched instantaneously like the hackles on a dog's back.

"I didn't think about it."

"I'm asking your mother's daughter."

"Therese."

I whispered her name like a prayer. The dirt road kicked up in front, and we wound around the corner, the back wheels sliding. Driving so fast, our hair roping out the windows, I watched the retaining wall pull closer to us. Closer and closer the wall loomed, like God, and then his voice thundering metal.

"You survived, Jane. You weren't in the car with her. You survived her, and you deserve to be happy."

I didn't say anything. I wished I hadn't come. I couldn't stop my mother from dying each time like a new wound, her body pinned in the car, a malformed insect. Dust spilling through the window and mixing on the seat with the blood. I left the house and went to the orchards, sought out the mango grove, watched the myna birds hopping from branch to branch as if to test the resolve of each tree.

III

"I've been asked to tell you supper is ready."

Grey had sneaked up behind me without disturbing the birds.

"You lost the coin toss?"

"Is it as bad as that?"

He crouched in the dirt next to me, the smell of salt on his skin, his hair still wet at the nape of his neck. Somehow, Grey seemed to belong to the orchard, his body perfectly at ease among the trees, and the blue block of sky. I felt more alien for his familiarity.

"No," I answered at last. "The house is so different. It's like I don't belong here anymore."

"It's called visiting, Janie. You don't have to stay."

"Did Dad surf with you?"

"Your fucking dad was ripping it up. Jesus, so that's where you get all your speed. Em and I were tearing after him—not a prayer of catching up, man. There were eight people in the water. Can you believe that shit? Eight people! I'm moving out here."

"Yeah, it's paradise. No movie theaters, no museums, no library, one UPS drop, no shopping—"

"If I could live here, I'd do it in a moment: this orchard is a world completely removed. You don't need anything here, just tending the trees and surfing."

"Maybe that's what my folks thought too."

He waited as if I might go on. I felt his eyes moving over me, scanning for my exact meaning. He reached over and pinched my belly.

"We've got to eat, kid. You can't afford to skip any meals."

"Fuck off."

"Or we could just hang here and make out."

I stood and looked down at him, crouched in the dirt like a peasant. His teeth were startling against the practiced tan of his face, and he grinned up at me with flinted eyes. God damned Hippie Gap Model.

"I'm afraid of nuns."

"Me too," he said.

He held my hand as we walked toward the house. From the trees bulbul birds swooped and wailed.

Grey kept us laughing all through dinner, recounting his mis-adventures skating uninvited in the pools of the ultra-rich in Hawaii Kai during the early eighties.

"We wanted to be the Z-boys of Dogtown—these rene-gade characters from California—but we were just a bunch of skinny surf punks running around with fat boards we could barely maneuver, these nasty burns on our legs from repeated falls."

"Keep in mind," Emily said, "that this is the eighties and Ryan wanted long hair like everybody else."

"Right, but instead of getting longer my hair just kind of fro-ed out like John McEnroe."

"Oh god, that's horrible."

"Think Gene Wilder in the early years, but curls instead of frizz."

"So this one cop is chasing us from this anonymous house one day and he's yelling at me: *Young lady, you get over here right now.*"

"No!"

"I thought I'd never live it down, yeah, Em? People were repeating that to me in the halls at school for months."

When she spooned seconds onto my plate, Therese leaned over me and rubbed my back. A truce. We'd called a silent truce. Dad and Therese offered to drive Grey to the airport when we finished dessert.

"You two can stay behind," Therese had said, squeezing my arm. She looked over at Emily and added, "To clean up."

The kitchen still smelled sweet from the bul-go-gi mari-nade. Halfway through the dishes—my head light with whiskey—I grabbed Emily and kissed her mouth. Wresting a plate from her hand, I pushed her against the counter and went on kissing her, my wet hands in her hair, all my grief pooling inside our mouths.

"Stop," she said.

I yanked her shirt up and clutched her breast, a groan inside me deep as a lioness'.

"Honey," she said, her voice a warning: "Stop."

I dropped to my knees, and pulled at her shorts as though I didn't understand the concept of button fly. She squirmed sideways pushing my arms away.

"Stop it. Stop."

I dropped onto my back and covered my face in my hands. Was there no comfort anywhere?

"What? Jesus, what?"

"Is that why I'm here? To fuck you when the house is empty?"

"Oh god, please. I can't handle another scene today."

"I'd hate to inconvenience you."

"Jesus."

"I know we're being discreet about seeing each other. We both wanted that, but this is ridiculous. Ryan is going to find out sooner or later, and your parents know you're a lesbian."

"They aren't my parents."

"You know what I mean. Are we just having sex? Is that all we're doing?"

"We're not even doing that."

"Fuck you, Jane."

"Wait," I sat up and grabbed at her calf. "Wait."

She stopped at the foot of the staircase, refusing to look at me. I stretched my arm up to her.

"Please."

She kicked the bottom step and slapped my hand away.

"You have to give a little, honey. You have to have some confidence in me."

"I'll tell them if it'll make you happy."

"They already know—and no, I didn't say anything. This morning, Therese told me to move my bags into your room. She apologized for separating us."

Don't you deserve it, too? she'd asked me, her face strained with worry. I allow we deserve it. Even I.

"My mother died when I was fifteen. We don't talk about it. We've never talked about it. Coming home has been really complicated for me. I didn't mean to hurt you."

Anxiety, like a spent candle, extinguished from the room. She sat me on the counter in front of her and cradled into me, murmuring something unintelligible, something lost. Outside in the dark, the trees must have shimmered under the moonlight, their boughs grappling ever higher.

XIV.

Paul's face blistered whenever he spoke in class, though he looked right at me to give his answers as if determined to see the thing through properly. Not one of my students ever called me Jane, nor did they use my surname. Instead, most of them simply caught my attention by other means, then began talking, although a few would call *Miss!* if I happened to be looking down at my transparency and had not noticed the insistent wave of one of their hands. But Paul, a thin, pale young man with long dark eyelashes, and a sculpted effeminate face, always addressed me as Professor. He was the closest I ever came to having a crush on one of my students, except admiration took the place of any erotic notion: I felt a maternal pride in his quick able mind; pleased each time I graded his test to find he'd scored perfectly again; listening specifically for his voice whenever we ran declensions as if he were my gifted soprano.

"Professor," his hand raised above his forehead as if in salute, he blushed when I met his gaze. "I've been wondering—I'm not sure it's appropriate for me to question—but I've been wondering about the translation exercises."

Here he paused, glancing around the table at his nearest peers as though seeking their support to continue. I waited, curious.

"Well, it's just that more than half of these translations include some form of rape. And I've ... well, it bothers me."

He looked around the table again, then up at me, with a worried expression as if he'd been disrespectful. The rest of the students had turned from Paul and were now watching me closely, apparently sharing Paul's anxiety about an impending reprimand. I admired Paul; I was almost sorry to tell him that we have to live with our stories.

"It bothers me as well," I said. "To use primary source material is preferable whenever possible, and these myths are more interesting than financial records, but you're right to be bothered. Elements of these myths, the violence and the punishments, are often both shocking and distasteful to our modern sensibilities. It speaks to our evolution as human beings that this is true. The Latin gods, thieved from the Greeks, were frequently vindictive, selfish, amoral creatures who preyed upon the populace—sometimes at random."

I scanned the class, then met Paul's rapt gaze again: "But we study these Latin myths and poems because they give us insight into an age of great progress. Certainly they seem antiquated to us in the final years of the twentieth century, but the Romans made determined advances for their time period, not only roads and aqueducts, government and law, but in art and literature."

"You're suggesting that I'm taking these myths out of context?" he asked calmly.

"I'm suggesting that in studying language we are also studying a people, a society, a culture and it is foreign from ours in many fundamental and important ways. Should we censor myths that offend us? Remove any reference to incest, rape, torture, or murder? Should we study only the enlightened periods of history? And who would decide which periods are enlightened? I don't mean to make light of your question, Paul, it's a complex and provocative question."

He shook his head slowly: "You haven't made light of my question, Professor. I suppose I have taken them out of context. They're myths, after all."

Returning to the office after my last class, I found Delvo sitting at my desk in the dark.

"How now, Mercutio?" I greeted her.

"My dear Elliot," she said as if someone were choking her.

"What's happened?"

"I haven't any idea. I'm supposed to be at the hospital right now, waiting in a cold impersonal stock room while my sister releases her first child. But I haven't the nerve; I really haven't. I hate hospitals, Elliot. Those squeaky floors and the pajama outfits on patients and staff alike, the intercom system, the rooms full of saws and needles."

I leaned backwards against the closed door, the knob digging into my spine, and swallowed the burst of laughter that gripped at my chest and throat. Hardly visible at my desk, her profile thickened as though she'd been sketched in chalk, and her voice rasped urgently on about the unyielding cold of stethoscopes, white masks, stretched latex gloves. I'd imagined some horrible tragedy, rather than an ingrained phobia.

"Delvo, it's only a building, an institution very much like this one."

"I am not trapped in a building with gurneys and a morgue here."

I smiled in spite of myself, hoping she couldn't see my face clearly.

"Shall I go with you?"

"Oh no, no, I've quite made up my mind: I cannot go. I'll see the child when they trundle it home. Babies all look like blind mice at first anyway. No doubt there will be pictures. My brother-in-law commemorates everything."

Now I laughed heartily, masking the knock on the door behind me, so that the door opened into my back, knocking me forward into the dim room.

"Professor," said Paul. "I'm sorry."

"No worries, Paul."

He stood awkwardly in the doorway, clasping his bag in his hand as if it were a floatation device and he in grave danger of drowning. I switched on the overhead light. Delvo went on mumbling from behind my desk.

"What can I do for you?"

He cast Delvo an anxious look, then said: "I've been thinking about what you said, Professor, and I think I understand. It's like *Huckleberry Finn*. At the time it was shocking—revolutionary—to think that a black man was human with complex emotions and value. And Mark Twain wrote his argument from the perspective of an uneducated, mistreated Southern white boy, as if to say, 'If this kid can get it, then anyone can.' Now, of course, when you read *Huckleberry Finn*, you cringe through most of Huck's racist observations, but that's because the book's out of context today."

He stopped, face flushed, voice trembling and I grinned at him.

"That's exactly right, Paul. Your example is much more precise than my explanation to the class this afternoon. I'll borrow it, if you don't mind, for the next time the subject arises."

Despite his shyness, he beamed at me. "I don't think the subject will come up again. No one else seemed bothered."

"Most of them, I suspect, were just as troubled. Not everyone is brave enough to express concern to a roomful of his peers."

Still beaming, he backed out the door, stammered he'd see me in class the next afternoon, then hurried down the corridor with his bag swinging dangerously at his side.

Delvo appraised me from my desk.

"He was worried about rape in the myths."

"Ah," she said. "I tell them, just wait until we get to the histories."

"No doubt they find that comforting. Come on, Delvo, I'll buy you a drink. Can't have you camped out all night at my desk."

"Excellent," she said, climbing slowly to her feet. "Excellent. But I warn you, Elliot, any discussion of babies or hospitals is strictly prohibited."

Without any inclination to broach taboo subjects, I locked the door to the office, and we followed, like a delayed echo, Paul's footsteps down the corridor and into the night.

XV.

Sometimes I imagined myself the mistress's mistress, housed in the servants' quarters behind the mansion, the murmur of rain in the thick stalks of the banyan trees, awaiting a visitation from my lady. I never once slept with Emily in her own room. The rules for the affair were strict, implicit—we never shared them with each other—and integral to the survival of our relationship both as friends and as whatever we had morphed into.

Rule 1: No one knows. (Amendment to Rule 1: Or anyway, as few people as possible and certainly not the guy you surf with.)

Naturally, this is one of those rules that you hope, rather than expect to keep. A woman having an affair smells different, her body more resolutely sexual, more confident—a bolder laugh, a more relaxed gaze—a kinetic pulse between her lover and herself. Though some of these attributes may be interpreted as simple happiness, in the company of your lover the body confesses every secret. Ryan Grey, then, as our closest mutual friend, was our greatest liability.

Late one night in February, I hogged the couch at Grey's place, where we were watching *The Philadelphia Story*, my legs cast across his lap, feet tamping his forearm whenever he stopped massaging whichever foot I'd pressed into his palm. Begrudgingly, he jabbed his thumbs into my footpad and arch while his fingers slid along the top of my foot.

When he chose, his dexterous fingers gave a powerful soul-transforming massage, but you had to catch him in that moment between distraction and absorption to suck up every ounce of pleasure.

Concentrating on the movie—he was laughing at all the jokes, which made me love him all the more—he neglected my feet until I began to prod more insistently. Finally, after indiscriminate kicking failed, I paused the movie.

"Play the movie."

"What?"

"Play the fucking movie."

"Sorry, I didn't catch that. What was it you said you wanted?"

"Give me the remote," he said.

Since he already had my feet in his hands, it was fruitless to resist.

"Fuck that, bitch," I said. "Come and get it."

Spinning me onto my belly, he pounced on my back to prevent me from scrambling off the couch. Before I could stuff the remote down my shirt, he'd already pried it from my hands and was rewinding the film, one knee still etched into my back; I pulled the hair on his leg and pinched any skin I could touch. The couch was supple leather and it seemed possible I might inhale half of the cushion before he released me. Finally the whirr and click of the rewind stopped, and he set the remote on the table. The weight of his not inconsiderable body concentrated between my shoulders, I had decided to give.

"Can you speak?" he asked.

I couldn't. I couldn't even fucking breathe. Plotting desperately for some retaliatory kung fu master reversal of his death hold and coming up blank, I focused on not suffocating against the leather.

"Enough with the kicking. OK?"

I groaned in assent.

"We're going to watch the movie and you're going to behave. OK?"

I drooled onto the couch. He lifted off me, and I lay still, checking my reflexes for paralysis.

"Jesus, dude, you fractured my fucking neck."

"Watch the movie."

I pushed into a crouching position and massaged my neck, shrugging my shoulders backward and forward, an old boxer. My pulse as rapid in my throat and temple as hummingbird wings, I tried to catch my breath without gasping.

"Jesus."

"Watch the movie."

He started the film again, his attention immediately absorbed as Tracy and Mike ran out of frame for a moonlit swim. I felt nauseous and a little dizzy.

He watched the screen as if he weren't aware of me, though I was staring at him as defiantly as a child. His face and neck were flushed from exertion, but his breathing was normal. I had an impulse to pummel him senseless, batter his Hippie Gap Model features until I had to pull teeth from my knuckles. High on my impulse, I hurled into him, driving my knees into his gut as our heads slammed together and we both pitched off the couch onto the carpet.

Now I really couldn't breathe. Sucking air into the pinprick of my esophagus, I tried to focus my eyes on the wood grooves in the ceiling (did that wood knot really look like a leopard?) until the pounding in my head (was that my heart or my brain?) ceased. I'd found a quick fix to the fuse of my anger: self-slaughter. The plush carpet beneath me not quite plush enough, I was a rapidly deflating balloon.

"Fuck," Grey groaned.

He'd propped himself against the couch, both arms wrapped around his stomach, his head resting on his knees.

"Jesus, Janie."

Taking deep breaths like a diver, I finally rasped: "Sorry. Ten years ago when all this started, I was just kidding around."

"You don't get enough of this from Emily?"

"Enough of what?"

"A beating."

I was too tired to attempt a diversionary reply or even to explore his question further. *Did I get enough of a beating from Emily?* I let the whole scene go and settled my breathing instead. But my brain kept sneaking the question in, palming it carefully like a Rubik's Cube: why *beating*? Why had he chosen such a word? To ask these questions of oneself is to violate all rules, and I had trouble enough: Rule 1 had broken; Grey knew.

Rule 2: Live present tense.

Affairs do not exist in future tense. *We, someday, promise, together* are abstractions—vague and unsteady—not to be applied to affairs, and you must keep alert despite happiness, sexual fulfillment, emotional connection and compatibility because all pleasure is momentary. You must live like a puppy.

Present tense frees you as well from your past. Lovers deserted, places fled, the self you shed like a pair of jeans have no context here. You are a new self, a present self, a self without history or complication, existing in the simple light of your own presentation. Do not complicate present tense by telling lies—you never went to medical school or worked for the Peace Corps—you withhold the past and stall the future to exist in the now with the lover you desire beyond all reason, temptation, or sacrifice. This is present tense.

So I don't tell about the dentist from Belfast whose family wanted so much to love me, or the years I submerged myself in her skin with every intention of adapting to the conditions. I don't tell about Rita from Chicago with her red, red hair and the black boots that reached her knees. How her mouth was perfectly shaped, the bottom lip with its single devastating freckle. Their hair in my hands, their bodies as different as stories and how they sculpted me even as the men did—how many times have I been reconstructed?

I don't tell Emily about my mother's orange Camaro because that daughter is not this girl with her tongue testing the resolve of a bellyring. These hands on the broad, speckled shoulders, brushing back her soft hair, resting in the pool of her collarbones, these hands belong to a different girl entirely. And I sift my fingertips across the scar beside Emily's eye to remind myself that she is delicate, that the story of her hipbones is in my throat like the memory of flavor—that spring in seventh grade when I first tasted honeysuckle—that to exist in present tense I must be a girl without a suicide mother because this woman who has not yet said our affair will never be anything more will say that our affair will never be anything more and when she does, I don't want to leave more of myself than I take.

Of course, this ties directly into Rule 3: Confessions are landmines.

You see why this is, of course; if you have to retrace your steps, you might be blown to pieces. And so the most dangerous moments often follow the most blissful: lying in bed in the cool of the pre-dawn with the sheets wrapped like a python around your lover and her face tender with an expression akin to love, you must be vigilant—wary as her fingertips linger on your belly, her mouth brushing your lips.

As I climbed back into bed, the candle on the end table cast ghoulish shapes against the walls. Emily lay propped on two pillows, her hair in a brown tangle around her neck and shoulders, her brown eyes less intense in the near dark though no less cautious. I lay my head on her belly, just above the silver ring with the blue knob; her fingers ran softly through my hair, coaxing me toward hypnosis. A frog croaked outside.

"How were midterms?" she asked.

"They went well. My students all scored above eighty-four percent; Dr. Adams was pleased."

"I thought about you in class today—imagined you in front of a group of glossy-eyed kids, chanting incantations like a witch. I'll bet you blush when you teach. You do, don't you? You're so excitable."

"Am I?"

"Yes, like a kid. Do any of them have a crush on you?"

There was a girl, Judy Suzuki, a petite slender girl with shoulder-length black hair and puffy bangs, who stopped by my office a couple of times a week to chat about the translations and vocabulary lists. She had a habit of pulling her chair very close to mine and touching my shoulder like an exclamation point while we looked over whichever assignment she'd questioned. Lately, I'd developed an anxiety about being alone with her.

"They're too preoccupied to have crushes."

"Bullshit. I had a couple of serious crushes when I was at U.H., especially the German professors. I had a German professor for Greek History who would get so excited during class that he'd start writing his notes on the board in Greek and German instead of English. He had this huge white beard with no mustache and was tall and thick ... absolutely beautiful man."

"You sleep with any of your professors?"

"One. I thought it would be transcendent—seriously, that's what I was expecting. But I was really bored."

She started laughing, remembering, evidently, how

bored she'd been. I was distinctly aware that we were no longer in present tense.

"Did you ever sleep with any of your professors?"

"Yes."

Her fingers stopped brushing my hair.

"Male or female?"

I'd slept with two of my professors: a shaggy-haired poet who wore tweed jackets and carried a leather briefcase, was pompous, extremely funny, and wrote some of the most beautiful odes I'd ever read. The second professor was an actor.

"Male."

"And?"

"And what?"

"That's all you have to say?"

I stared at the candle shapes instead of answering. Confidences were no good here in the desert, where a mirage transformed easily into the oasis I wanted so desperately.

"What do you miss about Ireland?"

A girl who read aloud to me in the evenings, flawlessly, as though she'd spent the day rehearsing: the caesura just so, the dialogue exact and clear, the descriptions fluid. How the stories took shape in the air between us—all those worlds we wandered through—her voice a rope I bound myself to. Or the train, commuting from Belfast to Dublin five days a week for three years: I'd memorized the hum of each station; the reliability of town after town and the sea; the passengers one came to recognize and the lives I invented for each of them. Or the pubs with their jovial madness—always the fiddle, drum, and flute—the old people who knew a thousand stories, a million songs, and still drank Guinness though all the kids downed Budweiser (and more's the pity of it).

"The pubs."

She hit me with one of the pillows.

"Liar. You're such a liar. You vanished just now, remembering what you loved."

"Glorious redheads."

Another pillow.

"I'd say that's more likely."

I think I underestimated Emily then. I mistook her quietness for wary distance, but she might have been responding to my own terror. She might have been trying to love me. On the bed that night, she shifted so that she could look into my face, her wide eyes like wells that I wanted to drink from. She smirked at me.

"One of these days, I'm actually going to learn something about you. I hope I survive the shock."

Sessions with Dr. Mya: Day 3

Dr. Mya expelled me from our morning session, remarking that I'd wasted enough of her time for one day. She'd been questioning me about where I grew up, and my earliest memory from childhood. What that had to do with my fucking coma, she wouldn't say, although she'd speculated my past probably had more to do with my present than I could fathom. When she said I needed to find a path back into my memory, and plunged into some diatribe about childhood guilt, I became belligerent and unreasonable; anyway, that's how Dr. Mya characterized my position. I don't remember the point I was trying to make, but I know it was valid.

These headaches are ruining me. I get anxious over nothing. This morning, I couldn't get my blanket to cover my foot and I just freaked out, ranting and raging like a nasty little kid. I want Audrey to find me. I want her to sense that something has happened and seek me.

My appetite is back. I'm craving something spicy to burn through my sinuses, something like the curried dinner Audrey prepared for the Montana dykes their first night in Honolulu.

That evening, Audrey took another sip of wine and continued shredding the coconut. She'd been cooking for hours, meticulously preparing couscous, pitas, spicy tofu curry, and hummus. I'd set the table and done most of the household chores—including dusting, which I abhorred—and finally joined her for a glass of wine. Her three art buddies from grad school had flown in from Missoula earlier that day for a fortnight's vacation. They'd taken off for the beach, but were expected back within the hour.

"Should I jump in the shower?" I asked.

Audrey glanced at me and nodded. Her face glowed from working at the stove and her shirt was spattered with some greenish substance. I'd never met any of her school friends before. I took a long drink of wine.

"You should hurry," she said.

I showered quickly but stood, staring into my bag, trying to figure out what the hell I should wear in front of these Montana dykes. Khaki slacks seemed so pretentious and oddly formal—yes, I teach Latin, have I mentioned that? Surf shorts seemed too casual, too obvious.

"Babe? What are you doing in there?"

I grabbed my black tank top and threw on a pair of khaki shorts, furious with myself for letting what I wore matter to me. Audrey glanced at me when I returned to the kitchen, but she didn't say anything.

"What?"

"I didn't say anything."

"So say something."

"I can see the burns."

I looked at my wrists. The burn scars were still obvious, ridged and white like some bizarre tribal bracelet. I'd become comfortable enough lately to go topless around the house, but certainly guests deserved better than to be exposed to my scars. I carried the bowls of tangerines, raisins, shredded coconut, and peanuts to the table.

"You want me to change into a long-sleeved shirt?"

"Do what you want."

"Fine, I'll change."

Instead, the front door opened and the three of them swarmed into the room—one, a short spiky-haired girl with

123

a paunch and stunningly white teeth was already bright pink from the first afternoon—laughing loudly. They each kissed Audrey in greeting, smiled at me, and asked how they could help.

"It's finished. You guys, sit. Jane, will you bring another bottle of wine to the table?"

I brought the wine and sat between the spiky-haired girl and her partner, a thin, tall chick that didn't wear makeup or need to—her face flawlessly crafted and her recessed brown eyes expressive and quick. Hopelessly, I tried to smooth my hair. The third chick, one of Audrey's ex-girlfriends, was petite and competent-looking with shoulder-length black hair and a silver ring on each finger. Her name was Fiona. The other two were Gloria and Glenn, but I hadn't yet figured out which was which.

"So, Jane, you surf?" Fiona asked, after we'd finished loading our plates.

"Yeah, I longboard."

"Any chance you'd be into taking a newbie out sometime this week?"

"Sure. I'll take you out. We could do Queens tomorrow if you like: surf's probably about four feet or so this time of year. Just you?"

I hoped my question didn't sound as anxious as I was. I looked at the other two. Spiky-hair smiled at me and asked if I had boards for all of them.

"I'll call Grey and between the two of us, there'll be plenty of boards and instructors, too."

"Gloria, your face is totally fried," Audrey said. "Didn't you guys bring sunscreen?"

Glenn and Fiona started laughing. Spiky-hair glared at them.

"I fell asleep on the beach with my hat covering my face and *someone* thought it would be hilarious to remove my hat. No one's telling who it was."

124

My money was on Fiona. They spent the next hour charting who was dating whom, who had split from whom, and how each split had reverberated through Missoula's gay community. In an effort not to exclude me, they'd give an abridged history of any couple before detailing the drama:

"So Sammy and Trace—Sammy's brother is gay and they used his sperm to impregnate Sammy's girlfriend, Trace—have this kid right, and she's such a beautiful baby—blond, silly, a complete sweetheart—and what does Sammy do? She starts having an affair with this ski instructor from Wallace. It was so evil. Trace confronted her about it—I mean, people had seen them together—and Sammy actually denied it. Unreal. Trace finally threw her out, so now she's got to deal with raising the kid by herself."

I ate and listened, and wondered at the idea of a community where you had no private life. Apparently, everyone knew everything that happened to everyone else. It sounded like some Orwellian nightmare to me. As much as possible, I tried to obscure my wrists from view. I envisioned the three of them returning to Missoula with tales of Audrey's freaky scarred girlfriend.

Into our fourth bottle of wine, we'd moved to the couches and I lit a couple of candles around the room. Seated next to me on the couch, Glenn asked how long I'd been with Audrey. Was it months now, or years?

"I don't know, awhile."

"She was so hot at school. She was the chick everyone wanted. It's funny because she was always too driven for a relationship then. Yeah, even Fiona. That was just an affair. She seems really settled with you, though. It's amazing how different she is."

I looked at Audrey—laughing at some undoubtedly witty thing Fiona had said—her white T-shirt still stained pea green on the belly, her hair disheveled, the curls random and puffy. Her face red with wine and excitement, she appeared quite different from the pixie I'd first met. Had she settled? She smiled at me then as if she'd heard the question, but denied to answer.

These girls all seemed so comfortable in themselves and with each other. I felt my tagline streaming across my forehead: orphan, professor, bisexual, masochist, coward. Why did I seek out Nick? What perversion in me hunted the perversion in him?

The first time he'd tied such a bad knot, my wrists kept slipping loose and we'd both started laughing—the whole situation chalked as another meaningless failure. I don't know how it got away from us: how it mutated into something monstrous. I didn't blame him. Not entirely.

Audrey crossed to our couch and leaned against me. I rubbed the small of her back, until her head collapsed against my chest. Mumbling drowsily, she said she'd have to be carried to bed. Why had Audrey chosen me?

On the floor in the corner, Gloria had fallen asleep, the pink of her face illuminated by candlelight. I shuffled Audrey to bed, then returned to give the girls some extra pillows. They spread their sleeping bags on the floor and blew the candles. From the hallway, I watched Glenn tuck Gloria into her bag.

God is half altar, my mother had written, half say. Was Nick my orange Camaro, or my first razor? Audrey couldn't settle for me. I wouldn't let her. When I left, how much would I keep? Her crooked grinning sarcasm, that tough character she wore effortlessly like broken jeans, her small, calloused hands. Hadn't the feel of her name in my mouth changed me?

I'd expected Audrey to be asleep when I crawled into bed, but her hand slid along my thigh, pulling me on top of her. Her mouth tasted tangy and acidic. I lifted off her shirt, sifted my fingertips down her sternum, and rolled her to trace her spine. She shivered as I continued down her thigh,

126

brushing my nails against her skin as if to name her. As if to etch into her the end as I saw it. We both knew I was never gentle.

Later, when she moaned, I cradled her into me, memorizing the strawberry scent of her hair, the soft haven of her throat.

As Lucy waddles into the room, I know that something has altered, transmuted—broken the mystery of my case wide open. Her smashed pug face can't repress its sneer of delight as she records my temperature in my chart. No doubt she draws a little smiley face inside the degree symbol. I let her fester as I continue to stare out the window at the edge of blue building and drab condominiums my view affords.

"So," she says finally, looking down at me with a hint of triumph in her grunting pronunciation. "You've got a visitor."

I nod as though this were perfectly reasonable, expected even, a visitor after more than a month.

"Feel up to seeing this visitor?"

Ah, what a coy little ape. I stare at her and then blink twice. After a fleeting dirty look, Lucy turns away from me and toddles for the door.

"I'll send your husband in then."

She casts this sentence back like a stone and doesn't wait for my reaction, though certainly my reaction would have gratified her. *What fucking husband?* From the hallway come the murmur of voices—a rare event indeed at Kapiolani, where no one ever thinks to lower the decibel of her voice for the sleep-deprived, body-ravaged squatters hunkered in these dismal rooms—and I strain to remain detached, to continue to stare out the window as if a visiting husband were truly something ordinary.

How would Dr. Mya react to the news of a husband finally come to claim me? Her porcelain face forced to express an emotional reaction for the first time in her starched life. *A husband! Why, Jane, I misjudged your situation entirely. This changes everything.* A husband would almost be worth the opportunity to fuck with her mind.

A moment later Nick walks, unescorted, into the hospital room—his orange shirt a beacon in the fluorescent-drenched sea of white and pastel—and stands several feet from the bed before he braves the distance to lean over me. His hand grazes my neck like the blade of a knife:

"Hey, kid."

His voice, a pitcher of water tipped over my mouth. I have a vision of reckoning yanked from some black and white Western, where the hero returns like Odysseus to reclaim all that seemed forfeit. Husband. Husband. I want to believe.

"Where have you been?"

"San Francisco, then Seattle. I just arrived home this afternoon to a machine full of messages from the hospital, the police, supervisors from UPS and U.H. ... Everyone freaking in this high-pitched mayhem—it was surreal, listening to message after message. I kept waiting for the one that said this has all been a terrible mistake. If they'd called the studio instead, my secretary would have gotten word to me before."

Before: such a sad, comfortless word. He looks pale and thinner as if he has become adolescent somehow; his head shaved to a fine stubble that accentuates his nose even more dramatically and the startling green of his eyes. Sliding his hand under my neck, he looks down at me and then scans the room, taking in the obscure view, the dark television, the IV stand, and the hospital paraphernalia littered among get-well cards (from the ramp crew at UPS) before he finally lets his gaze settle on me again.

"That nurse told me you've been here over a month."

I nod.

"A coma?"

"Briefly."

"And the other injuries?"

"Splinters and breaks. I'm on the gauze and morphine treatment program."

I wave my left hand dismissively, careful not to hurl the IV stand at my husband.

"That nurse said your condition's still serious."

"She's a meth fiend."

"Yeah, she doesn't like you, either."

He brushes the hair from my forehead, his hand resting longer than necessary on my widow's peak.

"Husband?" I ask.

"My house still smells of you … the cupboards, the clothes."

Before.

"They're worried about the scars on your back and wrists. That nurse said …"

"None of this is your fault."

"Why hasn't anyone come to visit you? Why haven't they called your dad?"

"I'm OK."

"She said your injuries were so serious that—"

"Nick."

"Where the fuck is Grey?"

"In Washington, divorcing his wife."

"And Emily?"

"Paris with her mother."

"Your dad?"

"Not like this."

"Jane, this isn't like your sexual preferences, you can't keep your accident from everyone. You have broken bones, for Christ sake. This isn't a fucking government secret. Let me call your friends and family."

My friends and family. I let the idea simmer in my head

129

like a migraine: Nick phoning my scattered comrades to report the accident, my condition, my hospital status; Nick acting liaison to my recovery; Nick making everything right.

"I'm tired."

I shift lower into the bed, exorcising him from view. Dismissed, I want to tell him. I'll survive this as well. Run away to the Mainland. Let me keep what I will.

"Jane."

Calm again, he crouches beside me, fingers sifting smooth against my dry lips. I want to weep for us, for the decline of empires.

"Does it hurt?"

"The morphine, remember?"

What had it taken for him to come to this hospital room? Had it taken courage after so many months of absence? Could curiosity alone have propelled him here? Was this the same prodigal boy touching my face?

"The nurse told me they haven't given you morphine for several days now."

"Then I must have another kind of delusion."

He smiles then, almost tenderly, or maybe it is tenderness and the fluorescent lights make it difficult to recognize. Clearly I had expected him to come to the hospital, to keep my secrets and his own. What prompted this faithfulness from either of us?

A girl used to go to the edge of a cliff every day to watch hawks swirl and dive. For years, she stood and watched until even the slightest movement in their musculature became apparent to her, until she could anticipate the purpose of their movements, until she could emulate those movements. Then she jumped.

"I'll come again tomorrow, alright?"

I blink twice.

I I I

After that first evening with the Montana dykes, my mind, so purposefully resolved to liberate Audrey from the ordinary of our relationship, faltered. We had planned a trip to Maui to stay with Therese and my father for several weeks that summer. We'd agreed to chair a beach cleanup rally in September. She had more art commission projects and needed my help with supplies, logistics, supervision. We had obligations. We had this scaffold of a life girding our commitments, our habits, our sleep and waking; who would bring her tea to the studio in the evenings, steeped exactly four minutes? Who knew to buy the brand of vegetarian baked beans that did not contain gluten? How her fingers opened and closed when she dreamt, her fetish for frozen bananas, the way she whistled whenever she was nervous— I wanted more than the memory of these peculiarities, I wanted the peculiarities themselves.

Glenn and I had surfed every morning the chicks stayed at Audrey's. Eventually Gloria and Fiona had tired of the guys in canoes trying to railroad newbies into the reef that edged Queens like a picture frame. They'd opted instead to spend their mornings hiking with Audrey before testing our favorite cafés for breakfast. Glenn surprised me, she was so hardcore. Granted the waves at Queens were only four–six, but a lot of aggressive surfers competed for swells and hesitation was costly: they'd fucking mow you over if you didn't seize or vacate. Glenn blitzed: arms like rotor blades propelling her into the swell, her long legs dragged along the board's surface in a single motion, before crouching, body cocked to spring, to break the wave. Her tremendous upper-body strength seemed completely incongruous to her slender poet's frame until, several days into their visit, I'd discovered that she owned a climbing gym in Montana and was a nationally ranked climber.

In the cold outdoor shower, we blasted salt from our hair, skin, surf shorts, bikini tops, and, particularly, from our mouths. Since I didn't drive, Glenn had rented a minivan for their last week, and we dried the boards as thoroughly as possible so they could be scuttled in the van while we ate crepes with fresh mango and blueberries at Solstice Café, drinking several pitchers of water to rehydrate and counteract the six cups of coffee.

"I'm going to miss Oahu," Glenn said between mouthfuls of sliced mango.

I smiled at her, a fleeting scene of piled snow and black ice flashing through my mind. Montana seemed as foreign a concept to me as the Alaskan wilderness, and somehow the re-introduction of wolves coupled with the idea of territorial grizzly bears spoke more to the journey of Lewis and Clark than the reality of this rogue model with her achingly sculpted skeleton. Climber or no, she just didn't look like a granola girl to me.

"I'm going to miss surfing with you," I told her. "You're a natural, man. Seriously, you're fucking fearless. You scared the testosterone out of that canoe crew, and those bastards would bludgeon their own mothers."

We'd thrown long-sleeved shirts over our bikini tops, and the watermarks on our chests gave the impression of Mickey Mouse ears. Hanging with these chicks comforted me, and the longer the girls had been at the house, the more I envied their community in Missoula, in spite of bears and blizzards. In fact, I marveled at Audrey's ability to leave that community for the isolation of Oahu. She must be lonely.

"I was really worried about this trip, but I've had a great time."

"Worried how?"

She spread syrup and powdered sugar around the plate with her fork. Her nose had started peeling, but the rest of her body had tanned a brown as deep as her eyes. Solstice Café's tinted windows lent a moody shade to the yellow and blue interior. Disjointed impressionistic paintings from several local artists hung on the walls. I stared at the piece behind Glenn: in red and blue streaks, a woman appeared to be screaming, her mouth shaped like a violin, her hands dissolving into white.

"Gloria and I have been together a long time—nearly five years—and sometimes monogamy has been really challenging. Gloria had a lot of affairs before she started dating me and from her perspective monogamy is a hetero convention, you know? We live in a community of ex-girlfriends. I mean, she and Fiona used to date. She's had to redefine her perspective to stay with me. Sometimes I feel really terrible about needing a monogamous relationship—like it's a failure on my part."

"Why do you feel like it's your failure?"

"I don't know. It worries me to confine another person. Who am I to say what's right for someone else?"

"You're just saying what's right for you. That's not the same thing as confining someone else, is it? I mean, everyone has boundaries."

"I've only dated four girls since I was sixteen."

"Seriously? How is that possible?"

"See, you think I'm a freak too."

"No, not a freak, just, I mean haven't you ever had an affair?"

She shook her head, finally meeting my eyes for the first time since we'd begun this peculiar conversation. I tried to remember the last time I'd been monogamous. The dentist probably, unless letting a guy feel me up at a dance club in London counted as an affair.

"Every once in a while I'll be hanging out with someone and there's this spark, right, there's this pulse between us, but I've never acted on it. Not even during grad school when gallons of liquor eliminated all inhibitions. Honestly, I find denial much more sensual than skulking around behind my girlfriend's back."

133

She'd tucked her hair behind her ears, which were bright red, presumably from the subject matter; her fingers fluttered nervously like a startled dove.

"So, you've had the impulse before but you've denied it. Is that what you're saying?"

"Yeah. I mean, I have the impulse right now."

I felt my face go warm, my eyes widening despite my best efforts at nonchalance. She cleared her throat, her eyes darted to mine and back to her plate.

"I'm not trying to seduce you or anything; I'm just illustrating my point. To me, it's much more interesting not to have an affair. No drama, no casualties, just the ache, the friction of being with a person you're into and denying yourself the chance to experiment."

"So you're an emotional masochist."

She frowned, considering my accusation. I'd finally recovered from her sucker-punch confession and felt I'd gotten one of my own off.

"I'm not sure the denial is painful," she said finally, "but on some level, I see what you mean. Anyway, the whole reason I started blabbing on and on about this is that I worried about taking a vacation with Fiona and Gloria—there is no predicting what Fiona will do at any given moment—and seeing Audrey again was a test as well."

The waitress removed our plates and I asked her to bring us a couple of beers. Glenn raised her eyebrows, settled back in her chair, and stretched her long legs beneath the table.

"You and Audrey had sparks?"

"I always thought so. But, of course, I had a girlfriend, and … Audrey's one of those instantly fascinating people. I mean, well, obviously you know what I mean. Anyway, I've watched the two of you together and it's just so cute. You guys are so cute."

"Cute?"

The word seemed desperately out of character for both of us. Glenn's voice had pitched into a little girl singsong when she'd uttered it—*twice.*

"Yeah, she's so obviously in love with you. I just hadn't expected that. I've known Audrey for years and I've never seen her in love. That first dinner at the apartment eating tofu curry, there was this amazing sexual energy between the two of you that just crackled."

The waitress brought our beers and another pitcher of water. I tried to reconcile cute with crackling sexual energy. Clearly, Glenn had meant it as a compliment.

"You'd think," she went on, "I'd feel really staid and domestic by comparison. Instead, I feel hopeful. This trip has reinvigorated my perspective and made Fiona's choices seem more like failure than my choices. That probably sounds really petty. OK, it is really petty, but I've worried lately about becoming almost filial with Gloria, you know what I mean? That easy comfortable feeling you develop after you've been with someone for a while that may signal passion's demise. I'm not worried about that anymore."

I nodded, gulped my beer. Somehow cute had inspired hopeful, and as improbable as that seemed, I knew exactly what she meant. Raising her beer, she smiled at me.

"Anyway, it's been a good trip. Thanks."

"No worries. I've enjoyed it as well."

Maybe the woman in the painting didn't scream, maybe she sang. Glenn peeled the label from her beer, her expression absorbed in the meticulous un-sticking. I had no idea how old she was, but she seemed very young to me, her moods always so apparent on her face as if she hadn't learned to hide exactly what she thought or felt. Was it innocence? Was that what made her so appealing?

"What was Audrey like at school?" I asked.

She glanced at me and shrugged, "Same as now in a lot of ways. She lived in Missoula for about six years, didn't date much—a few affairs—but then Audrey has always been independent. She generated a lot of buzz in the community, you know? The mysterious artist is always sexy. I guess the biggest change about her is you. She was the perfect climbing partner: focused and self-reliant. We went on a few extended climbing trips and I swear we spent whole days together never exchanging more than fifty words. I always dug that about her: the stripped utility of her company.

"I've wondered about that silence thing. Sometimes she makes that a frightening weapon."

"There's nothing worse than the silent treatment. Give me a shouting match anytime, man. I can't bear neglect."

She laughed into the neck of her beer, finished the last sip. I paid the bill and followed her to the parking lot. Outside, the sun had scalded the minivan, creating dangerous weapons of door handles and seatbelts. After rolling down the windows, Glenn let the van idle, and stared at me.

"I want to ask you about something," she said, "but I don't want to spoil anything."

Concern had drawn her eyebrows together.

"Ask me."

"Your wrists," she said haltingly, "and your back. I, well, I wanted to ask about—" Her face agonized over the proper phrasing and though I felt guarded for the first time since I'd met her, I stretched my arm toward her reassuringly, trying to make the scene easier on both of us. Sleeve pulled back so she could scrutinize the lines on my left wrist, I palmed the armrest nervously with my free hand.

"Contact sports," I told her.

She didn't understand. Blushing, she rubbed my wrist with her cold fingertips as though she might find the answer in my skin—intuiting that my body had always been more forthcoming than my mind.

"I'm sorry," I told her, and was.

How to explain? Her fingertips brushed along my wrist burn, reminding me of that first night with Audrey in her lavender flat. Drowsy, intoxicated, aching—and if I lived by Glenn's rules, I'd have denied myself the slow, tempered kiss Audrey gave me, I'd have withheld myself because of Nick.

"I'm a masochist, and a while ago the situation got a little crazy. I let it get a little crazy."

And if I lived by my own rules, I'd leave Audrey soon despite holiday plans and voluntary commitments because that easy filial comfort was hard to diagnose—sometimes it wasn't bliss but death. And maybe I didn't want either.

"Before Audrey?" she asked.

"What?"

She held my wrists, not answering, and I finally deciphered her meaning. Had my injuries predated Audrey? That was really the essential question, reduced in the stove of that minivan in the little dirt parking lot on a backstreet in Manoa by a stunning climber from grizzly land.

"Yeah," I said, "long before Audrey."

XVI.

Lit with hanging lanterns, the room felt as intimate as a park in the moonlight—the sake burning through us like laughter. Our table in the bar sat alongside the koi pond and our reflections in the mirrors that lined the walls ate even as we did. Grey, Emily, and I were downtown at Aki's Sushi Bar. Outside, rain battered the pavement, rows of posh sedans, the glass-encased bus stop.

"So, next weekend," Grey said, "is my parents' fiftieth anniversary. You guys are coming, yeah?"

"Jesus, fifty years," I said.

"I know, it's crazy. I was the only kid in school, I think, whose parents hadn't split up, yeah, Em?"

"Split up or died."

"Dead is split up."

"Your wife coming?" Emily asked.

Grey stuffed a piece of eel into his mouth and chewed slowly. Emily glanced at me as she shoveled down a mouthful of fried rice. She'd pulled her hair back into a bun so tightly that it looked painful, the skin around her eyes stretched toward her ears. Forsaking the lavalava for a short black skirt and sleeveless silk shirt, she looked stunning, her brown eyes resting on me a long moment while we waited for Grey to feed us a new and utterly unreasonable excuse for his wife's absence.

"She couldn't make it," he said finally.

I drank my sake in tiny sips, the flavor not quite palatable in my mouth. I took a bite of ginger as an orange-speckled koi flicked past in the pond to my left.

"I can't imagine what it would be like if my parents had lasted fifty years," Emily said. "I don't even remember what they were like together when I was little."

"Oh yeah?" I asked. "Not even if they were happy or if they fought all the time?"

"I don't know. They didn't argue—at least, I don't remember any fighting—but I don't remember much affection either. Mom worked every night and my dad was away for months at a time. I remember their absences more than anything, their ambition. Whenever my dad left, he used to wake me the night before to tell me good-bye—to avoid delays or a scene or whatever the next morning—and this one time he forgot. Mom said I was inconsolable for weeks."

"Poor little heiress."

"Ryan, don't make this evening ugly."

"And spoil your outfit?"

"I didn't know she wasn't coming."

"No?"

"That's why I asked."

"I'm sure, Em. I'm sure you expected her to come."

"Didn't you expect her to?"

"You're such a little bitch. Don't try to make fucking innocent with me."

"Grey, calm down, man. She was just asking. Seriously, you're freaking out."

"I'm freaking out? I'm freaking?"

"Yeah … a little."

"Oh god, I'm so sorry to freak out. It's only my parents' fiftieth wedding anniversary, not an important milestone or anything for my wife to attend. It's not like the TV cameras will be there, for Christ sake. I mean, if she came, who would give the senator his blowjob?"

His voice was rising and, despite his tan, Grey's face

burned. I slouched in my chair, my chopsticks extended before my face to ward off his temper.

"Jesus, Grey."

"Oh, am I embarrassing you? I don't mean to embarrass you ladies in your Rodeo Drive outfits. This is a nice evening right, a celebration of friendship and camaraderie, so we should just kick back and drink our fucking sake."

He drank the rest of his cup and poured another. He'd spat *friendship* at us like a poison dart. Emily raised an eyebrow and watched Grey pour his drink. I drank the rest of my miso soup and observed him over the rim of my bowl: his face tight with distress, his eyes glassy as though he might cry.

I ate my sushi rolls quickly, spreading a thick coat of wasabi over yellow fin tuna, unagi, and tako rolls so that they burned my sinuses with each gulp. We'd planned a festive dinner to catch up since we'd had few occasions of late to surf; my school schedule was still wigging me out despite the fact that we were in the last half of the spring semester. Though my students were exceptional and diligent, I wanted to prove that I could teach graduate classes and was spending more time with lesson plans and student conferences than strictly necessary.

With my focus on work, I'd missed Grey's distress. It was evident now as he slouched over his fried rice, glaring into the ceramic interior of his sake cup: the scales of his even temper were no longer balanced. Grey always joked about his wife's absence, about their non-sex; I'd never seen him get upset about her, or anything else. It seemed to me as I looked from Emily to Grey, that we were all liars—holding pieces of truth back from one another like businessmen—and I felt sick that I had never told them about my mother's wreck. That any secret existed between us seemed false and cowardly. And though I had never mentioned to Grey that I'd slept with Emily, nor did I think she had confessed to

140

him, I felt no urgency to impart that information. Only the death of my mother taxed my conscience.

Grey finished the bottle of sake, waved at the waitress for another, and stared stupidly at his plate. This youngest child of old parents, I wanted to comfort him. A red lantern above Emily's shoulder swung in the wake of the waitress' departure. What was the value assigned to family failure: did a suicide mother trump a shitty wife?

"My mother had an orange Camaro—a present from my father. She drove it into a cement retaining wall the spring I was fifteen—on purpose."

It was the *on purpose* that opened inside me like a wound, this ill-advised betrayal of my mother—this sad summing up of a family tragedy. And suddenly I couldn't go on. Baby, I thought, you fucking baby. Having already confessed so much, I told the rest of the story to my startled priests.

"I was eating gingersnaps on the kitchen floor, waxing my board. I didn't notice she'd gone. I don't remember the last thing she said. It was late that night when the police came. The older one patted my shoulder and asked my dad to come out on the porch with him. Dad didn't say a word when he came back inside. I knew, though. I knew when she wasn't in the orchard that afternoon."

Grey's face had drained of pigment and temper; he looked like he'd been punctured. He held his cup of sake clenched in his fist and stared at me with dilated eyes. Emily winced as though I'd struck her. I felt hollowed in the silence, a traitor to my mother. The pond gurgled beside us. I tasted bile and chugged the clear burn of sake down in two gulps to suppress the taste, to fill my mouth with a different sensation. It was the sake that stung my eyes.

"Jesus fucking Christ, Janie."

Grey reached across the table and grabbed my hand, smashing my chopsticks into my palm. I resisted the urge to pull away from him, to leave the table, the restaurant. Emily hadn't moved or fixed her face; her eyes still winced despite the tears. She'd ruin her shirt if she didn't stop. I wanted to comfort both of them, to hold as the grief passed through our sieved bodies.

"Fucking hell, Janie," Grey said. "I'm so sorry."

He looked over at Emily and then back at me.

"Jesus," he whispered. "I'm so sorry."

I'd never told anyone before. Not even the Belfast dentist. I hadn't wanted my mother to exist like that between us. I held tight to Grey's hand. Emily hadn't moved or spoken. How could I comfort them and not myself?

We sat like that a long time, statues of people at rest, eerily lifelike under the lanterns.

XVII.

Shivering and tightly huddled, I lowered myself into the scald of bathwater, and stretched my aching legs, my crippled back. As I'd biked up the winding climb of Tantalus, the light rain had become a torrent and then a howling, blinding deluge: mud-caked, my thin layer of clothes sopping, even my bones felt brittle. I'd wrecked twice, the back tire skidding away, my leg burned from the pavement and seasoned with gravel. I'd peeled my spongelike clothes off, climbed into the tub, all the while cursing Dr. Adams, that collaborator, kowtowing to treacherous, pedestrian bureaucrats.

She'd left a note for me to visit her office for a quick conference and I'd caught up with her during one of my afternoon breaks between classes. Preposterous, thimble-sized slices of watermelon dangled from her ears.

"Oh, Dr. Elliot, I'm sure you know all about the imminent teachers' strike, so it won't surprise you at all, I'm sure, when I tell you that next year you'll continue to teach second-year Latin."

"*Imminent?*" I said. "I don't know about an imminent strike. My students tell me every year there's a strike rumor and nothing ever comes of it."

She paused, her face filled with a kind of wonder at my evident incredulity—were those earrings whimsical?—then she went on as though I hadn't interjected.

"It's possible we'll have to cut some of the assistantships

too, which I refuse to consider right now. Anyway, I have to keep you where I have you."

She went on to explain that every department in the university was under budgetary pressure to minimize course offerings and terminate subjects considered to lack "real-world application"; so we in Classics must continue to bolster our numbers in the introductory courses—to reinforce our students' superb performance—and thereby the legitimacy of upper level and graduate course offerings.

"You've achieved so much with the students and the coursework, it would be idiotic not to exploit the students' response to you. I know it's a disappointment, Dr. Elliot, but you and I will reevaluate each term and hope for better accountancy."

And that had been the quick conference. I'd been type-cast. It was illogical to be stalled in my position because I did it well, because some asshole with a pie chart refused to understand that enlightenment and meaningfulness aren't random and miraculous by-products, but the primary objective of teaching: the *purpose* of education. On my voice mail at work, Emily had left a message canceling our plans for dinner—for the third time in a week—so I'd determined to bike Tantalus in the rain instead of going straight home to another dinner of cereal. A brilliant day all reckoned.

By the time the water had become tepid and I was debating whether it was better to stay and shiver or grasp my way out, I heard Emily's voice in the studio.

"Honey? What the hell happened to your bike? Jesus, look at your clothes. Jesus, look at you. What the hell have you been doing?"

It all seemed self-evident, so I didn't answer as she set down the pizza box she was holding and helped me from the tub.

"God, your leg looks nasty; do you have betadine?"

I pointed to the cupboard. After she'd applied the ointment

to my leg and roughly toweled me off, I threw on my sweats and crashed on the futon. She surveyed me a moment, then went to the kitchen to plate the pizza. Outside, the rain had stopped.

"I didn't think you could get away tonight," I said.

Emily and her partner had taken over production of a documentary about local photographers and she'd spent the previous three months—cell phone plastered to her ear, fax machine whirring bids and contracts—piecing together the funding to keep two film crews working. Relying on credit cards, the director had gone wildly over budget: he'd been following four photographers on three different islands intermittently over a period of fourteen months to capture as complete a picture as possible of each artist's process. One of the Oahu photographers, Nick Reinhart, had called Emily when the project had stalled; it was precisely what she and her partner had been looking for, but it was also a financial catastrophe.

She sat in the chair across from me, her plate in her lap, and twisted her hair back into a tight bun that she re-secured with chopsticks.

"I've been feeling like a complete asshole about rainchecking with you all the time. I'm sorry, by the way. You've obviously had a crap day."

"This pizza is definitely the bright spot."

"Well, I'm sorry about that too. Things are just crazy for me right now. I know I said I wanted a local project, but I should have been more specific. Anyway, the director has promised me all he needs is six more weeks and I've given him three, so we'll see how it goes. But I don't want to talk about work, and I don't want to have to apologize to you anymore—"

"You don't have to apologize—"

"No, I mean, I hate that I feel lousy about neglecting you and I think it's only fair to say that for the next few

145

months I'll continue to neglect you, so instead of having to apologize over and over and feel shitty and neglect you, I think it's better to tone down."

The pizza stopped tasting delightful. Tone down? Emily was talking too fast. I sat up on the futon; in the large room of the studio, she sat ten paces from me. Her eyes looked red, her slacks rumpled, and her black heels torturous.

"I've got the Spark to manage and this nimrod director and I hate to do things badly and I don't want to do you badly, either—I mean, to suck—I don't want to suck at my job or my relationship, so it's easier to be upfront and just eliminate the possibility of failure in the one place I can, right?"

If anyone knew about eliminating the possibility of failure, it was me. Through my wretched tiredness, I smiled at her. And then it occurred to me.

"Why not just get someone to manage the Spark for a few months? Tanya, she'd be great and you've worked together for years."

Emily picked the mushrooms from her slice and nodded absently. She had yet to take a bite.

"Yeah, I don't think I want to turn management of the Spark over to anyone else ... even short-term. It's mad busy at the moment and this summer it'll be even more intense."

This was beginning to sound like another quick conference.

"So we'll tone down: taupe or maybe even beige; something to go with your heels."

"Yeah, so this is going well."

Emily kicked off her heels, stood, and began pacing in front of the bookshelves. I didn't have the stamina for this: the rest of my muscles were sore, why not my heart too?

"Tell me," I said. "Tell me what happened."

Emily quit pacing and began a story that I stopped listening to after the first sentence.

"There's this guy—one of the new bartenders."

For a while she talked and finally I felt her hands on my shins and realized she'd sat on the futon beside me. But my punishing ride had inured me, I was only weary.

"Come on, roll over and I'll give you a massage."

I rolled onto my belly. At some point in the night I woke, the lamps dim, plates cleared away, the girl gone.

XVIII.

I met Nick Reinhart at the wrap party for Emily's documentary film eight weeks after we'd been toned down. I knew his work: curious brown-tinted photos of hula dancers at rest, a sea turtle gliding with elementary school kids in a cove in Koko Head, young men cruising North Shore with their boards strapped to the roof of duct-taped cars. The photos had an impromptu sense of catching the subject's secret self—an exposure of a fierce, snarling character that most people manage to shield from cameras. Because the photos were aesthetically beautiful, the light somehow manipulated like a Vermeer painting, the subjects were even more intriguing, sadder and richer.

I had seen many hours of footage at the production studio with Emily—Nick was the second photographer shadowed on Oahu—and was enraptured by Nick's quick satirical commentary, his lack of interaction with his chosen subject, and the days of meticulous work he poured over each photo—altering the texture of the image so significantly that often the source of the photo seemed wholly unrecognizable from the finished piece. He seemed more like a painter to me than a photographer. Dressed in blue jeans, deep-colored oxford shirts, and black Doc Martens, he was the last thing you'd expect after seeing his Hawaiian-style work. Also, the fact that he was exceptionally, even shockingly pale and wore his hair shaggy and unkempt like a skater, was in direct contrast to his prep-school style of dress. I told Emily I had to meet this guy.

"Nick? I dated him in college … briefly. Egomaniacal. We were doomed."

"Jesus. You dated him, too? No wonder he knew you were good for the funding."

"It's a small island, honey. You have to learn to expect these things."

Naturally. What was I thinking?

"What's he like? I mean, besides being egomaniacal."

"Really smart. History fanatic, addicted to popular culture. The guy could talk intelligently about any subject. You know how quickly people like that get old."

I looked back at the screen: Nick in the dark room, perched on a wooden stool, his head half-cocked as he looked directly into the camera; his features illuminated as if by firelight. I had to meet this guy.

At the wrap party in Kahala Hotel, the posh event was catered: two tables of local-style grub (chicken katsu, poi, mahi mahi, etc.) and a sushi chef wielding several large knives and a remarkable dexterity with seaweed. The party boasted an open bar, and I was helping deplete resources as quickly as possible, gulping whiskey while hovering just outside the hum of the party.

On the off chance I might meet the gifted photographer, I'd worn my little black dress with my open-toed black slides and had actually attempted to control my hair with a comb. Well into the evening, he was still mobbed by the crew, their spouses, several of the elite investors Emily had set on him, and his assistant, a stunning Japanese girl with straight shining black hair that swayed along her waist. I'd never seen anyone in real life with shining hair; it was deflating and gruesome. I had a vision of sheep shears and sobbing.

Emily popped over whenever the mobs relented, but for

the most part, I felt out of context. In the end, I walked outside the hotel dining room and wandered the courtyard, settling finally in one of the metal chairs gathered around the pool. The moon stalled, lonely in the pale of the sky.

I'd been out there so long that I grew chilled and was considering sneaking away all together when I heard footsteps on the cement behind me.

"Mind if I smoke?"

It was Nick. Honestly.

"Go ahead. I was just about to shoot some heroin."

He laughed and sat down in the chair at my right. He smoked Marlboro reds. There was a time (high school), when I would have found this terribly sexy, but after Ireland, where everyone smokes Marlboro reds or brown cigarillos, I'd learned that sexiness is more complex than a brand of cigarettes.

"How are you connected?" he asked.

"I'm with the sushi chef. I've always had a thing for knives."

He looked worried, or possibly confused: his brow furrowed and the skin above his nose scrunched; his eyes seemed sharper and more intense. They looked green on film, but must have been hazel. He took a drag from his cigarette and settled his expression.

"You're joking. You're connected to Emily, right? I've seen you with her at shoots a couple of times."

"Yeah. I live in the studio behind her mansion."

"Some place, yeah? I always felt like a fucking thief in that house, waiting for the butler to box my ears and throw me out the servant's entrance. I took some pictures of the house but haven't ever done anything with them. They looked kind of eerie, like maybe the house wasn't right. Those banyans in the back, you know, giving the place this grim atmosphere? This crazy sort of hovering, and that's what the camera caught. It was really bizarre."

He brushed his hair back from his eyes and smiled at me. He was drinking Heineken. Around the perimeter of the pool, ferns waved listlessly. The pool had a diving board into the six-foot deep end, which seemed inexplicably sad. His cigarette burned away.

"The bats in the banyans are what I love. I can hear them at night before I fall asleep, flitting like heavy moths."

I thought about a church I'd found in Edinburgh beside a shabby little graveyard. Through the round-topped wooden door, I'd entered a striking Anglican sanctuary ornamented in white and gold, where an elderly congregation sang in fine style a song as foreign to me as the country. I was so lonely in their gothic city of gray spires. I wanted to tell the photographer about Edinburgh, explain how the church had meant something. I was so certain it had meant something.

"Your accent's weird. Where are you from?"

"Maui. I went to school in Ireland, though."

"Yeah? My mom took us all over the U.K. one summer when I was in junior high. Isn't it weird to see all the Roman ruins there? I remember being amazed by that. They made it all the way to England."

"It is weird. And the druids as well; all these people dragging massive stones around to build temples and shrines, from Egypt to Ireland. I suppose it was some primitive form of the skyscraper."

"Commerce instead of religion?"

"There's a difference?"

Nick grinned at me as if to let that one go. Beside the pool now, he lit another cigarette and it seemed unaccountably important to describe the church in Scotland, I wanted the photographer to understand: the garish gold, the bright white, the perplexing song.

"I have this thing about graveyards."

Suddenly he was laughing at me, and in my confusion I couldn't remember what I was saying, so I stopped and watched him. When he laughed, his eyes squeezed shut and his mouth opened wide as his shoulders shook uncontrollably. It was more like convulsions than laughter and made me nervous.

"You're a trip," he said. "Ever posed?"

"Hmm?"

"Have you ever posed for a photographer?"

"No."

"Would you pose for me? We could take some shots at Punchbowl, since you have a thing about graveyards. I've wanted to do something with Japanese graves. I dig that concept of leaving food and liquor for the dead; it seems so much more useful than flowers. And you have a really interesting body—sort of angled and sexual—sinewy—like your fuck is outside your clothes."

"My fuck?"

"You know how people wear their fuck?"

"My fuck is outside my clothes?"

"Some chicks wear their fuck in their face, a lot of guys wear theirs in their eyes, some people wear theirs deep in their bodies, like you'd have to root for it, yeah? You know, your fuck, that sense of sexual awakening? You wear yours outside yourself like it's an orbit around your body. Call it a sexual glow. You've got a sexual glow."

I'd blushed. I could feel my head going red like some goddam convent girl. So I wore my fuck outside my clothes. So maybe that explained something. Didn't we all leave ruins behind to mark our place here? I thought of an archaeologist finding my bones with the photographer's beside this pool. So they would burn these white sticks in homage to the gods and to create an awkward euphoria. The women covered very little of their bodies. Tense and primitive creatures, they crafted cement containers to hold undrinkable water.

The archaeologists could not know about his eyes,

152

though. How the hazel color would sometimes darken into a remarkable green, like this moment as he attempted to convince me that he was not an ax murderer, not even a pervert. I'm just a photographer, his eyes assured me, an interesting guy you should get to know.

To alleviate feeling like a coward, I agreed to the photo shoot and gave Nick Reinhart my work number. Because I was a coward, I left without telling Emily goodbye.

XIX.

Nick called me four days after we met poolside. The photographer was at ease on the phone and made me laugh despite my best efforts at gravity. He told me about a fencing match he'd won the previous evening.

"Fencing?" I repeated.

"Yeah, I fence in an amateur league."

"You mean in the bee suit with the wiggly sword."

"Bee suit and wiggly sword are technical terms. We're very informal at our matches."

"Seriously, you fence? I thought fencing died out when men stopped wearing white gloves and plumed hats."

"There are a few of us beekeepers left. I'll bring you to a match sometime and you can give us pointers."

"Wow, a fencing photographer. They should have put that in the documentary."

He'd been scouting locations at Punchbowl and had found the perfect gravesite—beer, lanterns, incense, sushi rolls, and sharkcake—if I still wanted to model for him. This time, he made the proposition sound completely natural, not in the least perverted.

"There's just one thing," he said.

Apparently, normalcy was too good to last. My skin tightened around my throat.

"Yeah?"

"I don't date my models."

He paused. It felt like I was supposed to speak, but I had no idea what to say.

"OK."

"It's too hard on the reputation. So this'll really just be me taking pictures of you. I don't want a crew out there affecting the mood of the piece or making you uncomfortable. Usually I don't even mention this sort of thing, but I wanted to make it clear that I'm not trying to seduce you."

"Of course not."

"So I'll meet you at Punchbowl Friday morning at seven."

"What do you want me to wear?"

"Anything but black."

Had I come off as so desperately interested that I had to be told there was no chance? I stared at the phone, looking for some confirmation. What the fuck? What was the deal with people making all these weird rules for human interaction anyway, as if no one could be trusted? I didn't want him to seduce me. I just wanted to be involved in his process. I wanted to be his subject.

I biked to Punchbowl Friday morning with a change of clothes in my bag so I could go straight to class afterward. The graveyard was deserted except for one of the groundskeepers who manipulated the sprinklers for full exposure, his landscaping tools secured in a Rubbermaid trashcan in the back of a golf cart. I changed from my biking shoes into Birkenstock sandals and chained my bike outside the Visitor's Center, planning to wait for Nick in the parking lot.

I had a view of the road from the lot and watched an orange car navigate the curves toward me. Wide and shiny in the bright, clear morning, the car drew nearer; a peculiar burn lit in my belly, a recognition. When the car stopped in the parking lot and Nick climbed out, one arm extended in a quick wave before he began pulling his equipment from the trunk, I felt my body shiver. He drove a vintage orange Camaro.

"You biked here? No wonder you have a killer body."

He stopped smiling when he saw my face, let his bags slide to his feet, and rushed forward to grab my arm.

"Are you alright? Has something happened?"

He looked around wildly as if to find a villain escaping into the immaculately pruned shrubbery. I concentrated on his face, determined to keep him in focus, the green of his eyes startling against his red oxford shirt. My grip on his arm all anchor.

"I'm OK, just startled."

"By what?"

"My mother died in that car."

I pointed to the parking lot, my eyes never leaving his. A wild notion rushed through my head that maybe she lived. Maybe she had taken her car to Oahu. Maybe she was safe and had another family here. Maybe she lived.

"What?" He hung on to me and something like terror flooded his expression.

"My mother died in an orange Camaro."

Suddenly I was crying against him, sobbing heavily so that he had to gather me into his arms to keep both of us from collapsing. His beekeeper arms firm and thick, though his shoulders were not nearly as wide as Grey's. I wept against him loudly, shamelessly, the certainty that my mother did not live here or elsewhere as deep in me as marrow.

"OK," he whispered. "OK. I've got you. You're alright. I've got you. You're alright."

Fuck. I put my hand up as if to touch his hair which fell around his face like loosed cord, but didn't. Up close, his nose had a large bump on the bridge; his eyebrows thick and dark; his lips thin as grass blades. Without wiping my face, I stepped away from him.

"Now I look like a proper mourner," I said.

156

A smile flickered across his face, and I turned toward the cemetery. He grabbed his bags with his left hand and kept his right on my arm as a brace against further explosion. Not for a moment had it occurred to either of us to abandon the shoot. He guided me down the central staircase to the core of the crater, looking over at me occasionally to reassure himself that I remained stable. Deep into right field, we stopped at the site he'd chosen. Beyond the huddle of gravestones, trees cut to resemble the sparse bend of a bonsai swirled and bowed.

While Nick set up his equipment, he asked me to kneel in front of the grave and just observe. Sliced and fanned on a narrow green plate, the fishcake and sushi arched like a rainbow. A fat Buddha, incense at his feet, crouched beside the elaborately inscribed stone, commemorating a World War II soldier who'd died in 1944.

"Can I borrow your lighter?"

Nick tossed it to me and I lit the incense. Sitting before the grave was an intimate gesture—like reading someone's diary or watching a guy zip his fly—and guilt spread over me even as peacefulness did. Kneeling at this grave felt like peeking behind the veil to the little fellow with the levers, and I imagined the man honored here, gone for more than fifty years. I imagined being his widow, his daughter, his mistress. He'd died at thirty-three, his body still firm, hair still full and dark. Or maybe not, maybe he'd been bald and wiry. It was impossible to say and did not really matter. Opened miniature kegs of Orion beer in front of the stone revealed enough. That morning, I sat for hours as Nick worked around me, oblivious to most of his process save the click of capture, letting the incense gird us as the sprinklers droned.

"Can I take you to lunch?"

"I've got my bike."

"We can throw it in the—"

"I should get to class."

"I thought you didn't teach until one."

"What time is it now?"

"It's not even noon."

I nodded. The smell of sushi had made me hungry, but not hungry enough to ride in his car.

"I'll tell you what. How about I take you to dinner this evening instead? That way we won't be rushed. I've—I've got a Chevy Impala I'm restoring, and I'll pick you up in that, OK?"

"You don't date your models."

"I haven't paid you yet."

"Don't quibble."

"Let me take you to dinner. I'm just going to worry about you all day anyway."

"Don't. God, please don't worry about me. I feel like an idiot. I don't need pity or a guardian. I was surprised, you know? I was overwhelmed and I wigged out. It's not a chronic condition."

I felt the lie the moment I said it. Wasn't grief my chronic condition? Who the fuck was I kidding? Nick dragged his hair back from his face and looked at me steadily. He knew the lie as clearly as I did. He'd been so perfect all morning—suppressing any curiosity he had about the circumstances of my mother's death; letting me weep like a fucking child and not once mentioning any of it; not pressing me—and now he refused to argue.

He watched as I changed my shoes and unlocked my bike. The beekeeping photographer and the girl-freak—my T-shirt smelled like incense and I wondered if his did too.

"Destroy the film."

"What?"

"Expose the film now and I'll go to dinner with you."

"It won't change anything that happened today."

I wasn't sure what he meant. *Can't I change the way we'll*

158

remember this: a girl at a gravesite; a coffin car; eyes the color of chlorophyll? I wanted to punch his nose, to flatten that bump on its bridge. We've always kept a record of mourning and struggle. I thought of Sisyphus rolling his stone uphill forever. Don't we ever progress?

"Expose the film."

He unzipped his bag, pulled five rolls of film, and knelt on the pavement before me. Later when Emily asked, *Why Nick? Why then?* I thought about that moment in the parking lot as he drew film out one handful at a time, the exposed frames spiraling onto the pavement, bouncing cheerily: all his hours of work, the morning spent at his feet. Nick worked deliberately, his eyes narrowed with focus, his dark hair often sliding across his face until he snagged it behind his ears in one seamless gesture. When he finished, he secured his bag and faced me.

"You aren't a vegetarian, are you?"

"No."

"Good. I'll pick you up at eight."

I biked out of the parking lot, and when I looked back, he was still watching me.

XX.

Light glared through the pale greenhouse of my classroom, sifting among us as though it were hunting, or scavenging for roots. My class rattled off their third declension nouns as I listened to the symmetry of repetition and chorus: two dozen twenty-year-olds chanting a language that hung in the room like perfume.

Language so clear, so defined that during recitation only the verbs were out of context, the present imperfect. Kyle fumbled with his translation of Ovid, surfer bangs riffled with a nervous gesture of his hand. During a debate about the meaning of Achilles' fate, a British Lit major, Annabelle, who'd scored perfectly on each exam and homework assignment, drummed a pencil against her lips and stared out the window onto the common. Here we could talk like the dead: *epulatus eram, epulatus eras, epulatus erat, epulati eramus, epulati eratis, epulati errant.* Here we spoke of love potions and sons of centaurs with deliberate formality. Here treachery translated to *proditus,* a harmless enough word in Latin. Emily had said I frightened her, the way nothing moved me.

XXI.

Grey and I arrived early at Catacombs for the Flapper Party—men in tuxedos, women in short, loose-bodied dresses with cigarette holders and chic, feminine skull caps—to find the dark bar crowded with freaks. We had hoped, at 6 in the evening, to be among fifteen overzealous people seat-saving for two exclusive sets featuring the slick croon of Diana Waelly, The Remake Queen, in this swank and enigmatic jazz cave. Instead, descending the stone steps into the dim, smoke-clouded cavern, we collided with swirling teenyboppers, tourists, and way too many old men in top hats for my taste. But we pressed through to the bar anyway, counting on a couple of whiskeys to make us more social.

Grey was wearing a tuxedo for the first time in my memory and looked ravishing. Every girl in the place—as well as a number of men—glared at me insinuatingly as if only blowjobs could keep such a guy at my side. I'd worn a sleeveless rouge-colored dress, a black headband with a peacock feather, slingbacks, and my best intentions. The queue to order drinks stretched back for centuries.

"Every chick in here hates me," I told him.

"I hate you too."

"That's what I said."

"You actually combed your hair tonight, didn't you?"

"It won't last. My hair has a mind of its own."

"You look really good, actually. Taller."

"You're darling. Are we staying here?"

"Have to," he said. "The gang's all coming here and I volunteered us to be place-holders. I'm not getting stuck at some table by the men's room. We're going to be close enough to see the sweat on Diana Waelly's upper lip."

"You should have fed me. I'm in a filthy mood."

"We can get something to eat here. Shit, grab that table and I'll get the drinks."

Four elephantine girls had labored off their stools, and begun the slow procession toward the door, so I snaked their table and waved down a waitress to order a plate of calamari and two house salads.

"Service is delayed tonight," she began.

"No worries, I'll pass the time with some whiskey."

"That's the spirit," Grey said as he handed me a glass and smiled at the waitress. "I knew you couldn't stay filthy for long."

With an intrigued look, the waitress merged back into the haze.

"The bartender and I went to high school together," Grey said by way of explaining the quick drink service. "He just told me Diana Waelly doesn't come on until nine, but some quartet will take the stage at seven."

"Nine? What the fuck?"

"Hey, do you want to sit at a table by the men's room? You can't leave this kind of reconnaissance operation to Kimo or Karen."

"What's with you and sitting by the men's room?"

"Look, you said you were happy to come along early with me, so no bitching now."

I'd agreed to come early with Grey in order to tell him privately about Nick, but somehow the opportunity for my disclosure just hadn't appeared. Nick was supposed to have been my coffee break; my Rex Stout mystery; the popcorn movie to distract me from beige days and another term of

162

second-year Latin. I'd left Ireland for this? Delvo had tried to console me when I told her that Dr. Adams' strike fixation had consigned me to another year teaching polliwogs: "Focus on summer school—you and I will be the only instructors—no departmental meetings, no frenetic teaching assistants, no more discussions about the merits of fat-free ranch dressing."

Instead of a meaningless affair—a couple of dinners, a tour of his studio, his bedroom—the photo shoot at Punchbowl had charged the air for me: I kept returning to the image of him crouched in the parking lot with the film unspooling; and his hands, the way he'd gathered me up and held me. So for the past two months, I'd tried to figure a way to tell Grey and Emily that I'd toned up with a guy they both knew in isolated past tense. Amazingly, I had never found the right opportunity to explain about Nick, so I'd decided to ambush the whole scenario by inviting him to join us for the Flapper Party.

"The thing is … I invited someone here tonight."

"Yeah? Someone from school?"

"No. The thing is I've been seeing someone—a guy. I've been seeing a guy."

"Yeah?"

Grey watched me closely as he spun his coaster around the tabletop. My mouth couldn't keep up with my brain; I had the numb of Novocain anesthetizing my inputs.

"Yeah. The thing is you know him: Nick Reinhart."

"Sure I know Nick—the photographer who dated Emily in college—he was in her last documentary."

"Right."

"So you've been seeing him?"

"Yeah, for a while."

"Well, that's interesting."

He didn't sound interested so much as pissed.

"Yeah, the thing is it was difficult to explain—"

"Well, that's shocking, really amazing. I've never met a chick who kept so many secrets, so many deceptions and ruses—not even my wife. Your whole life is a masquerade ball. Are you incapable of honest human interaction? Is that the fucking problem?"

"What are you getting so upset about? I wanted to tell you, but things are so complicated with Emily and everything—"

"Right, complicated with Emily because you've been having an affair with her for months, but God forbid you talk to me about it. What's your deal, Jane; can't you be open with your friends?"

"Grey, what—"

"No, don't accuse me of overreacting. I have a right to expect honesty from my friends. Honesty may be the only thing we can expect from other people, and I think I deserve it."

"I haven't been dishonest with you."

"Oh my fucking god. What are you talking about? You have to tell lies to keep secrets, Jane. Especially you: you'd tell a lie before you'd ever betray yourself."

"I don't have to expose every aspect of my life for us to be friends."

"I'm not talking about exposure; I'm talking about honesty. You've been telling me your classes keep you so busy five nights a week, and that's not true, is it?"

"I'm trying to explain about that—"

"About how that's not dishonest?"

"Grey, can I please talk?"

"Sure, just don't develop a habit of it."

"Oh god, you're so infuriating."

"I'm infuriating?"

"Shut the fuck up for Christ sake and give me a chance to explain. I'm sorry, OK? I'm sorry I didn't tell you I was seeing someone. It was just supposed to be a harmless affair, you know, no casualties. We got serious so fast that I felt like an idiot trying to explain—I feel like an idiot trying to explain about not telling you before."

Grey concentrated on each ice cube in his glass, crushing his coaster in the deliberate collapse of his right palm.

"Ryan, I'm sorry. I'm really sorry. I should have told you before."

"Why didn't you?"

"I don't know."

That was another lie. I hadn't told Grey for a number of reasons: if he knew, Emily would be more likely to find out; Grey and I spent so much time together that dating another guy felt traitorous; I worried Nick and Grey might not get along; and I worried too about the way Grey might take the news.

I felt my face flush when Grey met my eyes.

"Don't lie to me anymore," he said. "Why didn't you tell me?"

"I felt like a traitor—seeing someone else—and that's completely irrational because you're married. I'm not with you. I can see whomever I want."

"Have I ever said different?"

"No, but that's not the point. I'm telling you how I felt."

"Jane, you know I'm attracted to you. Have I ever acted on that, have I ever made a move on you, or made you uncomfortable?"

"No."

"Why is that do you think?"

"Because you're married."

"That's right. You're the most interesting chick I know and I love to hang out with you; I made a choice to be with you and never to act on any impulse—never to let anything interfere with us being friends. That was my choice and I've been faithful to it. Gang references aside, truthfulness is about respect, and I think I deserve that respect from you.

I'm not asking for graphics of your sex life or an incursion into your privacy, but would mentioning the fact that you're seeing someone and that it's serious violate your self-imposed confidentiality clause?"

"I should have told you before."

"That's all I'm saying."

"I'm really sorry. Honestly."

"So how's the sex?"

"Asshole."

"No, seriously, you're having sex right?"

"Is Emily going to be as upset as you are?"

"Worse, I'm sure. But you know, you could have spared all of us by—"

"OK. I've got it."

"Actually I can't wait to see her face; it's going to be beautiful."

His olive-toned face was pink with excitement as the waitress slid our salads and the plate of calamari onto the table. Grey ordered two rounds of drinks before letting her vanish again.

"May be years before we see those drinks," he said, "so it's best to have an extra pair. Jesus, the quartet's playing. I hadn't noticed."

On the other side of the room, three young men in thin ties and dark suits wailed away on the piano, saxophone, and guitar. A tall woman in a scoop-necked dress fingered the thick strings of an upright bass. They played quick, wildly overlapping notes that had the crowd head-bopping practically unawares.

"They're crazy," I said, grinning.

"If they can keep that up for two hours, I'll be impressed. Do you mind telling me how Emily didn't find out about this guy you're seeing?"

"I told you things are complicated with Emily."

"Yeah. What does that mean again?"

"She told me this spring that she didn't want to get too serious—she didn't want to be exclusive—with me. She said she wanted to tone down. Meanwhile, she's seeing one of her new bartenders. I wasn't sure how to read that exactly—you know, curtain or intermission—later I understood she'd meant intermission."

"And that was OK with you?"

"No. No that really sucked. The thing is Emily's ... well, we exist by her rules, you know?"

"Yeah, I remember."

"So I met Nick at the wrap party and ..."

I shrugged my shoulders. Grey's eyes were lit, his mouth wide with amusement.

"That's classic. I hope she appreciates the irony."

"I'm not sure why you're so gleeful."

"I like the idea of Emily learning about commitment while you're learning about honesty."

"You really are a bad hat."

"Thank you. So you pulled the curtain?"

"Not exactly."

"Ah. Then this may not be much fun after all."

"No. I'd hoped that you would be happy for me, and that would set the tone for the evening, but my projections were off a bit."

He nodded, trying to appear sober and empathetic as he shoveled calamari strips into his mouth.

"What time's Nick getting here?"

"Nine."

"So how much does he know about this?"

"Less than you."

"How much less?"

"He knows I rent the studio behind Emily's house, and that the three of us surf together, that we're friends."

"Jesus, you're amazing. It must be something to keep all your different characters straight, yeah? Don't you ever get confused, assuming your various roles with each of us?"

"There is a line, Grey, that even you can trip over."

"Try that one on Emily when she threatens to rip your heart out and see if it works any better."

"Don't be nasty. I don't want him to meet you when you're nasty."

"To protect him or yourself?"

The waitress materialized to drop off four tumblers of whiskey-cokes and collect our plates. In front of the raised platform on which the band played, a couple of shaggy-haired hippie chicks gyrated to the syncopated rhythms. Around the bar, heads and shoulders nodded to the bass beat and the band began to hold the audience's attention with their complicated arrangements and funky rhythms.

I wanted to start the night over. It had been a relief to talk to Grey about Emily, a relief to stop the charade, but I had no skin for his vindictiveness, no calluses to protect myself. I drained one of the tumblers—the startled burn—and stared at the band, willing Grey to be calm and reasonable. He fidgeted next to me, shifting his emptied tumbler to the edge of the table, and glanced up with a sly grin.

"So inviting him to a costume party is symbolic, right?"

I fingered my peacock feather, "Yes. I'm getting rid of all disguises."

"Brilliant. We can all pretend to be our best selves. We're certainly dressed for it."

I nodded. His tuxedo was ravishing; it lent him the appearance of a grownup.

"Guard the table while I get us another couple of rounds."

The dance floor spread like a contagion until anyone who wasn't queued for drinks at the bar was flopping around in front of the band; heads bobbed like waves through the smoke fog. Eventually Grey and Emily's classmates arrived and I was able to leave the table to dance with Grey. By the time Nick showed—wearing a smooth black tuxedo with his hair slicked back so he looked like a gangster—the rest of us were sweaty, well buzzed, and giddy.

I should have known better than to worry about Grey and Nick getting along; they spent the intermission between bands entertaining the table on any number of topics from the political repercussions of the word *squaw* to the extent of ozone depletion as a result of methane gas produced by cows, to an uncanny rendition of the African or European swallows debate from *Monty Python's The Holy Grail*. Nick's dry wit was a perfect foil for Grey's outrageousness, and they were obviously struggling to hold straight faces quite as often as the rest of us. When Diana Waelly's set began, at nearly ten, her honey-fused growl poured over the crowd, lending our drunkenness a regal quality as we pitched and swayed.

Well into the second set, Emily still hadn't arrived and Karen Cho—International Finance—and Kimo Howerton—Investment Banking—were both ringing the Spark on their cell phones without getting an answer. No doubt we should have been worried, but Grey and I had been drinking steadily since 6:00 p.m., we'd all danced and laughed to stupor, and the music had shrouded us in a bubble of happiness that no one wanted to burst. We didn't know about the paramedics and cops summoned to the scene of a bar brawl at the Blue Spark; the number of people in gurneys or handcuffs; the bouncers who'd had to be restrained from killing a couple of military guys who'd groped a waitress.

169

XXII.

In July, I met Nick's mother. Nick's father had been an army engineer; upon retiring from service, he'd started a construction company that made barrels of money in the real estate swoon of the nineteen-eighties. He'd had four sons, three wives, and had died on the operating table during a bypass operation in 1990. By that time, he and his third wife, Verity, a Hungarian woman he'd met while stationed in Frankfurt, were sleeping in separate rooms.

In his final year of film school, Nick dropped out and returned home to take care of his mother. It was a decision that he did not make entirely on his own, or for that matter, entirely selflessly. A great portion of the father's estate had been left to Nick, along with the house in Aliamanu, and the condo in Maui. To his other sons—only two were still living—he left controlling interest in his construction company. His wife got nothing.

Nick used his father's money to open the photography studio; had the basement of his mother's house remodeled as an independent living space with kitchen and laundry facilities so that he could live near enough to watch over his mother while giving each of them a semblance of privacy. I thought his devotion to his mother old-world gallantry of the noblest sort until I met her.

Verity Reinhart, dark and diminutive, with a curt accent and short thick waves of gray hair, was a spiritualist. During my first meeting with her, she walked me around the living room, encouraging me to hold this rock or that statue and experience its aura. She routinely sited alien ships, had been visited by gargoyles in her sleep—"a heavy weight on my chest and I felt the clawed feet sinking into my flesh"—claimed that her connection to the ethereal world (as she referred to it) came at the expense of her health, and she belonged to a sort of club of spiritualists who met every year in some foreign city where a hubbub of spiritual activity had been report. The city she was bound for that year: Cairo.

We met for drinks instead of dinner—presumably because Nick anticipated exactly what occurred, unabashed antagonism and revulsion on my side and whimsy from his mother. She thought me the most interesting of Nick's troupe of girls—"so many that I never can keep them all straight, but, my dear, your accent is delicious!"—and when she found out that I taught Latin, well it was exactly what she'd expected: I had a predisposition to understand the ethereal world where she lived most of the time.

Honestly, I didn't try very hard to be polite. The three of us had cocktails together and then Nick and I left to have dinner at John Dominis. After several months of dating, Nick wanted me to move in. Meeting his mother had been a sort of test for our relationship and I had the impression that I wasn't the first girl he'd brought to his mother for approval, but she'd raised serious questions from my perspective—obviously his mother was unhinged and did I really want some wacky woman who entertained gargoyles living a flight above me?

Then, of course, there was the alternative: to stay in the studio behind Emily's mansion and observe the decay. After the Flapper Party, I'd gone home with Nick and hadn't discovered anything about the brawl at the Spark until late the following evening. When I came back to the studio, Grey had left a note tagged to my door outlining what had transpired and I'd run up to the main house to check on Emily.

171

I found her in the kitchen, mobbed by her friends. Emily's nasty glower assured me that Grey's response to Nick would pale to what I was about to experience. Obviously, her friends had told her that I'd gone home with Nick—you know, that really funny guy you dated in college—which was a shock in itself coupled with the brawl, then compounded by the fact that I wasn't home to console her in the wake of these events, nor had I bothered to appear until nearly nine o'clock; certainly, my case looked bleak.

"Can you believe it, Jane?" asked Karen Cho. "A brawl at the Spark, and we're all dancing at Catacombs completely oblivious. I feel terrible."

Still looking at Emily, I nodded. Terrible. Yes, that was extremely compassionate of Karen to feel terrible about a bar brawl that had required medics. The rest of the room nodded assent, as they had been doing all day no doubt, empathizing with all their little hearts: swooping in vulture-like to commiserate, their soulful masks obscuring their delight. I felt sick looking at them. The rest of the room, finally attuned to the fact that Emily, drawn with rage, had not taken her eyes from me, tensed as they leaned forward, waiting to catalog the drama.

Emily didn't look at them, annunciating deliberately as though English were her second language: "Thanks so much for coming, all of you. I'm tired now."

No one moved to leave. Emily looked up dazedly and smiled at them. Karen glanced at me and backed toward the French doors. The rest of the group followed until the doors banged closed, icing us in.

"Are you OK?"

She didn't answer me and I realized it was a dangerous question.

"Were you hurt?"

Even worse. My stomach wrenched. Our conversations were always desperate—I couldn't relax and talk plainly about Nick or even what I felt for her—charged with sexual tension and something ugly, something insinuating that frightened me. Maybe I hadn't come home on purpose. Maybe I knew something had happened when she didn't come to the bar, and I wanted her friends to tell her about Nick first so that I wouldn't have to. Maybe her fury would make leaving easier.

"Were you trying to hurt me?" she asked.

"I meant the brawl."

"Were you trying to hurt me?"

"No. I wasn't trying to do anything. Seeing other people was your idea, remember?"

"Yes. It was something I talked to you about, not something I did behind your back, not something that you had to hear about from other people after conceivably the worst night of your life."

"No one else knew until last night, I was going to tell you when you came to Catacombs."

"So it's my fault."

"No. I should have told you sooner, but I'm saying I meant to tell you before your friends did."

"Oh, you meant to. Oh well that's all right, then."

"Don't. Don't twist everything—"

"I'm not twisting anything. You fucked this guy for months and never bothered to tell me about it. Never mentioned a thing and that's so irresponsible, that's so fucking sick and deceitful, that's so miserably weak. When I heard it, I wanted to rip your fucking heart out."

"Because you would have felt better if you'd known I was fucking someone else? You just wanted to know, right? Then it would have been OK. This is really about keeping you out of the loop. This isn't about how much it hurts to have someone you love fucking somebody else."

"I don't love you."

"Then why are you so upset?"

173

"I thought you were better than this."

"I am better than this. I'm better than you and us and this whole fucking scene."

She'd jumped up before I could get to the door and slammed me against the counter, my back arching awkwardly as her full weight heaved into my hips. I swung once and caught her in the jaw. Her head twisted back, a look of horror opened her eyes as she retreated from me and raised her hand to her face.

"You fuck."

I reached my hand out in a gesture of peace and shock, not believing I'd just cracked my knuckles against her face. She flinched.

"Don't fucking touch me. Get out."

"Emily, I'm—"

"Get the fuck out of here."

I returned to the studio, my hand aching, not certain if I should pack and leave, return to the house, or wait for Emily. I'd hit her in the face, lied to her about Nick, failed her violently, treacherously. I couldn't be the same self. This wasn't me.

She didn't come to the studio that night, or that week, or that month. I didn't pack and move because it worried me to leave her; I thought that might be worse than staying. I mailed the rent check to her and slept at Nick's more regularly.

Grey and I still surfed, met for drinks, or watched movies at his place. When I told him what had happened in Emily's kitchen, his face paled, but he tried to reassure me that she'd rushed me and it had probably been a self-protective impulse to sock her. I'd tried that argument before, but it didn't play. If self-protection was my impulse, why hadn't I just pushed her away?

When Emily left for California to visit her brother, we hadn't spoken to or seen one another for more than six weeks.

174

At John Dominis, Nick ordered a bottle of Bordeaux and a starter of escargot. He'd cut his hair so that it fell above his shoulders, though the bangs were still long and a little wild. He kept smiling at me but refused to say why.

"So your mom's going to Egypt in August?"

"Yeah. Last year it was Bali."

"She has money of her own?"

"God, yes. Her family was extremely wealthy and she's an only child. They left everything to her."

"That makes it less awkward."

"About my dad, you mean? Yeah."

"And your other brothers, they live here?"

"California."

"Do you ever visit?"

"Never. They're from his first wife—an extremely nasty divorce. Those kids weren't allowed anywhere near my father. It was a slick trick, though, leaving a controlling interest in the construction company to them: highly profitable, but extremely time-consuming, the perfect barbed gift."

"And the brother that died?"

Nick had mentioned his brother's death before, but had never gone into specifics. Meeting his mother—he'd tolerated her irritating affectations with remarkable forbearance—had given me the urge to inquire about every detail of his family; I had some experience with real madness and posturing eccentrics irked me.

"He was from my dad's second marriage—she was an alcoholic—my dad got custody, so Andy and I grew up together. Well, sort of, he was six years older than me. He helped me restore my first vintage car: a gorgeous 1948 Chevy Coupe."

"So you were close?"

"He really looked out for me."

I didn't press him, knowing he'd tell if he wanted to. I

took a sip of wine and smothered a snail in butter before popping it into my mouth.

"My dad was one of those extremely brusque men—testosterone heavy, foul mouthed, typical ex-military guy—who thought Humphrey Bogart had the right idea not letting his wife ride in his sports car: dames are bad luck. My dad used to try to get me and Andy to watch porn with him—not like he was going to hurt us or anything—he just thought stuff like that was funny, guys sitting around watching porn. It was kind of creepy."

I nodded. He sounded lovely.

"So you can imagine what it was like for my brother to grow up with a father like this and—and he was gay."

"Your father?"

"No, my brother. I didn't know until he visited from college. He was going to school in Jacksonville and when he came back for Christmas break his sophomore year he brought a guy with him. This tall, fit, extremely good looking guy; and I just thought they were buddies, you know. I mean, who doesn't want to come to Hawaii? But my dad was suspicious right away and nasty to both of them. So they left and spent the rest of their vacation at a friend's place in the U.H. district."

Maybe I didn't want to know this after all. I was suddenly very grateful that the father had died before I had the pleasure of meeting him.

"That was the last time I saw Andy. He wrote me all the time. Last letter came postmarked from New York; he wrote how I should look him up. He died of AIDS my senior year in high school. I don't know who was with him or how long he'd been sick or anything."

"God, that's horrible. I'm so sorry."

"He was a good guy."

Our main plates had come and we ate in silence for a long time. During filming of the documentary, Emily had

176

taken me to a gallery show of Nick's work. His eye was unforgiving—in one photograph a beautiful young Polynesian woman hands a smiling child to another woman; the young woman's face is a profound expression of resentment, despair, and a despicable slyness. It shocked me, that expression. Throughout the evening, I'd gone from one image to another horrified, entranced. By catching the complexities of character in the faces of his subjects, he seemed both to perceive and reveal their essential selves. Nick set his fork down and cleared his throat.

"I want to ask you something."

"Yeah?"

"I've told Mom that I'll fly to Cairo with her. They usually attend these conference things for about three weeks and she dragged me to Egypt when I was sixteen, so I don't really care to hang out there the whole time, but I've never been to Venice. So I was wondering: do you want to meet me in Venice for two weeks in August? You'd be back before start of term. I'll fly back to Cairo to collect Mom at the end, but you can just fly in and out of Rome and take the train to Venice."

I was dumbstruck. I'd had this alarming sensation at first that he was going to ask me to attend a cult meeting in Egypt—not bloody likely—and then it had flashed through my head that I'd be asked to watch Jake (the mother's Cairn terrier) while they were gone, but meeting Nick in Venice had not occurred to me. How much would a trip like that even cost?

"You kind of have to say yes because I've already bought your tickets for the plane and the train, and booked the hotel in Venice."

He smiled and passed me the plane ticket.

"Have you been to Italy?"

I nodded, my body rushing toward the ceiling.

"Rome. I've been to Rome and Florence."

"But not Venice? Well this'll be perfect, then. I mean, if you're interested."

I started to laugh and didn't stop for so long that the other customers must have been nervous. Suddenly a mad mother didn't seem quite so insurmountable.

Sessions with Dr. Mya: Day 4

While the pug is taking my vitals, I examine my breakfast tray: pancakes, bacon, and a couple of withered slices of cantaloupe. Why don't they ever serve oysters in hospital? I've been craving oysters now for several days; maybe this means I'm recovered. I'm tempted to ask the pug.

Dr. Bocek, my neurologist, visited before breakfast and advised me again to be patient with the raging temper, the panicky confusion and nervousness, the sarcasm. Patting my good arm, he'd added chummily, "Don't be too hard on yourself, Jane. You took one hell of a blow to the head."

I am improbably comforted by Bocek, a jittery, quipping little man. If he'd give me some fucking morphine, I might love him. Since his visit, I've spent the morning laughing. Grey once told me, months previously, that all of his failings were moral ones. I'd wondered at the time if that meant my failings were immoral.

Audrey and I had arrived at Grey's house for an impromptu cookout that Sunday afternoon in July with a giant glass bowl, and the ingredients for sangria. Under the covered porch, Grey and Emily played table tennis amidst a constant exchange of vulgarisms, while some feet away the grill smoked untended.

"Audrey," Grey greeted her with a kiss. "Take my place."

Audrey took his paddle and hunkered down to return Emily's serve. When Grey passed me to check the grill, he punched my shoulder.

"What the fuck happened to your face?" I asked him as I mixed the sangria, pouring each of us a glass.

"A goatee. The chicks love it!"

"Don't believe anything you read in men's magazines."

He grinned at me, swigged from his glass, then gestured to the grill, "Oysters, ahi, and grilled vegetables for Audrey. She likes sweet potatoes, yeah?"

I nodded. Sweet and red potatoes roasted beside kebobs of mushrooms, squash, tomatoes, yellow pepper, and broccoli. The rice cooker on the table steamed. I refilled our glasses.

"Very nice," I said. "So what inspired all this?"

"Just wanted to kick back with some honeys."

"We're the test market for that fucking goatee, admit it."

"I bought a foosball table, so I had to invite some people over. Challenge later, you and me versus."

"You are a man who loves his toys, Grey. The yard's looking as lush as ever."

Grey had paid thousands of dollars for a landscaper to remove any trace of grass or flowers and terrace his backyard with rocks and rubber trees. The yard looked both stylized and decimated, as though it could serve as the backdrop for a kung fu fight.

"Low maintenance, man. That's all I'm after."

The ping-pong ball scraped against the cement at my feet and Emily shrieked *fuck* five times. Audrey grabbed a glass of sangria from the table, and said, "Game," as calmly as any ass kicker.

"Rematch," Emily hollered, still clutching her paddle.

A moment later, the ball knocked across the table, and Grey giggled as he turned the oysters, "Who'd have thought the chick could wail at table tennis?"

"You should see her play pool."

He sat beside me on the cement and looked out at the yard, stretching his bare feet atop the rocks. Unruly, his hair shagged around his ears, and down toward his shoulders.

Maybe the goatee lent him a haggard appearance, but the slumped posture and the wrinkled T & C shirt didn't help. His surf trunks had a hole in the crotch.

"You sleep in your clothes?" I asked.

"Rough night, man."

"Yeah?"

"You know, I had a dream about you after that first party at Emily's. I dreamt we were in this insane theme park and it was derelict, swamped over: moss covered the Ferris wheel, vines wrapped around the roller coaster, and we're wandering through the place at night. We climbed to the top of the water slide and slid down on our bellies, both of us shrieking like little kids. Just before we hit the water, we saw crocodiles swarming around in the pool, ready to ambush us. The water went over my head and I woke up, completely disappointed that our dream-selves were wrestling crocodiles instead of fucking."

I smiled, though his voice sounded more solemn than playful. The oysters popped on the grill and Grey sprang up to plate them. Behind us the paddles thwacked, and Emily had started grunt-squealing in an effort to swallow her curses. The overcast afternoon seemed like a prelude. I watched Grey work at the grill, flipping vegetables and ahi filets, worried suddenly that I'd missed the portent of whatever he'd been trying to tell me.

Grey carried the plates to the table, and scooped rice onto his and mine. We prepared our oysters with chopped jalapenos, grated cheese, and shoyu. I refilled our glasses with sangria as the ping-pong ball sucked into the net and Emily squalled, "Motherfucker! Motherfucker! Motherfucker!"

"Rematch later," Grey said. "Come eat."

Emily brought her paddle to the table, her mouth a thin line of rebuke as she re-wrapped her hair into a bun. She threw a tank top over her bikini and prepared her oysters in stern silence, refusing to acknowledge Grey's query about a foosball challenge after lunch. Audrey's face was bright red—even her ears—and her expression of self-assurance catlike as she separated her vegetables from the skewer, murmuring delightedly when she bit into a sweet potato.

"Where's Jenelle today?" Audrey asked, ignoring the threatening glares from Emily and me at the mention of Jenelle's name. We'd had enough visits lately from Miss Hardcore to last four lifetimes.

"Working, I think," Grey said.

"That's too bad," Emily said. "We could have used some more testosterone at this picnic."

"You say the sweetest things," Audrey told her.

Emily smiled and asked for more sangria. A bee loped around the table's edge until Grey batted it with his spatula and sent it careening into the rock yard.

"Em," I said, "they're advertising for a four-man volleyball tournament at Magic Island this month. We should get Pete and Rookie and enter, yeah?"

"Rookie may have moved back to Washington. I'll talk to Pete about it Tuesday night. He only comes to the Spark a few times a week since he started dating that Filipino chick."

"The chick with the inflated arms?"

"Apparently he finds bloating attractive."

"Nice. Grey, what's up; are we going surfing anytime soon?"

"Will you guys call me next time you go?" Emily asked. "Fucking assholes never invite me."

"We were going Sunday mornings and you're always wasted after closing at the Spark."

"Go Monday, then," Emily said. "Shit, now that school's over, we can go every Monday until I leave for France, unless you're teaching mornings during summer school."

"Monday morning works for me; I'm teaching a class in the afternoon."

182

I looked over at Audrey to elicit her silent consent, but her attention had focused on Grey, who seemed to be reading his own palm. Above us, the sun stagnated in the windless sky. I scooped more rice onto Emily's plate and mine.

"Why didn't you bring anyone, Em?" I asked.

"Haven't you read the flyers, honey? I'm single again."

"You and me both," Grey said without looking up from his palm. "It's just like senior year all over again."

"What are you talking about?" I asked him.

"She asked for a divorce. I've signed the papers. There's a mandatory waiting period, and then it's over."

Calmly, Grey returned to eating his ahi and rice as though a landmine hadn't exploded at the table. The three of us sat staring at him until Grey added: "I've given notice at UPS, and I'm going to work for my dad at Mako Surf Company. It's time to quit fucking around."

"She asked for a divorce?" Emily said, trying to keep the astonishing revelations straight.

"I signed the papers last night. Feels like I've been single forever, now it'll be official."

"And you're going to work for Mako?"

"Yup."

"When did you decide all this, Ryan?"

"I've been thinking about it for ages. Dad wants to retire."

Emily looked at me questioningly, as if I might have known or anticipated any of this disclosure. I shook my head in response. Audrey continued to stare at Grey, her catlike expression had vanished, and now concern narrowed her eyes, creased her brow.

"I didn't mean to ruin the day," Grey said.

"When did she ask?"

"What?"

"When did she ask for the divorce?"

"I got the papers Wednesday."

"Jesus," Emily said. "I can't fucking believe it. I never thought she'd ask for a divorce."

"Ryan," Audrey said, "are you OK?"

When Grey glanced up from his plate, his face wreathed in shaggy hair like a disciple of Christ, I started laughing. I couldn't help it. He looked like John the Baptist. But swallowed beneath the torn shorts and *Gene Wilder: the early years* fro, I recognized the same Hippie Gap Model who had waited out his unfortunate marriage with a loyalty that I had never understood. He'd been faithful to a woman who had refused to give cause or gratitude for such fidelity and he'd maintained this devotion while drinking excessively and keeping time with sexually ambivalent women with a proud tradition of errant behavior.

I laughed until I choked, incapable of apologizing even as the tears ran down my face. My stomach cramped as I kept laughing until, inexplicably, Emily joined in, her expression as sanguine and unrepentant as mine. Grey, dismayed, looked from one of us to the other and then to Audrey, who appeared appropriately scandalized. I laughed until I thought I would vomit and then bent over the table and shook, hoping for some rational method by which I might make amends when I recovered.

Our faces swollen and damp, Emily and I finally quieted enough for me to say, "Seriously, this is good news, right? You've finally ditched the bitch."

"And you have the best support group around," Emily said. "Look at us: Jane and I have both had disastrous relationships—Jane survived a fucking sadist for Christ sake—and I survived Jane. Chicks will be fist-fighting us for your number once you shave, get a haircut, and buy some new clothes. You really need to toss those shorts, Ryan. My god."

At the head of the table, Audrey had finally caught our contagion and was trembling with laughter. Her little body squeezed like an accordion as she howled. No doubt it was the idea of Emily or me supporting anyone's recovery that set Audrey off.

"This is your chance, Grey. This is your chance to be happy."

He grinned then and dashed the last of his sangria. That evening, Grey and I challenged nine foosball games against Emily and Audrey and lost every one. They beat us two of the games without allowing us to score a single point. Some support group.

Later, while they re-matched at table tennis, Grey and I dragged chairs into the rubber trees and stared at the slash of moon. He'd grabbed a bottle of Jameson from the cabinet and we traded it like a compliment. From the neighbor's yard came the husky gulp of a toad.

"It'll be strange to be single," he said.

"Why?"

"Because you're no longer single."

I looked over at him, but he continued staring at the sky. In my hands, the Jameson bottle already felt insubstantial. The air colder now, I'd thrown a sweatshirt on and pulled my legs against my chest to ward off chicken skin. Still wrestling crocodiles, I thought.

"It's a moral failing," he said.

"What is?"

"Divorce."

"How can you say that? Grey, you two didn't have a fucking chance. You live in completely different places—figuratively and literally."

"I should have tried harder."

"Yeah, you should have moved to the east coast, where they measure lives in floor space and luxury cars. Miserable beaches, toll booths, three-piece suits; Christ, what a scene."

"I expected her to live here despite her ambition. I had

this concept of love and I refused to change it, even with both of us so miserable. She's getting remarried in September, some attorney at the Justice Department."

In the dark, the leaves of the rubber trees fluttered slowly like heavy wings. I know no way of healing, I wanted to tell him. You're better than all of us. You deserve a garden, and some rational girl.

The ping-pong ball pock-pocked on the table behind us and I heard Audrey laughing. Handing Grey the Jameson bottle, I curled my arm around his, partially from cold and partially because I felt so impotent. Beyond us, the frog croaked unpleasantly.

When the orderly rolls me into Dr. Mya's office, the doctor doesn't greet me or acknowledge my presence though I've arrived on time. At her desk, she sits in a slump, staring at the opened file, twirling her pencil through her fingers like a miniature baton. Hair flat and lifeless, her clothes disarranged as though she'd dressed in her car and randomly applied her makeup at stoplights. Could the good doctor possibly have a hangover? Or nicotine withdrawal perhaps— I thought once I'd smelled a faint trace of cigarettes when she'd walked past me. Spectacles in her right hand, she appears bleary-eyed and irritated.

"Who kicked your ass?" I ask cheerfully.

She gazes at me a moment before sliding her spectacles back on. Does she need them, I wonder, or are they simply another artifice?

"Oh, Jane, good morning."

Hesitantly she half-stands, then drops to her chair again. She has the symptoms of a hangover. I try to imagine a Benson & Hedges dangling from her mouth as she tosses back a double scotch with a practiced grimace, clad in Olivia Newton-John leather pants and a dirty cowboy hat.

Somehow that image won't reconcile with her knee-length navy skirt, cream silk blouse, and Girl-Scout sensibility, despite the fact that her hairstyle this morning parrots heroin-chic.

"Good morning. Seriously, what happened to you?"

She smiles at me wearily, closes the file in her hand, and moves around the desk to take the chair across from me. She isn't wearing stockings; maybe she had dressed in her car.

"Late last night, I was paged about your visitor."

"No such thing as off-hours for a mind doctor, huh?"

Her eyes flash at me overtop her spectacles—a grilling look as if expecting to catch me at something—so I grin at her. In her hand, the pencil chokes.

"Jane, your recovery team—"

"My recovery team? What is this, *Mission Impossible*?"

"Your recovery team has reached an impasse of sorts. Have you spoken lately to your neurosurgeon?"

"We don't really talk. He just tests me."

"He has recommended that you be transferred to St. Luke's Rehabilitation Center to begin physical therapy. This is a positive recommendation: he believes your recovery is progressing well—that your concussion no longer requires intensive monitoring. "

"Well, that's kind of him. So the impasse?"

"Your orthopedist believes the pins in your right leg should be protected by a cast, after all. He wants to remove the intramedullary rod and have you in a cast for at least two months. In his opinion, physical therapy can't begin in earnest until the removal of the casts."

"Sounds like I should be discharged, maybe with a large prescription of codeine. How about it?"

"From a certain perspective, Jane, where you go once you leave this facility is your problem. But as far as your recovery is concerned, where you convalesce is vital."

"To be strong, to be well."

"What?"

"Convalesce. It's really a beautiful notion."

Dr. Mya runs her pencil along the edge of the file in her hands. I fight the urge to smooth her hair. Her office smells of anise. Behind her, the wooden blinds drawn over the windows inhibit even the semblance of a world outside the hospital.

"Despite your impressions, Jane, a number of people involved in your case have adopted a personal interest. The circumstances have been so unusual as to pique even the most jaded among us."

"How's that exactly?"

For a moment, I think she's going to burst out laughing, but she manages to swallow it back down.

"Jane, it can't go on forever."

"What can't?"

"Think for a moment: two insurance agencies, the hospital's accounting department, a university, and a renowned package delivery company are all involved here; these people take their financial records very seriously. They'll find out how to contact someone who's missing you. This charade can't go on indefinitely."

She pauses, waiting for me to interject something. I consider telling her I'm a covert operative, but haven't got the energy to play through. So I shrug.

"When the police became involved, they uncovered nothing: no driver's license, State I.D., phone listings, or affiliation with any community group. The two addresses on your emergency contacts list have been checked multiple times, of course: at one house, an older woman claims never to have heard of you; at the other, no one could be located until this last visit, when a gardener refused to speak with the officer beyond stating repeatedly that her employer is a woman named Emily Taylor who is currently traveling abroad."

Nick's mother really is a perfect bitch; the woman believes in a parallel universe, but *I* don't exist. (I'd used Nick as the emergency contact on my UPS application.) No doubt Hiromi refused to cooperate with the police believing that she was making a stand for civil disobedience—giving Emily's name in place of name, rank, and serial number. Hiromi has an immigrant's distrust of the police, which is lucky since she also has Emily's contact address and phone number in Paris on the notepad in the kitchen.

"Your colleagues have been interviewed a number of times and not one has ever been to your residence nor can any recall your mentioning a friend or relation—except for a former supervisor at UPS, and we have been unable at present to locate him as well. Somehow you've managed to live on this island for years and leave no physical impression."

"That sounds very sad."

She readjusts her legs.

"As I said, it can't last. Early this morning, I met with Dr. Grace Adams at U.H. We talked—she's only in town today and tomorrow before a conference in D.C.—about your work at U.H., and Dr. Adams gave me the opportunity to review your employment application."

The moment she says "review," I know she has found the crowbar to jimmy the trunk. My passport application, which I filed the year I turned eighteen, has my father's address in Maui on it. Now there will be no protecting him from the inevitable official notification: Sir, I'm sorry to inform you there has been an accident. Your wife, your daughter … there has been an accident. I cannot bear for him to know how I am broken.

"Your passport," she says. "You used it as picture identification on your applications at U.H. and at UPS. This morning I called the police and asked them to procure a copy of your passport application from the State Department. Naturally, this process of retrieval will take longer than anyone involved would like, and I'm telling you this in blatant disregard of my own instincts, as well as the recommendations of my colleagues. Even now, with discovery unavoidable, I don't believe you'll help us."

Her eyes search me with a pleading hopelessness, a look that seems to ask me to be better than myself, to rise above the resolution of secrecy I've maintained like a holy vow. She wants my confession and I find to my horror that I want to confess.

"Listen, the guy who came to see me—"

I stop. It isn't right to tell it like this, to drag Nick into it as if to hold him liable for my choices, to start the story in the middle. How can I explain to her that I have alienated myself from everything vital? That I walked through Manoa the night before the accident and decided to burn paintings, documentaries, surfboards, photographs like leaves in the street.

On a cul-de-sac that night, I saw a flash of red and found another way to make my bonfire. It had seemed so simple then as I crossed the yard, and now in the room with Dr. Mya fixating on me with her serious brown-rimmed spectacles— wanting so much—I find that I can't explain any of it, not rationally anyway. Hadn't the accident been a bonfire of its own? Hadn't it raged beyond any method of control?

"I can't—"

She prompts me: "The guy who came to see you—"

I shake my head. I'm standing in the cul-de-sac in the rain. Behind me, the screen door slams. Suddenly my leg burns so badly that I nearly cry out. When I look over at Dr. Mya, I find she's talking. Something about a meeting Nick was supposed to have had with my doctors, but he never showed. I concentrate on the pen in her hand, and will myself to track what she's saying.

"Even during my brief interview with him last night, he seemed agitated and reluctant to give any helpful information about your case."

"How could he have given helpful information?"

"He might have explained why no one knew you were married, or why the address he gave us was the same one inhabited by the older woman who'd claimed never to have heard of you. He might have told us about any other existing family members or why you've been in the hospital for a month and this is the first we've seen of him. He might have explained about the scarring on your back and wrists."

Her face has assumed the stern mask of a parent. She has taken a personal interest in my case. I can't explain why this surprises and terrifies me. In fact, at this moment, her expression raises my blood pressure. My leg prickles as though it has been asleep.

"Will you explain, please, about the scars on your back and the burn marks around your wrists?"

Oh god. My head feels swollen.

"Can you think of a single reason why I should?"

"More than one. Those scars indicate serious and repeated prior injuries. Given the extent of your current injuries and the time required for rehabilitation, it is essential that you recuperate in a safe and supportive environment. Those scars, coupled with the fact that you have guarded your private life fanatically, suggest to me that your home life will be neither."

Animated and sanguine, her argument spurs at her. I feel suspended between my horror of her accusations and my sense of their feasibility. Her version of events—more than plausible—illustrates how dangerous Nick's visit has been for me and for him.

"This morning during my meeting with Dr. Adams, she told me of the informal investigation conducted last spring as a result of concerns about your withdrawn and erratic behavior. She'd suspected drugs, but as you well know, found no evidence to support that supposition."

Around my mind I have the distinct impression of a vise

closing, squelching any chance of a logical rebuttal to Dr. Mya's hypotheses. Rage, a throbbing beehive, hums through me: images of Nick in handcuffs, police interrogations, and a squalid trial—newspapermen barking at us, insinuating the extent of our depravity—flicker through my head. As though I've had a stroke, my mouth and brain stem refuse to function properly. In the cul-de-sac, it's raining. I see a glow of white and think I may be sick. Something is trying to tear off my leg.

In my aching head, the cul-de-sac leads to a courtroom: the judge perched above me wears a tremendous white wig and blood-red robes; the executioner with his gimp mask and blunt ax stands motionless in the corner of the room. My clothes are wet. I can smell rain even indoors. A drop and a glow of white as my leg is torn from my body.

"Listen," I finally shout at her.

Dr. Mya says my name. She's pressing a button on her phone.

The smell of sweat and sex permeates the air around the jury; an attorney with a harness in his hand preaches about the sick, desperately immoral pit where I've made my bed; the judge strikes his gavel like a knell. But it isn't a gavel, it's a screen door. I'm running down the cul-de-sac in the rain, and then I'm on the tarmac, approaching the plane. I've levered myself below the cargo door and am just about to turn the latch.

"Listen to me. Listen for Christ sake. Listen."

I keep shouting. I can't stop.

XXIII.

I'd had insomnia for six nights in a row when Grey came to the house one Sunday morning for our road trip to Pali Lookout. Scraped raw and burning, my nerves traitored my calm demeanor.

"No sleep?"

I shook my head and threw my pack onto the backseat of his Honda. True to Grey, he'd packed water bottles, sushi, Funyuns, and fishcake to tide us for our half-day adventure.

We'd spent an inordinate amount of time, just the two of us, traipsing all over the island since the Flapper Party, each avoiding the lack of Emily by talking a little more excitedly than was natural for either of us. Grey seemed more like a brother to me now than ever before and I clung to him—I know I clung to him—with all my selfishness.

"I know it's early, but I want to beat the tourist buses up there. When I was in high school, we used to drive the Pali at night all the time. That stupid myth about driving to the Lookout with pork and getting hacked to pieces by the guy with the claw; man, we wanted that to be true. I got laid a bunch of times by the Hawaiian altars."

"Serious batchi."

"Yeah, and now I'm married to a nun. See what happens when you defile the sacred sites?"

"How is the nun?"

"I haven't spoken to her in a while actually. How's the heiress? Any word from the dark mansion?"

"Nothing."

"She's giving me the cold as well, but I've heard that she's going to Europe for a couple of months this fall."

"Maybe we'll meet up in Venice."

"Sure. Why waste all this hostility when you could share it with other countries as well?"

"You're so supportive."

He passed me the bag of Funyuns as a peace flag.

"Meanwhile, Delvo tells me the strike may be serious after all. She's been attending teachers' meetings and they're talking about a state-wide strike—all public school teachers—kindergarten through college."

"For money, of course."

"Of course."

"Is this why you haven't been sleeping?"

"I like money, Grey, and I need it to live. Professional instability I don't need. Even the moderates think this strike could last six months."

"That's alarming."

"Yes, it is."

I opened the fishcake and bit off a chunk as the car cruised up the Pali, and the lush green of the trees began to canopy us, parceling the sun into thin, random beams. U2 played on the stereo. I gave Grey my mother's rabbit story:

So there's this boy who discovers a burrow of baby rabbits early one morning. He crouches beside the hole, studying the five hairless bodies, and debates. How would he feed five bunnies, and what if their mother returned and found the nest robbed? He decides to hide farther along the path, and wait to see if the mother rabbit returns.

All morning, the boy waits by the path; occasionally the cry of one of the rabbits would disturb the forest. As the morning wore on, the cries became less frequent and less hearty. The boy decides to give the mother rabbit until midday.

The sun arches and begins its descent. Along the path,

the boy returns to the nest. Four of the rabbits are stiff and cold. The fifth twitches strangely. Cradling the last rabbit in his jacket pocket, the boy returns to his home.

"What the fuck kind of story is that?"

"It's a story of hope."

"It's a story about dead rabbits."

"It's a story about a boy who saves a rabbit."

"No way, that rabbit doesn't live."

"He's alive at the end of the story."

"You don't know that. The kid might have been cradling a corpse home. You know how hard it is for humans to feed bunnies? The little dropper and everything."

"You're outside the context of the story. In the story, the boy returns home with the last living rabbit."

"You poor sucker. You can't really believe that rabbit lives. It was twitching strangely, for Christ sake."

"You can't read into every story."

"I'm not reading into the story. 'Twitching strangely' was your line, remember?"

"I'm saying that stories aren't necessarily art. That story is about hope and rescue. The last rabbit lives according to the story."

"According to you it lives. The story isn't specific."

"About that single event. It's specific about the rest of the deaths."

"Yeah."

"So you see my point."

We pulled into the parking lot at the Pali Lookout, where three tour buses had already unloaded their groups. Grey groaned. Japanese couples were climbing all over the Lookout, taking photos of each other perched above the sprawling valley below this vantage from the Koolau Mountain Range.

"Is it true the winds here can support a human body—keep you from falling from the ledge?"

"Emily never told you that story?"

We locked the car, and skirted past the throng around the altar, through the curved courtyard to the wall on the right by the iron gates. The sheer cliff rushed to the valley below, which was covered in dense greenery. Kamehameha and his soldiers had pushed a rival army from this cliff, thereby securing victory in that particular war. Such a tumble against sharp rock—or worse, a plunge straight to the ground 70 meters below—raised the battle to mythic proportions.

"What story?"

"We were dating then and sometimes a bunch of us would come up here to make out, yeah? So this one night we come and Emily's amped up—hopping out of her skin. We're just hanging out in the dark, trying to freak each other out, and she runs to the ledge and leans toward the valley—fucking just hovers there like a kite—the wind rushes up her shirt and kicks her hair into a cyclone. It was a mad scene; we were all screaming and running to pull her down. I thought for a second, that second I was rushing her—so far past panic, adrenaline screamed through my body—I thought she'd vanish before I could grab her; I had this vision of her body shooting straight off the ledge into the sky like an egret. Wigged everybody out; we stopped coming here."

I looked to the valley below with a new fear now. What if that rabbit didn't live?

Emily had taken me to Tantalus one summer afternoon before we'd started sleeping together. The road up Tantalus wound in sickening curves and sharp bends that stretched the talent of many drivers (and cyclists) and the will of many vehicles. Emily pulled to the side of the road at one bend and told me about Driver's Ed her sophomore year in high school.

She'd been paired with this geeky haole boy who happened to be the bane of the instructor's existence. For their final training exercise, Emily drove the first half of Tantalus and then switched with the geek. When he'd closed the door and readjusted the mirrors, he asked the instructor which pedal was the clutch and which was the brake. The instructor lost his patience, reminded the geek that the car was an automatic, and threatened that another such question would mean failure of Driver's Ed. The geek drove straight into the rock wall after rounding his first curve. Emily said all she remembered was screaming and the orange finger-like petals of a trumpet vine. Exhilarated from the crash, she'd started laughing, even when she saw the geek's head bleeding so profusely blood poured down his shirt.

We'd climbed from the car so she could show me the mark on the rock that the car had left all those years before. It all seemed like bullshit to me; even the orange trumpet vine that grew just to the left of the impact mark felt staged in its brilliance. When we switched places so I could drive home, I took the bends as fast as her Miata would curl.

XXIV.

In Venice, Nick and I might have been flawless forever and lived in the deteriorating city of waterways, sending postcards to the jealous bastards too cowardly to live in Europe, who knew gondolas only as romantic clichés from obscure foreign films. We'd scoured the city each day—the cathedrals and exhibits, the tiny bistros and tenements, the gaudy shops—and returned to the same café each evening for olive bread and cheap red wine. The bread round and brown and warm in our mouths like forgetfulness, we were glamorous ex-patriots deconstructing the Salvador Dali exhibit we'd spent two days devouring. I thought of *Reflections of Narcissus*—the whole landscape melting and Narcissus forming two creatures from two perspectives— and wasn't it like that for us? The shape of the known world distorted in the landscape beyond us while we stood unharmed at the epicenter, radiating a bold self-reflexive light. Only later would I understand this light was happiness.

What if I had lived like that for twenty years? Forty years? What if I had finally outrun my unfathomable capacity for rage, dissatisfied girlfriends, and thwarted sexual relation-ships? What if we'd learned Italian, grown old eating olive bread, vanished from our lives? Could that happiness have been sustained?

In our hotel room, Nick stood on the threshold to the balcony and stared at the edge of city. He wore boxer shorts and looked terribly lean—shockingly lean—with his arm raised, hand resting on the top of his head, smoking Marlboro Reds. For the first time, he'd noticed my insomnia. Determined to stay up with me each night, he suffered in a way that I had outgrown, in an effort to—I wasn't sure why—to ease my loneliness? It was fruitless, of course: to go without sleep for a week is an irritant; to go without for years, a lifestyle. But the gesture moved me. I thought then, watching him on the balcony that night, struggling to keep pace with my sleeplessness that I could forgive him for anything.

At the end of the second week, he put me on the train to Rome and kissed me in the tender, tongueless style of old movies. I kept waiting for the fade to black as my train pulled away: girl looks wistfully out window; sound of laughter from the back of the compartment; hum of train; girl smiles; dissolve.

I didn't smile, though. Something ached in me for the whole of the train ride. Though I tried to read, I kept staring instead at the random world across the window, unable even to organize my mind into a single stream. Maybe I already sensed that dissolve had more than a single context.

When we left that skin in Venice and came back to our jobs, my ex, his mother, the titles on our bookshelves, meat jhun with kim chee, everything ordinary and familiar, did we forfeit that other self, that other life? That fall, I couldn't come when we had sex. The obvious solution was to try harder, more frequently, and we worked away: Nick shifting my body around like a sack of grain, purring, coaxing, teasing until the inevitable moment where he lay in exhausted fulfillment and I felt shredded. We fucked in his office, his Impala, posh hotels, the beach; me on top, him behind, sprawled on tables, standing in the shower. We role-played; we talked dirty. We became tired porn stars striving for some semblance of realism, anything to make it feel less staged and predictable. Oh right, here's the moment where she doesn't have an orgasm. And here's that moment again—failure on instant replay. Somehow my insomnia had infiltrated my sex life—the acute sense of dislocation permeating my brain and nervous system—leaving my body hollowed, restless.

And I thought again of Nick on the threshold in Venice as if he had been sculpted there. His hair crumpled and disheveled, his back bare, pale, hairless. How was it that the memory of him slouched against the doorframe held so much hope for me? The circumstance of his posture, was it, the fact that my insomnia had kept him up as well? Wasn't his carelessness part of his appeal, the slovenly unkempt sexiness of him at that moment in that ruined city where the two of us would always be young and symptom-free? I might have loved him there. Maybe it was as simple as that.

Work was supposed to be my outlet, the simplified, professional part of my life where sleep and orgasm had no effect. But anxiety about the strike swept like a brush fire through the university—rumors from the administration about slashed budgets, antiquated departments, and staff downsizing weren't encouraging, either—a mounting hysteria, worrying staff and students alike.

Chanda Prader, a Chinese girl with a journalism major, dropped by my office, fidgeting with the hem of her skirt, and talking randomly about her trip to Canada over the summer.

"Actually, I really came to ask you about the strike. Is it true? They're saying this might mean a six-month delay to graduating. Can that happen? Should I transfer to a school on the Mainland? I don't know what to do."

I didn't know what to do either, so I certainly couldn't

advise my students. I'd spent the previous spring reading all the graduate course textbooks and plotting my teaching strategy, only to be told I'd stay where I was put. If layoffs became necessary, I'd be the first to go from our department despite the popularity of Latin courses.

Delvo, shaken by the rumors, had taken a part-time teaching position with the women's prison several evenings a week and had encouraged me to do the same before the job market flooded with teachers.

"A contingency plan, Elliot, that's all. Not a panic situation yet, but these meetings have become dire, quite dire—I don't mean to alarm you—but it might be advisable ..."

Grey, in an effort to distract me, advised a night of drinking at Fat Tuesday's—an open-air bar in Aloha Tower Marketplace. He'd spent the previous two weeks in San Francisco with his family and was sporting a new prep-school shirt.

"So your wife showed?"

"Noticed the shirt, eh?"

"Obviously you like it."

"It's expensive and trendy. She could purchase for Banana Republic if she ever leaves politics. She came the last weekend."

"How'd she look?"

"She looked good. She always looks good. If seeing my wife a couple of weeks during the year were enough for me, I'd have the perfect girl. What's going on with you? You look frantic tonight."

"I'm light years beyond frantic. Honestly."

"Is your officemate giving you more cheery news about the strike?"

"If we strike, how will I pay rent?"

"You could live with Nick."

"Yeah, so there's that."

Grey flagged the waitress and ordered vodka shots. He

pulled my shirt sleeve to drag me around to his side of the table.

"OK," he said. "What's happened?

"God, I don't want to talk about it. Let's get drunk and forget everything."

"Sure, since that's the sensible thing to do."

We slung back the drinks, round after round, until the giggles set in. Some horrible alternative band played on the short stage to a crowd of moshing college kids. A breeze blew in from the pier, but both Grey and I were sweating.

"OK," I said, "so I can't come."

"Where?"

"In bed."

Grey grinned at me and leaned closer. Oh, the delicious failings of our friends.

"Ever?"

"Of course not, just this fall. I have no idea what the fuck's going on."

"Is he … does he suck?"

"No. God no, it used to be amazing. It's me. Something's wrong with me."

"Maybe you're a lesbian."

"Why would you say that?"

"Why would I say that? Hmm, because you recently broke up with a girl you were crazy about and had been seeing for months. And we've never talked about it, but I assume Emily wasn't your first."

"I'm not a lesbian."

"You say that like I accused you of being a leper."

"That's not what I mean."

I took a drink. What the hell did I mean? The spins had set in. I drank half my glass of water and focused on the mosh pit. Did that girl have green dreadlocks? Freaks crawled all over the bar, bobbing around as if the floor were a trampoline. The drums thundered in my head in the room, drowning out even the squeal of the guitar ... focus, focus.

"How do you know you're not a lesbian?"

"What?"

"How do you know?"

"Because I'm attracted to men, too, Grey."

"Attraction is all well and good, but if you don't enjoy the sex, that's problematic."

"It's a phase."

"Are you sure?"

"Jesus, I don't know. It's not like there's a litmus test."

"How many women have you dated?"

I gulped the rest of my water. Seven, eight, who remembers exactly?

"Eight, I think."

"How many men?"

"Twenty or so."

"Really?"

He looked puzzled, in complete contradiction to his confident prep-school shirt. As if the numbers had anything to do with it. I wasn't even sure they were accurate. Ultimately, I saw myself as bisexual, and how I saw myself was definitive, wasn't it?

"This band sucks, Grey. Let's take a walk on the docks."

We settled the tab and floated, though the music crowded us all the way to the water's edge. Against the piles, the black lapped and rolled like a great dog.

There was a girl once who would shed her skin and disappear into the night, formless. She crept among the trees like a leopard on the hunt until the night weakened, then she'd climb into the highest branches to watch for daylight. Leaving your skin is dangerous, but the girl continued her wanderings for many years, terrifying her neighbors and living among the dark predators. Late one night, she returned to the spot where she had hidden her skin and found nothing. Panicked, she tried to track the thief, but could smell only her own scent. She raced through the forest into the village and scoured for any sign of disturbance while in the east a faint glow shimmered. Suddenly dawn poured over her and her spirit vaporized. This is the risk when you leave yourself.

XXV.

Every Sunday morning, the Belfast dentist and I would drive to a stretch of beach to walk along the shoreline. White stone littered the ground where dozens of gulls swooped and hopped as the wind tore through the place, coaxing swirls into the dunes as the water swallowed our footprints, covering any trace of us, any memory. Occasionally someone ran along the beach, but most Sundays we had the sprawl to ourselves, especially in the late fall and winter when the horribly arctic wind blasted through our coats and sweaters through our very substance.

On the drive home with the heater roaring, we'd stop at a farm for duck and chicken eggs to make omelets of fresh mushrooms and tomatoes while we read the Sunday paper at the wooden table in the light-soaked kitchen. She would bake coarse brown bread in her T-shirt and panties or scurry around the flat, murmuring to the plants as she watered them, gently massaging their leaves.

She'd brought me to Christmas at her parents' home our first year together, having announced to her family beforehand that she was bringing her significant other. I didn't realize she'd told them anything until the shock on their faces registered. They were angels to make me feel welcome despite their grief, and their kindness made it easier for us with the two boys, Kieran and Thomas. Catholic and rigorous, her parents prayed, I have no doubt, hourly for our immortal souls, but we sat down to goose dinner quite merrily as the wine and whiskey loosed all awkwardness until we sang together a number of tunes I had never heard before, though the verses went on so long it was a simple matter to memorize the chorus.

Honestly, I'm still dismayed by her family's welcome, by the effort they put into accepting our relationship, into accepting me. I hadn't told any of my mates from school, or any of my colleagues from work, not even my father or Therese. I wasn't brave like her; I wasn't strong enough to love her fearlessly. And I left while she was in Greece on holiday with a group of her friends from dental school, packing my things hurriedly like any scoundrel, though I'd already interviewed with Dr. Adams by phone and had known for some weeks that I was leaving—had the one-way plane ticket to Honolulu and the cash from my bank accounts stuffed into my backpack.

That last Sunday in Belfast, I followed our routine, driving to the beach for a solitary walk along the channel, stopping for two duck eggs; I even watered her plants, stroking them like she did. Instead of reading the paper while the bread baked, I sat at the table and tried to write her a note, hoping not to justify my actions so much as elucidate my motives, but in the end I wrote only what allowed me to leave—what would make it impossible to return:

Gone home for good.
My best,

j

XXVI.

When I woke that Saturday morning, I heard grunting and thuds coming from the back corner of the garden; the sounds one expects during a murder or a birthing. I threw a shirt on and scurried through the French doors to find Emily's aged gardener, Hiromi, trying to break her body in half. A supplier had dropped two truckloads of red rock the previous day, and Hiromi now threw heaping shovelfuls from the rock mound into three wheelbarrows that were staggered along the pathway just at the edge of my studio.

"So sorry," she said as soon as she saw me emerge into the mist of the morning. She gestured to the pile by way of explanation.

I nodded, turned back into the cottage, and threw on a pair of boots before returning to take the shovel from her.

"I'll shovel the rocks in and out of the wheelbarrows if you'll clear the areas where you want them laid."

She scowled at me and tried to take the shovel back.

"I'll shovel the rocks into the wheelbarrows; we'll both take them to the area where you want them laid, and you can scatter them. Yeah, we'll split the work—be done in half the time."

She grabbed for the shovel again, but I held it over my head.

"Split the work. Grab another shovel; then we'll both fill and distribute the wheelbarrows."

Finally she relented. We filled all three wheelbarrows and began the treacherous job of guiding them over the rutted, marshy pathways to the kitchen side of the house. By lunchtime, we'd humped twelve loads to the areas Hiromi designated, filled holes in the paths, and spread the rocks as evenly as possible. In the back corner of the lot, the heap of rocks, still tremendous, seemed to scoff at our work ethic. Hiromi returned to her own house for lunch and I stretched against the doorframe of the studio, massaging the tight strain of my hamstrings.

"It's kind of you to help her."

I turned around so quickly that I jerked off balance and tumbled toward Emily. She stretched her arms out and would have caught me if I hadn't leaned backwards instead, nearly tumbling again.

"God, are you OK?" she asked.

"Mm-hmm. Legs are a bit tight is all."

"I've made lemonade. Thought I'd come out and lend a hand if you guys could use me."

I looked toward the insolent mound and nodded. *What the fuck?* sang through my head as I tried to think of something to say since evidently we were speaking again.

"Would you drink some lemonade?"

I nodded. Emily walked back toward the house to get the pitcher. Cups, I thought suddenly. We'll need cups.

"I'll grab some glasses," I called after her.

When I returned with three glasses, she was standing in the yard before the doorway as if barred from entry into the studio. I stepped out and handed her a glass.

"We could drink it at the table," I suggested.

She took the glass, filled it, and switched me for an empty one without moving toward the studio. OK. So we were speaking, but we weren't going indoors. It was just a matter of figuring out the rules.

"Have you surfed lately?" she asked.

"Grey and I caught a couple of nice sets last weekend—wicked crowded, though."

Her legs looked pale in her cyan sarong. Piled on top of

her head, her hair seemed anxious to pitch toward the thin straps of her bikini top. If I had extended my arm, I could have touched her, but the distance felt insurmountable.

"I surfed when I visited Charlie in California: lousy waves and cold."

"Yeah, I've heard that."

Standing in the grass, she kicked her foot absently as though juggling a soccer ball. After gulping the last of my lemonade, I lay on my back and stretched my body on an imaginary rack. Pulsing against my skin, I felt my hamstrings expand in painful millimeters as the slothful vines of the banyan trees loomed overhead.

"Why did you stay?" she asked.

I studied her, though her profile, like her tone, confessed nothing.

"It seemed worse to leave you," I said finally.

As soon as the "you" slipped, I wished it back again. *It seemed worse to leave.* Yes, so much cleaner without the presumptive you. After all these months, I still couldn't speak to her properly.

"I've debated that as well," she said softly as if to herself: "Has it been more painful knowing I could cross this garden to you?"

A strand of hair tumbled down her throat and nestled across her collarbone. Though the sun straddled the sky, our corner of the garden, shaded by the banyans, felt cooler, protected.

Hiromi returned with her giant peasant hat and extra gloves, tried to protest Emily's help but quickly quieted when Emily threatened to send Hiromi home and finish the job herself. All afternoon, the three of us cleared weeds, filled ruts, humped pile after pile of red rock around the property as the sun pitched overhead. Emily and I worked in bikini tops, heads bound in bandanas, grateful that the rains had finally relented.

At six, a delivery of Chinese food came and we scrambled to finish the last load before our food went cold. We ate at one of the little tables on the back balcony. It hurt to lift the fork to my mouth.

"You're taking the rest of the week off," Emily told Hiromi.

Hiromi said nothing, though I knew she'd be at work the next morning as usual, hours before I awoke. How an old woman could handle this, I couldn't fathom. My lower back had knotted as tightly as the core of a golf ball.

Emily passed another beer to each of us and we ate in silence as dusk collapsed into night. Hiromi left, patting Emily and me on the head as she went, disappearing noiselessly into the garden.

"Thanks for dinner," I said.

She nodded.

I finished my beer and wished for another, for some reason to draw out the evening, though it hurt to sit, to move, to breathe. I'd been too tired and hungry to throw on a sweatshirt and shivered now in the dark.

"Will you help me clear this up?" she asked.

I grabbed the bottles and boxes, separating for recycling and garbage at the far side of the house. Something might have happened. I'd wished for something to happen all afternoon, working alongside her in the garden, our bodies like pivots among the tendrils of vines and shrubbery stretching always skyward as though they had some memory of heaven.

With the table cleared, and no sign that she might re-emerge, I returned to the studio. *Has it been more painful knowing I could cross this garden to you?* I filled the bath with scalding hot water, and knelt against the tub; uncertain whether I had the strength to climb in.

XXVII.

Early on the last Saturday morning in September, Therese and I raced mountain bikes on the trails, skirting occasionally along the road and through adjoining fields, until finally we caught a path running parallel to the shoreline. From the sea, a breeze kicked past, but the sky spread before us clear and bright. We rode hard for over an hour, shifting gears and grunting against the slope, nailing roots and rocks while guiding the bikes with the hovering lean of our bodies. Therese led, and whenever I looked up I noted the tense strain of her back muscles as well as the cut of her triceps. She looked good, as hard as the Marin she piloted like a schooner over the trail.

Although I biked everyday, often riding for hours, I had become accustomed to city streets and quick sprints between passing cars; mountain biking required a different set of muscles. Instead of keeping my head up and watching around me, I had to keep my head down and force my bike over the ruts I would always avoid on the street. By the time we reached the turn-around point, I was aching.

"Swim?" Therese asked when I caught up to her.

I nodded, draining my water bottle. We shouldered the bikes and sprinted down to the beach. Tossing our bikes on the sand, we stripped and ran into the water. It was tit-numbing frigid, but I felt my muscles relax after a couple of minutes as my sweat washed away.

"You were mad up there. How often do you ride?"

"Nearly every day."

"God, I haven't been on a trail since Ireland."

"Just street biking on Oahu?"

"Yeah. I bike nearly everywhere. Not the same, though, this is killing me."

She looked over at me and smiled, pleased to have challenged me so thoroughly. Her hair slicked back from her forehead, her beady eyes flickered at me beneath her sparse strip of eyebrows. Her body quite taut; she didn't look anything like middle aged.

"We'll ride tomorrow too, if you decide not to surf, yeah? I enjoy having the company."

"Is it company when I'm so far behind? Tomorrow I'll ride harder."

I climbed out and shook as much of the water off as possible, then soaked my shirt, sponging my body. Shouldering the bikes from the beach up to the trail took a determined sprint, but the ride back to the house was easier for me since I anticipated some of the twists and pits.

Back at the house, I climbed the stairs to shower, determined to dwell in scalding water for at least twenty minutes, but I'd only just stepped in when Therese knocked once and stuck her head in the room.

"Hurry up, yeah, and meet me on the back porch."

I glanced through my lather and rinse, shivered the wet into my towel, and squirmed into my T-shirt and shorts, before hurrying down the steps. As soon as Therese saw me, she turned and walked toward the barn. She led me through the landscaping tools, buckets, and piles of hose upstairs to the loft. There were three large trunks and several stacks of boxes in the loft, along with an old tandem bicycle and some of the crates of toys I'd long since outgrown.

"Your mother's things are in the trunks and a couple of the boxes."

"I remember this stuff. I went through some of these before I left for school. I felt really guilty about it."

Therese stood at the top of the staircase and watched me move into the memorabilia. I looked up at her when she spoke: "It will be different to look through them now."

I nodded, stared at the trunks. Had she had so little? I heard Therese descending the staircase.

In the first trunk were her clothes. They smelled and felt coarse to my fingers. Some of the shirts seemed familiar, but none of the pants. Had I seen her wear any of these clothes? Several flair-rimmed hats sat atop the clothes, and I remembered the orange straw hat as her favorite. She'd worn it often in the orchard if we walked in the afternoon. Nothing smelled like her, though; the clothes, old and musty, belonged to an ancient tribe.

The second trunk held trinkets: porcelain cats, two strands of pearls, an assortment of handheld fans, a tea set with elaborate black Kanji symbols, several Japanese lanterns, yellow and red silk robes, cloisonné pieces, and miniature landscapes with one white crane, one traditional dwelling, and one tree encased behind glass. A number of bowls—sea colors of greens and blues—held small change from each foreign city she'd visited throughout her life. She'd had a story for every coin; there were dozens at rest in the bowls—their faces and symbols worn now, their sheen dulled.

I remembered each of these pieces and fingered them gently, as if I'd been left alone in a museum. When had Father put her things away? I'd felt her physical absence so keenly that I couldn't distinguish any sensation of loss beyond her. That seemed right to me, though, and I was relieved that I associated the pieces with nothing so much as her.

In the final trunk, I found the mother I knew from the stories she'd told me. On Guam, she'd headed the Language

Program at the high school on Andersen Air Force Base, and had found the most effective way to teach students to speak foreign languages was for the students to write stories. If they had to think about using the language to convey original ideas, they were more motivated and invested in the outcome.

For variation, they wrote and acted plays and also delivered spontaneous news broadcasts of real and imagined current events. When she married my father, she brought with her to Hawaii an old chest full of plays, posters, and kooky stories scrawled in the lopsided, ambitious handwriting of ninth graders. I was now scouring that very chest.

Packed away with her students' work, were two journals my mother had used to draft teaching plans and sketch ideas for her classes. Her footnote on the first page read: "Language at basic level always symbol: the stroke of letter, the picture of word, the line of sentence. This stands for me: this 'I'; kono watashi. And god is half altar, half say."

In the loft, I sat staring at her handwriting, the delicate curl of her *g,* the tight round of her *a;* each stroke ornate and purposeful. I read through what I could decipher of her journal—she had a habit of lapsing into Japanese when she wrote hurriedly—laughing at the bizarre pictures she'd doodled in the margins, until my father climbed the staircase to let me know supper was ready. When he found me on the floor with piles of my mother's papers and trinkets scattered around the floor like a paper tsunami, he stood for a moment and smiled.

"Therese said she'd left you up here hours ago."

"Her journals."

"Will they be useful to you?"

I nodded, one journal balanced as carefully in my hand as a glass of wine. Without really considering, I had expected my search to irritate him; somehow I'd felt he might disapprove of what I myself regarded as an intrusion into my mother's belongings. But he didn't mind; in fact, he seemed pleased that I'd found anything of interest. Was I such a stranger to my father?

"Take anything you choose."

He walked across the loft and knelt near me, his brown arm stretched to ruffle my hair. His favorite gesture, this quick mussing of my hair—all of his tenderness made evident in a single reach of his golden-haired arm. When had he grown so old?

"How do you find Therese?"

"She kicked my ass on the trail today."

"Strong that one, she'll live a thousand years and still not have a wrinkle."

His grooved brown face broke suddenly into his crooked grin. I followed him from the ruins.

XXVIII.

The trade winds vanished and the last, unseasonably arid days of October festered in the withered grass, scalding pavement, the blinding climb of buildings, landscape parched with want of rain. Back just two months from the outdoor cafés of Venice, and the mythical contentment I associated with that crumbling city goaded me. Bubbies Ice Cream Parlor at University and King, a weekly stop on my bike ride home from class, had become a daily respite from the brutal, unholy weather.

Shirt soaked with sweat, Nick pressed the glass of his root-beer float against his face and leaned his elbows on his thighs. Though the air conditioner hummed above us, our clothes clung like wallpaper. Decorated with bizarre black and white photos and Bubbies-through-the-ages T-shirts, the narrow parlor seemed desperately out of time as though a leggy roller skater with fake eyelashes might drift by at any moment with an order of fries for a greaser by the jukebox. In fact, the parlor had a jukebox, and Cracker's *Low* bellowed out, a denial of every time-warp sensation.

"So, what's up?" Nick asked, wresting his bangs back from his forehead in an aimless gesture—they toppled instantly and covered his eyes. He'd been eating more of my mint ice cream than I had, and now he spooned some into my mouth as if I were a toddler.

7:00 p.m. on a Monday evening, three young men sat on the stools at the counter up front, flirting with the ice-cream chick. All four of them spurt-laughing in an effort to drown the sad finality of a spoon clinking against the bottom of an ice-cream bowl. Nick had come straight from work to meet me; I'd been practicing my speech for two days, and couldn't remember a word now.

"I've decided to keep the studio and continue living there."

He straightened, set his glass on the table.

"Really?"

"I don't like the idea of giving up my place."

"I thought you were worried about the money."

"I am worried about the money, but I've got this gig at UPS—"

He groaned. Grey had finagled me a job on his ramp crew, unloading packages from the belly of a 747 into dozens of white containers the size of walk-in closets, which we then wheeled around the tarmac on Toyota tugs and dropped at various sort zones in the Hub from 6:00 a.m. to 11:00 a.m., Tuesday through Saturday. Three weeks of work and I'd already browned darker, bruised deeper, and put on five pounds despite rampant heckling from the crew about my twiggy girl arms. For Nick, the idea of a chick with a Ph.D. in Classics crouched inside the cold slick belly of an airplane, heaving boxes onto metal rollers was beyond absurd—to him, it was prodigal.

"It's a job, Nick."

"A job that's beneath you."

"I'm keeping the studio."

He looked at his glass a moment, then smiled at me. Obviously he'd recalculated his strategy.

"Why not take the winter off, concentrate on your classes, conserve your resources?"

"I don't mind the work."

This was true. It felt like a gift, to dress in my second-hand combat boots, surf shorts and tank top, to drive a

Toyota tug with a three-cart load of thousands of packages around the hectic tarmac to jeers from a crew both riotous and crude. My yellow leather gloves lent the work a rodeo flavor—and always at the end of the morning a tangible sense of accomplishment.

"It's ridiculous to waste your money on rent when I have plenty of room at my place. What will you do when the teachers strike? How are you going to afford the studio then?"

"I'd face the same dilemma at your place."

"But you'd have savings to rely on because you won't need money at my place."

"Jesus, Nick, I don't want to be the chick that latches on to the money guy and stops working, stops paying to support herself. It's important for me to have my own place. I don't want to worry about disturbing you when I can't sleep or when I have to be up at 5:00 a.m. Don't you like the idea of choosing to sleep together rather than assuming we will night after night in some dismal pattern?"

"Some dismal pattern? What are we really talking about?"

I wanted to tell him that something had happened. My insomnia was worse; emptiness sprawled inside me like an oil spill; our sex never sated me anymore.

"We're talking about my staying in the studio because it's necessary."

"Let's get out of here."

I followed him outside into the oppressive glare, the noise of traffic and pedestrians no longer muted by the air conditioner, or the jukebox. A patch of sweat spread down the middle of his green oxford shirt like an inlet. He paused beside my bike, leaned close to me; his hand stretched out to touch my belly, and left a wet mark.

"Let me come to the studio with you tonight."

I nodded. I felt us ending there on the sidewalk as a shockingly white girl buzzed past on a pink moped.

This miserable October, even the banyans could not keep the studio cool. I'd cast all the windows open, left the lights off, the ceiling fans churning so that the main room felt almost bearable, the wooden floorboards cool beneath our bare feet. He'd never been in the room before, not in all the months we'd dated. I'd kept this much for myself.

"It's different from what I'd imagined—nearly empty, really."

"I'm not a collector."

"Not of things anyway."

He grinned at me. I handed him a beer from the fridge, unbuttoned his shirt and slid it off, the sleeves catching on his wrists. We edged backwards toward the futon but collapsed onto the floor by the kitchen table instead, his pants peeling away like skin from a mango. I wiped my face on his shirt, mopped it across his body—our skin slick with intention. My body: a slide for desire. We dragged through the room, tumbling candles, Latin texts, CD cases, attempting to excavate each other's body as if to recover something precious.

"Don't move your hands," he said, his hips punching into me.

He rolled me onto my stomach, pinned my arms behind my back and struck me—a quick slap. My impulse to laugh quelled by the second slap, the third; his palm hit repeatedly in the same place, until the skin numbed and burned, until I bit into my lip to keep from screaming, until my head dropped forward and he pushed into me deep enough to taste.

Something was agreed to that night, something decided, and Nick left knowing he'd return, knowing that now I wanted him to. As I ran a bath, I thought about my routine, all's well meeting with Dr. Adams earlier that week. Before the meeting, I hadn't bothered to reflect on the tremendous fiscal strain throughout the university, its effect on our department, and particularly on Dr. Adams. After the discovery of my mother's journals, I'd become obsessed with adapting her methodology to my second-year course, and in my enthusiasm I told Dr. Adams, imprudently and at length, that the prescriptive nature of the current course, the unvarying, unutterable boredom of the curriculum, were impediments to the study of Latin at U.H.—impediments easily overcome with a bit of ingenuity. She'd laid her pen down deliberately on her desk, fiddled with a steaming cup of tea, and finally glared at me:

"And what do you propose, Dr. Elliot?"

"I think a little variation to the lessons—something besides routine grammar and translation exercises—would really invigorate the students. The course can be rigorous without being dull. What if we had them perform a play, or even write one? It would be exciting to put Latin to practice, wouldn't it?"

Dr. Adams took a sip of tea, arched an eyebrow, and said wryly:

"Dr. Elliot, I don't think you are purposely imperceptive, so I will only comment that I can't afford any dissent in this department at present. We are facing a real crisis—not a theoretical one—at this university and crises are not the time for experimentation. Your role is to ensure the students perform at the eminent level we have come to expect from this department. If this were a time of plenty, Dr. Elliot, an exploration of alternative teaching techniques might be appropriate. As it is, however, this is rapidly becoming a time of famine, and I refuse to let any of us—staff or students—starve."

Even in the hallway I felt the wariness and displeasure that had fluttered between us like moths in the evening.

XXIX.

At Duke's Canoe Club, two corpulent Samoans, a guitarist and bassist, in bright red luau shirts played contemporary Hawaiian music, their harmonies sailing into evening outside the open-air bar in the high octaves of a boy choir, their fat fingers fluid on the fret boards through frequent solos. Drinking scotch, Emily and I sat on the outer edge of the bar where the music faded to background noise and Diamond Head loomed in the darkness beyond us like the hull of a great ship.

She'd called me at work, her voice pitched higher than usual, her sentences jostled together like train cars, to invite me to Duke's for drinks. We hadn't been out together since I'd returned from my weekend in Maui.

On our third round, I finally relaxed enough to look at her: hair pulled into a precarious bun, jabbed with chopsticks; purple lavalava halfway up her thighs; scar painfully white against her tanned face; her brown eyes glazed with alcohol and excitement actually meeting mine for the first time in months. Still gorgeous.

"So I have a plan," she said.

"Yeah?"

"Body piercing."

She paused, eyebrows raised, mouth agape, expecting me to appreciate the scope and grandeur of this plan. I grinned at her.

"Can you tell me anything more?"

"Nipple piercing."

"Ah. It's starting to click now."

"What do you think?"

"For you?"

She nodded. I thought about her nipples.

"They'll be off center."

Emily laughed, head tossed back, throat exposed like a displaying bird.

"Aren't you afraid of the pain?" I asked.

She held her glass up, "That's what the scotch is for."

"You're doing this tonight?"

"We're doing it."

"I don't want my nipples pierced."

"No, but you're coming with me. I can't go alone. You have to be there to hold my hand."

I almost asked why Ray the bartender wasn't going, but the selfish part of me didn't want to know. It pleased me to think I was the one she wanted.

"OK. So where do we go?"

"Hole Punch, where I got my bellyring done. I made an appointment for nine with Jai. We have time for two more rounds."

"I haven't eaten since breakfast."

"You probably shouldn't now."

This seemed logical, amazingly, and I continued on my shot diet until we left (slightly wobbly) for Hole Punch. Along Kalakaua Avenue the storefronts were a carnival: Japanese tourists in garish fluorescent colors, loud tinny music, cheap T-shirt racks draped with plastic-flower leis; the obese haole family wearing visors and sunburns gathered around the obligatory white guy shouldering a parrot for tourist photos, as though parrots were indigenous to Hawaii. Ten minutes from Duke's, the shop was on the second floor of a Samoan-styled bamboo building, shielded from the neon strip by a palm tree studded walkway.

Inside the shop a longhaired chick lounged behind the counter, four silver hoops through her lips like fangs. Her halter-top revealed the tattooed body of a dragon swiveling its body up her chest and over her shoulders. The walls were cluttered with photos of various body piercings: the ball piercing with or without chain, the nipple rings, the penis stud. And ring displays of gold and surgical steel: small, medium, circus-sized.

"Jai."

"The belly looks good."

Emily nodded, waved at me by way of introduction, "My support."

Dragon-girl gave me a look, and then told Emily, "$160. Cash only."

Emily gave her $200: "I want the silver hoops with the blue stud—12 gauge."

"I'll measure your nipples to make sure 12 gauge will work."

We followed her through to a sparse room with a single yellow table and more photos. The dragon continued over her shoulders and plunged down her back; what appeared to be a tongue flicked beneath her left armpit.

"Shirt off; stand straight."

Emily stripped her shirt and handed it to me. Her tits looked shockingly white compared to her tanned surf lines. Jai measured the circumference of each nipple and nodded.

"12s will work. So, your nipples have to be hard. I can do it, or you can."

After Emily pinched her nipples hard, Jai marked each one on both sides.

"OK?"

Emily checked the placement and nodded.

"Have a seat, I'll put the clamps on and grab a needle."

Dragon-girl swathed Emily's nipples with betadine before attaching the clawlike clamp. I started to feel distressed.

Emily's fingers cinched my hand and a tightness passed across her features as Jai maneuvered the needle into position.

"OK, it's important to keep breathing."

It was like a birth scene. I kept thinking I should be coaching her to relax her jaw and make open-throated sounds. Jai thrust the needle through and stoppered it with a piece of cork. Emily had made a low growl, then gone mellow.

"Breathe," I said helpfully.

My fingers were blue where Emily clenched them.

"You ready for the second one?"

Jai went on without waiting for an answer, repeating the thrust and stopper. Several seconds later, Emily gasped, *"Ow!"* in a surprised way, as if the pain had finally climbed through the haze of scotch to her brain and started kicking her nerve sensors. Focusing for the first time, she looked up at me: "Are they bleeding?"

I nodded. A couple of streams of blood slipped down her torso, and Jai used a swab to wipe them away.

"Em? You have to breathe, OK?"

"I had a fainter in here last night," Jai said. "Tongue ring. He looked fine and then he fainted in the doorway there. You can still see the blood on the doorjamb."

Crouched beside Emily, I put my hand on the back of her neck and leaned my face against hers.

"Em, you have to breathe, baby. It's almost over. The hardest part is over." I looked up at Jai, "Right?"

"Yeah, we just have to thread the rings and seal them. A quick tug you won't even notice."

She pulled a ring through the hollow of each needle and closed each ring with a blue ball.

"So, you're looking at a six-month healing curve. Use betadine to clean the piercings at least three times a day. I hope you brought a bra."

She hadn't, so I slipped mine off and helped Emily secure it. Her nipples looked raw and grotesque, still viscous with blood. Wrapped in her shirt, she huddled toward the door.

Jai grabbed my arm, "Help her get some ice on those. Makes everything easier."

Outside beneath the palm trees, I steadied Emily, and looked her over. Completely sober now, I'd realized that I had no idea how we were supposed to get home.

"Should I hail a cab?"

"That really fucking hurt."

"It certainly looked that way."

"How do they look?"

"Too early to tell."

"I want to see them."

"You should wait until I can get you home."

"You have to help me with this shirt."

She squirmed like a child from my grasp.

"Be reasonable. Wait until I can get you home. Just let me hail a cab."

She stopped struggling, leaned over, and hurled against the nearest palm tree. Straightening slowly, she spat and took the first deep breath in forty minutes. A street lamp blinked out.

"Jesus, that fucking hurt. I parked the truck at Duke's. You can toss your bike in the back."

"I'm driving."

"I fucking hope so, honey."

That night, all the high school kids on the island were cruising Waikiki in their tricked-out Japanese sedans, and low-rider paint-brushed trucks. We sat in traffic at every light, creeping along while the pedestrians outpaced us, and the hookers stalked past in their pantyhose and heels.

"I came closer to loving you than anyone," she said.

The jeep next to us, packed with five blond navy guys, swayed as they leaned out to harass the hookers. A six-foot

225

gumball machine took up half the sidewalk outside the truck window, where three small boys had gathered as if in homage. We'd drunk enough scotch that night to last a crew through to Antarctica. I thought of her butchered nipples.

"Well, that's something."

"It might have been. It might have been something."

"You're drunk."

"Don't change the subject. I may never be able to say this again."

She edged across the bench seat so that I'd have to shift into her leg if we ever moved from this stall. What good would this conversation do us now?

"Fuck, Em, maybe you shouldn't."

"You're in love with him?"

"Who's changing the subject now?"

"All this time and you're still afraid to talk to me."

"Don't try to bait me. I'm not afraid."

"You're in love with him?"

"I doubt it."

"But you were in love with me?"

"Yes."

"And you weren't comfortable with me seeing Ray?"

"No."

"Even though we talked about it beforehand?"

"I thought you should be able to do whatever you wanted—I still think that. My heart just isn't as rational as my mind."

We drove through two lights, then stalled again. Another obese family trudged past, wearing thick-soled thongs and chartreuse shorts. I wanted to punch the horn, drive around the coconut trees on the sidewalk, and get the fuck out of Waikiki and this truck and this conversation.

She laid her hand on the stick shift, swaying it back and forth in neutral.

"It felt like you might never trust me," she said.

"I trusted you."

"Not enough."

"Em, there's no point in doing this, really. It's been a tough night."

Traffic picked up again and we fled through the city, snaking between low-riders and sedans, blitzing yellow lights, until finally we cruised into the compact neighborhoods of Manoa. She'd left her hand on the stick shift, her arm moving in a jerky rhythm with mine. I pulled into the carport and cut the engine.

We sat in the dark cab and I understood that if I leaned over and kissed her, careful not to brush against her chest, that she'd kiss me back. Her wide mouth like a place of extinction I kept returning to, looking for evidence, for precedent, for some archaeological proof of my existence.

"I've been so angry with you," she said.

"I know."

"You were my only secret."

Reaching across her face, I smoothed her cheekbones with my thumb, sketching her nose, eyebrows, the soft curve of her eyes down her jaw line to her throat. She'd closed her eyes and tilted her head. I pulled the chopsticks out and let her hair tumble, sweeping it back from her face until my hand caught and I stopped, waiting for her eyes to open, for her to look at me.

Leaned over her, I brushed the outside of her thigh so that she trembled into me, her mouth wide like hope as my hand skirted higher. Even then I might have withdrawn, terrified of her new wounds and my old ones, wanting for each of us something better than this—something nobler than a drunken fuck in the cab of a truck. Her eyes opened then in the darkness, and I kissed her—went on kissing her until my mouth nearly bled.

XXX.

I'd been carrying one of my mother's journals in my bag for nearly a month before I finally caught Delvo in the office at noon. Amidst escalating uncertainty about the strike, she'd started teaching an afternoon class—rudimentary composition three afternoons a week—at the Women's Correctional Center in addition to the evening classes she taught there. How Delvo could brave a prison when hospitals paralyzed her with terror didn't calculate for me, but certainly these were lean times. Hair frazzled, rasping heavily, she greeted me with an eager embrace—I tried not to recoil when she inadvertently pressed the marks on my back—as if we had been apart for years. She wore a rather nasty fuchsia stretch top with her blue jeans.

"It's my day off from teaching at the prison. I feel like an actual human being. Next week we begin a new session of composition classes—the three-paragraph essay. It's pure joy, I promise you. Pure joy."

I handed her my mother's journal, opened to the page I wanted translated. She eyed the script assiduously as if I might have presented her with some rare black market forgery.

"How accomplished is your Japanese?" I asked.

"My reading is quite good, my understanding more so. My pronunciation is dreadful. Wait, I need my glasses."

After rummaging in her bag, she put on the thick lenses and began to read the page before her.

"Beautiful script here. Beautiful. God is half altar, half say."

228

"Yes, I can read that part at the bottom. It's in English."

"The Kanji symbol next to the English bit is the Japanese word for god, which is, in fact, composed of the symbol for altar and the symbol for say. It seems to be unrelated to the text above, however."

I moved behind her desk and watched over her shoulder as she ran her finger across each line of text. My mother's Kanji characters were drawn in the ancient, fluid style, the words themselves art.

"Hand me a piece of paper, Elliot. Yes, I know this. This is a poem. It's a translation of a poem."

She translated the first stanza into English, and began on the second. Muttering in a deep, random grunt as her pen halted repeatedly across the piece of paper. I watched as the poem took shape on the page before us.

"The title is *Going Blind*," she said triumphantly. "Do you recognize it?"

I read the first two translated stanzas and shook my head.

"No?" Delvo shook her head sadly, "And to think you were educated by the Irish."

"Is the poet Irish?"

"Good Lord, no. This poem is by Rilke."

She continued translating and finally arrived at the last stanza. I mouthed the words as they appeared:

> *She followed slowly, and she needed time,*
> *as though some impediment slowed her way;*
> *and yet: as though, once she was past it,*
> *she would no longer merely walk, but fly.*

"This is intriguing, Elliot. Where did you find this journal?"

"It belonged to my mother. She used it for lesson plans and reading notes."

"Quite a skilled translation. She taught languages?"

"English, Spanish, Latin, Tagalog, and Japanese."

Delvo took off her glasses, rubbed her eyes, and smiled at me.

"So you come by this naturally," she said. "That is a great relief to me. I hate the idea of drastic leaps in evolution."

"Oh, for Christ sake. You don't, either."

"I do, I assure you. Sometimes when I'm teaching my class at the prison—these young women who can't conjugate verbs in their native language or spell rudimentary words—I feel the distinction of education keenly. But radical evolution skews all of our notions of progress. Random genius is one thing, but a division is growing—a very real division, Elliot—between those who conceive a ritualized world of guns, gangs, and exploitation, and those who craft language and mathematics in search of truth and beauty. How long before the rituals swallow up the craft and we relive medieval times?"

I shook my head, leaned my shoulder against the drab cement wall, and mindlessly straightened one of the many precarious stacks of books on her desk: "That's spurious and terribly oversimplified and you know it. What do craft and ritual have to do with drastic leaps in evolution? Are you suggesting that egregious lawlessness is an evolutionary trait?"

"Never forget, Elliot, that academic institutions are insular. There is a wide world of evil and ignorance out there. Evolution, by its very nature, concerns the development of acute survival skills. In a single word: savagery. Consider why crocodiles and sharks are pinnacle predators—creatures that have reached the most sophisticated level of evolution possible for their species—and what that means. Savagery, Elliot, to be the strongest, fastest, most brutal creature in your environment, this is what the crocodiles and sharks have mastered. The only threats to their dominance are humans and each other."

I kicked the base of her chair, "Don't try to use crocodiles against me. Your theory underestimates the vital shaping power of intelligence."

"Not at all. I simply doubt its ability to limit the sprawl of criminal enterprise."

"You really need to give up teaching at the prison. It's fractured your mind. So you see fatalism in evolution? You see a prescient consciousness? What about the prey's evolution?"

"Evolution involves simply the struggle to stay alive through any means necessary. The prey evolves over time so that it will continue to outwit the predator. Therefore the predator's savagery inspires the prey's evolution, or the prey's extinction. I do, in fact, see fatalism in evolution. I will not mislead you. I believe there is a god, but he does not love us."

She guffawed good-naturedly and handed the journal back to me.

"A pretty poem for a tragic age, my friend," she said.

"I never realized the depth of your pessimism."

"You're right; I should stop teaching at the prison. One more essay from a nineteen-year-old who cannot spell *don't* properly and regrets above all else that she disappointed her children, and I will howl until the ice caps finally melt and end all suffering. I hope that Rilke is right and flight is our reprieve."

When Delvo had gone, I sat in the office alone, examining the sheet upon which she had written the English translation. Why this poem? What had my mother seen in the lines? Was it hope?

During my second class that afternoon, Amber, a bushy-haired haole in pre-med who had aced the last three tests, stopped reading her translation and looked at me.

"I hated this myth," she said quietly.

"Why?" I asked, noting that several of the other students had nodded in agreement.

"It's so evil. Actaeon just stumbled upon her. He wasn't some pervert trying to see her naked or attack her or anything. He was lost. He made a wrong turn."

"Our justice system holds people to a similar standard. You can be convicted of a crime whether or not you knowingly broke the law."

"Yes, but we don't let your dogs devour you."

The class laughed.

"The gods exact vengeance as they see fit. Diana is chaste. Any man is a threat to her chastity, no matter what his intentions."

Unconvinced, Amber shook her head, returned to reading the translation. Disturbance of a sacred place, a virgin, a god—these were heavy sins—though Delvo might have argued Actaeon was compelled to agitate Diana. That the Fates had already cast him as a stag in the final act, and the resultant savagery had been made inevitable by Diana's being stronger, faster, more brutal. I too was starting to transform: the wounds on my back precluded bikini tops, surfing, chummy pats on the back. I began to seem a different creature with my long-sleeved shirts and stiffened gait.

XXXI.

On the rainiest weekend I'd ever witnessed, Nick took me to the Honolulu International Film Festival to watch the day-long anime exhibit. Upended umbrellas clogged the aisles, their wire tips grasping at our pant legs as we scuttled down a row of soggy, shivering attendees. A rotund film critic introduced the anime shorts and explained the transformative storytelling vision of Japanese animation, where moral ambiguity made a clear bad-guy inconceivable and imagination took the stories from underground cities to flying pirate battleships.

Nick watched each film like a child—gasping with delight at the intense scope of the animation (the worlds of hyperrealism), sniggering at the silly characters and incidents (the chipmunks mating like humans), suffering through the often heart-rending experiences of the characters (the chipmunks parted when a hunter shoots the female). When an artistic young man was dragged away by the Establishment and tortured into believing he had never seen a mermaid, much less loved one, Nick clenched his fists and held his breath as if contemplating some method of rescue for the pencil-looking character on the screen.

In his basement flat, Nick had organized a giant home theater in which his collection of hundreds of movies could be viewed with superb acoustics and just the right amount of light to keep one from going blind after an 18-hour movie marathon. The first film we'd watched together, *It's a Mad Mad Mad Mad World,* had taken nearly six hours to get through since, in addition to numerous smoke breaks, Nick had stopped the movie repeatedly to give me background information on the actors, sets, cars, direction, etc. In the scene of the final chase through the condemned building, he stopped the tape and told me I was about to see the most beautiful thing imaginable. I nodded appreciatively and prepared myself. He'd been referring to the derelict, crumbled foyer of a once grand hotel, where the camera paused momentarily before ascending the staircase in pursuit of Spencer Tracy's double-crossing cop. Did I know so little about beauty?

During the festival's afternoon break, Nick and I sprinted four city blocks through the blitzkrieg of rain to a dive of a Chinese restaurant; he ordered beef broccoli and pork fried rice for both of us. Stripping our jackets, we dripped all over the torn cushions of our booth, and stole napkins from the next table to use as towels. From the walls, black and white porcelain cats glared at us. After several cups of hot tea, I felt the ache leave my fingers.

"I was born in Okinawa," Nick said. "My dad was stationed there until 1969, and one of my first memories is watching 'Ultraman' on television with Andy. Sort of a precursor to 'Power Rangers'—you know, a live-action robot warring with various monsters. Probably pretty cheesy now, but at the time we were insane for 'Ultraman'—had the action figures and used to act out the various fight sequences, sing the battle songs, I've dug anime ever since."

"I remember 'Ultraman'—the red and silver robot, yeah? I remember the boys at school collected each one. They had different masks or something."

"Different helmets. Yeah, each successive action figure looked tougher and more futuristic—different suits as well. I can't believe you remember that."

"God, it was all those boys talked about for months."

"What's your earliest memory?"

I thought of the orchard, and navigating the paths beside my mother. How the long grasses swayed like souls against her legs. Always the wind in the branches confused with the croon of birds.

"Walking through the orchard with my mother. But I don't think it's accurate."

"Why?"

"I remember her holding my hand, but she wouldn't have. She rarely touched me."

"What do you mean? She had to touch you sometimes."

"She was so intense, you know? Every movement, every expression, I had this sense of her, this awareness. I'd tuned into her presence, but she was removed, peripheral, like an electron orbiting a nucleus. I remember her stories, and being beside her in the orchards. I can hear her voice all these years later, and the smell of her, but I don't remember ever being held or kissed."

Nick leaned across the table and brushed my hair back from my forehead. Contracted under his thick eyebrows, the hazel seriousness of his eyes worried for me.

"You were so young, Jane. Maybe things were different from the way you remember them."

Could he not understand how that thought terrified me more than any other? The waitress brought our heaping plates and another pot of tea. Around us, the other booths had filled slowly so that the restaurant buzzed with conversation. Nick hadn't shaken his concern. With his chopsticks, he stirred his sauce in a whirl, tangling broccoli, carrots, and meat with the noodles.

I scooped the rice greedily into my mouth. In the booth behind us a man reported to the waitress that the rain hadn't let up as it streaked down the windows directly across from where she stood, waiting to take his order.

"Who's your favorite actor?" Nick asked.

"It's still Emma Thompson."

"Oh, I've asked that before? OK, what's your most embarrassing moment?"

"When I caught my hair on fire in the school cafeteria blowing out my birthday candles."

"Seriously? Which birthday?"

"My seventeenth. My buddies put too many candles on the ice-cream cake. Singed off my eyebrows, all the hair around my face, and burned these round sores into my lips. And Jesus, the smell—too horrible to describe—all this black smoke rising from my head in a dark halo. Everyone just sat at the table with their mouths opened, watching my head flame like a tiki torch."

He laughed at me: "Oh my god, that's classic. I wish I'd been there."

"I had to shear my hair to get rid of all the damage. Really sexy."

"You look good with sheared hair now. OK, first kiss?"

"Second grade, Michael Watanabe's bedroom closet. And then he showed me his little dick."

"Favorite band growing up?"

"Don't laugh."

"I'm not going to."

"Simon & Garfunkel."

He laughed.

"They were my dad's favorite," I said. "We listened to them all the time when I was a kid—wore the records out."

"I never would have figured."

We finished the plates, and reclined in the booth to sip the last of our tea as the restaurant emptied around us. Outside, the fog of moisture hazed pedestrians and vehicles.

"What was your finest hour?" he asked.

I thought of the day I'd graduated from Trinity, how the dentist had prepared a lavish dinner of Chilean sea bass with tart, spicy sauce and we'd drunk an expensive bottle of white wine that made me giddy and euphoric. I had loved her then. Her dark eyes pulling at me like the moon.

"When I was offered the research position at the Linguistics Institute."

"Really? But you left three years later."

"Still," I said by way of explanation, and shrugged.

I stretched my legs under the table, had an image of the dentist returning from her vacation in Greece to find my sullen note and nothing more. Nothing more. Scouring through his wallet for the correct amount to pay our bill, Nick's head bowed into his task, his lips moving as he calculated tip. I ate my fortune cookie, left the scrap of paper on my plate unread.

"So you ready for more anime?"

I nodded, clapped my hands: "Bring on the moral ambiguity."

XXXII.

During the mornings I worked at UPS on the ramp—with Grey wearing his requisite white shirt and tie!—the tough physical work was a relief to me after months in the classroom. For those five hours I didn't have to worry about cutbacks, Nick, tadpoles, or my own inadequacy. My body found a groove and I worked past exhaustion and pain to a sort of bliss.

"How long before I'm driving forklift?" I asked Grey one morning when he picked me up for work.

"You're unreal. I'll partner you with Chance Chang—he's my best guy. You'll be driving forklift in a matter of weeks."

During the fall semester, I had to shower at school Tuesdays through Fridays, but the extra money was worth it, as well as the added benefit of worrying less about the negotiations, then underway, to avert a teachers' strike. UPS had killer benefits as well and Grey—one of the few non-asshole supervisors—looked out for me. Partnering me with Chance made for a sweet time: the guy was hapa (white mother, Chinese dad) and had gone to the hippie Evergreen University in Washington, where he'd smoked pot and blitzed on mushrooms all the while avoiding the unpleasant constraints of a grades-dictated education as he majored in Philosophy. Two years out of college, he worked mornings at UPS for the benefits, and afternoons at the landscaping company he owned with a buddy from high school. Thin and lanky with scraggly, orange-tinted brown hair, he ate poi and tuna on white bread compulsively. When Grey told him I surfed longboard, Chance and I were buds for life.

"Longboard girl, oh yeah? Shoots, you come out one Sunday morning, yeah? 4:00 a.m., we surf Queens: get choice waves and no fucking tourists."

I'd seen Chance at Anna Banana's with some of his surfing buddies: very earthy fellows who were obsessed with grabbing each other's crotches, but they'd seemed silly and harmless.

"You teach U.H.?"

"Yeah, Latin."

"Ho, Latin? You're like European?"

"I went to school in Ireland. I grew up in Maui, on an orchard near Haiku."

That was my second score; Chance wanted to know every detail about the orchard and what it had been like to grow up among the trees. He would have loved my mother; listening to her stories in the mango grove would have been Chance's idea of nirvana.

Since the fall rains had made everything dismal, Emily and I started racquetball wars at her gym. I'd played tennis in high school, but racquetball was a different species. Certainly some people were adept at targeting low flat shots or wicked unrecoverable angles, but Emily and I simply wailed. I'd go into the musty echo chamber with my body knotted tight as cornrows, punish that sweet blue ball with my dwarf racket until I couldn't grip the handle anymore, and then break for water. We'd play best of seven and every set was like being reborn—all sins purged; we were purified.

A shocking amount of swearing and grunting droned through the room with a frequency to rival the winged ball. Emily played well, and what I lacked in skill I compensated for with aggression—hurling myself into the walls, diving across the wooden floor with my racket stretched optimistically toward the lowest of low shots, battering into Emily like a wrecking ball. All too often our rackets connected with our competitor's body rather than the ball (mostly by accident), heightening the level of tension in the swampy, tropical room where Emily had been reduced to playing in a sports bra and boxers. I kept my shirt on despite the sauna.

Emily and I had reached Appomattox—no one had disarmed, but we'd established a ceasefire. I hadn't slept with her since the nipple piercing. That night, she'd stayed in my bed, where I applied ice compresses wrapped in washcloths, vigilant and worn with the weight of desire, with ending. Since that night, we'd drunk beer in the garden, gone for breakfast or sushi, and played racquetball three times a week. A tension lingered, but only a variation of the sexual energy that had always complicated our relationship.

After we'd played for a solid hour, one Saturday in November, Emily slammed her racket into my back, catapulting me onto my belly. With a screech, my knees grated against the floorboards before I came to rest, the taste of sweat and dust in my mouth.

"Shit, I'm so sorry. I know that hurt."

She tried to suppress a wave of hysterical laughter that erupted when I groaned.

"Oh, you bitch!"

"Are you OK?"

She knelt beside me, coughing and spurt-giggling, as she rubbed the spot on my back where she'd nailed me. Having finally caught my breath, I'd meant to clamber up and redeem myself when my brain ignited: a feverish sting tore through my back from the press of her hand; as I writhed from her grip, I couldn't quite capture a reflexive yelp.

She recoiled, "What the fuck?"

Mistaking my yelp, she tightened her grip and forced me back onto the floor, straddling my body with her own longer one.

"Don't move. Jesus, I may have damaged your back. Stop squirming, honey."

"It's OK. Forget it. I'm fine, Em. I'm fine."

She'd already pushed my shirt up to examine my back, and then I felt it: she shuddered. I felt her shudder. Her hold on my torso relaxed, her weight shifted off me, and I lay there, eyes closed, waiting for her to say something. Christ, oh Christ. In a moment I felt her hand on my back again, lightly with a caution that might have been tenderness.

"Jane?"

I waited, still unable to move as if her hand on my back were a winch securing me to the floorboards. My body started to tremble involuntarily. She let go then and I stood to stop the trembling, to shake the chill that had spread over the room. Already the spot where her racket hit me had begun to tighten. I pulled my shirt down; a grimace slid like rainwater over my features and vanished.

"Jane?"

She hadn't moved: still crouched on the floor with her arm stretched out, hovering there over the shadow of my body. I wanted her to recover quickly, to ask something more than my name. Anything, I thought. Ask me anything.

"Look at me," she said.

I did. I turned and met her eyes and I was ready. I could have defended myself and Nick and the whole scenario. I could have been eloquent and impassioned. I could have changed that startled, horrified expression. At that point I wasn't afraid.

"Why?" she asked.

"It's complicated."

"Try."

"I can't feel anything. I can't feel at all. I can't remember the last time I slept."

Somehow this argument—neither eloquent nor impassioned—came off better in my head. It felt staged and

241

ridiculous in the middle of the racquetball court with the girl kneeling. I couldn't change the way she would remember this. We should have been laughing.

"Your back—"

Oh Christ, say it or don't, but all this hedging. I wanted to shake her. Guilt—mine, my own guilt, and strangely hers too—was a fireball in the dust-clouded room: so palpable, I thought I could smell it.

"What's he using?"

"A dress belt."

"I think two of them are infected."

She picked up her racket and looked at it. I realized we'd been whispering.

"You don't have marks on your wrists. How's he pinning your arms?"

"Did he do this to you?" I asked.

"Not him."

"A silk tie."

"It never lasts," Emily said. "They lose their shape and don't hold tightly enough."

"There have been complaints."

She spaced the strings on her racket absently with her fingers.

"He'll upgrade to rope. That's how it happens. Then the catalogs start coming and somehow the shock—the revulsion—passes. You acclimate to the idea. Somehow it seems perfectly normal to be looking at these medieval devices and deciding which you should use on your lover."

Emily's face was flushed with exertion; her hair had slipped loose from its braid and caught in the sweat around her jaw line, lending her the appearance of a sultry monk as she knelt before me. It seemed that she was the one who needed to be comforted.

"It's never what you think," she said. "You can't keep it in the bedroom."

She stood uncertainly on new legs, leaned over, and picked up the ball.

"I don't think I can play another game," she said.

In the hallway, Emily grabbed her towel and water bottle, then called back to me, "Put some betadine on those cuts."

I started stretching my back in the cool hallway outside the court. When I was five, years before my mother destroyed her Camaro, my father had hurried back from the orchards one evening with Therese and spent a long time in the bathroom with my mother. When he came out, he told me my mother was very tired and couldn't put me to bed that night. But I knew better. I had watched her that afternoon: as she sat, square-legged, in front of the long bathroom mirror, she'd run my father's razor down her palms until the blood dripped onto the floor and down her arms like melt from a strawberry popsicle. I didn't see her for several weeks afterward. Therese put me to bed and read me stories. Later I realized it was like we'd been practicing for when my mother was really gone.

Sessions with Dr. Mya: Day 5

When I wake this morning, a woman lays parallel to the bed in a cocked recliner that one of the orderlies managed to heave into the room without disturbing me. For some time I cannot believe it is Emily, and make an effort to sit upright, to lean closer, to verify the scar at her eye, the wide mouth, the sleek taper of her body: to obtain tangible proof that my untrustworthy brain has recognized this woman properly; that she actually exists in this chair beside me. If she hadn't started snoring, I might actually have rung for a nurse, but she does snore and I am certain now.

For a while, as she sleeps, I kick around a joke about her arrival from France—was she able to fit her dowry into a single coffin, did she have trouble clearing customs?—something in line with her story about the Casket Girls, but I can't think of anything graceful enough to overcome the maudlin aspect. She'd told me the story of their unusual advent innocently on our first morning together, and cannot have known how often I thought about it afterward. I want to tell her that I'm not one of those girls after all—carrying my legacy in a coffin—there's the orchard, the stories my mother told me there. The myth of her life among the mango trees, and we must be resident. We must live with our stories. My failings, inscribed as they are on my body, are my own. Somehow I've never been able to articulate this, though I came close with Audrey, as close as Icarus.

One summer evening, Audrey and I left Honolulu Zoo and walked along the tree-lined avenue as dusk gathered around us. From the pavement, the beach stretched to the murmuring shoreline. She held my hand; our fingers knitted together, her short plaid skirt typical and comforting. Under the streetlamps, couples sat on benches or strolled past with dogs on lead.

"Tell me about the girl," Audrey said.

"The girl?"

"The girl in Ireland. What was her name?"

"Moira," I said. "Moira Cunningham."

"Tell me a story about her."

I told Audrey about the Christmas the dentist had taken me to her parents' house, the goose they'd prepared and the Jameson we'd drunk, the way their voices waffled on the high notes when they sang. The mother's black hair cropped elegantly, her face creamy and full with the memory of beauty. The father, red-nosed and jolly, had shaken my hand seriously, earnestly, all the while patting my shoulder. They'd embraced me for Moira's sake, for her happiness against their cultural impulses, against their very inclinations. Still they'd embraced me.

"What was she like?"

I thought of the black-haired girl with her coarse country brogue, eyes dark as peat, her nimble mind so insistent on the precise word, the precise tool. Her flat always in disarray: some carpentry project here, some half-painted room there; our warm and simple life.

"She was kind," I said, "and certain of everything. It was remarkable how certain she was."

Even as I said this, I was struck again, by the similarities between them: Audrey and the dentist, so much sincerity.

"Remarkable?"

"Yes. It takes a lot of conviction in permanence to be certain like that."

Audrey stopped, looked at me intently, shook her head. How to explain? How to tell her that I knew nothing of that kind of permanence, that kind of conviction, and how it had terrified me.

"Do you know what it's like to live with someone like my mother?"

She shook her head again, kept my hand clasped in hers. A jogger padded down the sidewalk and into the night.

"She was gone and then back, gone and then back for weeks at a time. There were scenes and it got so you dreaded going anywhere with her. You had to hide the car keys, give her one pill at a time and make sure she really swallowed it. You had to check under her tongue. For a while we had a special locked drawer for razors and knives. You couldn't cut a fucking mango without first getting the key to that drawer so you could use the paring knife. Therese threw out all the hand mirrors, and then had to check the mirror in each bathroom, the picture frames, every window in the house and tool shed to make sure she hadn't broken off a piece of glass."

I said this in a low breathless rush, and found I'd crushed her fingers in my hand. I let go now and looked at my palms, the sand on the pavement, the rubbish bin beside the nearest bench. Somewhere beyond us the sea trembled and crawled; I looked at Audrey's troubled face, the curls childlike and beautiful. I might have touched her, smoothed the skin around her eyes and forehead; instead I told her the rest of the story: "You were always watching her and all the suspicion made her devious. She had to sneak around just to avoid being observed like a science project. And partly you hated her for being sick, for being weak and partly you wanted it to end—the inevitable end you'd sensed all along, that you were just prolonging stupidly, pretending to hope. It was a relief when she died. You were glad. You were glad it was finally over and you hated yourself. You hated yourself, and wondered if it was inside you too: the sickness; and thought you deserved it anyway, thought you deserved to be sick because you were glad she was dead."

I kept looking at her, convinced I'd see a change in her expression, convinced she'd pick this moment not to love me.

She stepped towards me, her hand on my face, and kissed my mouth. A startling kiss, as though she'd lifted me, and I felt my body unfurl—a curious lightening in my belly, in my chest—as I held onto her. Oh, I clung to her, there under the eucalyptus trees, afraid she might lift me too high.

In my hospital room Emily sleeps on, her head twisted at an uncanny angle until the pug turns up to check my vitals and starts humming some insensible show tune.

"Hey you," I say as casually as I can manage with the pug hovering like a pestilence.

Emily watches Lucy work around me, all solemn efficiency as she scribbles notes in my chart. After dragging the whole procedure out for as long as possible, she finally vanishes from the room and the squeak of her shoes migrates down the hallway to the next poor bastard's room.

Emily slides her recliner next to the bed and kneels so that we're level. She holds my shoulder and smiles at me, her eyes bloodshot and recessed.

"Hey you," she says.

"Aren't you supposed to be in Paris?"

Her fingertips run across my collarbone, making me tired and hungry simultaneously. Maybe I'm not awake at all.

"How do you feel?" she asks.

"Not so bad."

"Why didn't you call?"

The wells of her eyes—how often could I have drowned in them?

"Em, take a look at this fucking place: *I* don't even want to be here."

"If you'd called me, we could have gotten you out of here."

"They've had me under constant observation—because of the head injury—but it's really just a suicide watch. I've had to meet with this shrink—"

"Dr. Mya."

"So you've already heard this story?"

"I talked to her last night when I arrived. She's proof the experience hasn't been all bad."

"Don't bother, she's straight."

"There's hope for all of them."

"My head—don't make me laugh."

"Sorry."

She reaches up and touches my forehead like a blessing; I close my eyes and feel the sheet pulled away from me. Her hand slides across the plaster on my arm and stops at my hip.

"What the fuck is that?"

"A metal brace to hold the pins in my leg. They're supposed to replace it with a cast."

Tentatively, her head inclined, she runs her hand along the metal brace. Freckled and hesitant, her forehead lined with unease, she touches my body as if for the first time. I think I cannot bear this gentleness.

I know, of course, who told her.

"He called you in Paris?"

"He stopped by the house and told Hiromi. He said you'd been badly injured."

Has Emily seen this coming all along: me in a hospital bed? Her almond eyes pool for a moment, then she brushes her unkempt hair from her face and coughs.

"And Grey?" I ask.

"He'll fly in this morning. It took me a while to track him down."

"He's ditched the bitch?"

She nodded, "He's officially single again. Apparently he's been at his brother's lake place the last week or so."

Grey waterskiing across the shimmering surface of a lake; I imagine him with a couple of blond college girls driving the boat, admiring his form. How we unravel and gleam.

"Em, I hate being here."

She looks up at me, her lips compressed, her expression surfing through several channels before settling finally on anguish.

"I know, honey."

"They put me on fucking suicide watch."

"The scars."

"Em."

"It's OK now. You're going to be OK."

I swallow, my throat aching, and strain to collect myself. I don't know how to ask—how to form the words. Lying back on my pillow, I stare at the dull-white ceiling, steady my breathing.

"Em, will you do me a favor?"

"I've already called her."

On my first vacation to Italy, we'd stopped in Florence for a day trip to see the Uffizi Gallery and Michelangelo's *David* and so one of my mates could buy a cheap leather jacket. That day in the square, the students had staged some sort of medieval festival. The boys trudged about, hefting jousts and shield coats fashioned from burlap sacks, with coats of arms dragged behind them by aptly disgruntled serfs. The girls wore elaborately stitched dresses and ornate hairstyles. They waved long handkerchiefs at no one in particular from the pinnacles of their respective turrets. None of it made much sense to me.

I skirted the square and walked among the market vendors, looking for the entrance to the Uffizi, which I found behind a queue of hundreds of tourists, including a large group of bellowing middle-aged Americans. A girl with ice cream trotted past and I returned, dismally, to the market, searching for the ice-cream stand among the vendors. Policemen in threes strode around on foot, looking oppressively overdressed in their dark outfits and hard black hats. After taking a wrong turn, I ended up in an alleyway between vendors, and before I could turn a man stumbled into the alley from the other side of the market. He wore a crumpled white suit, no hat, and had blood pouring from his chest. He seemed to be walking on the tips of his toes, with his arms puffed out at his sides as if he might take flight. At first, I thought he was a performer with the students' festival, but then he fell backwards onto the brick of the alleyway and I understood he'd been injured.

While I stood there, not three meters from him, a group of people noticed the man and called for the police. I walked slowly down the alley, not looking at the man or the crowd, hardly noticing as the police rushed past me with their black sticks drawn. All I could think was that the man's suit had smelled of goat. Again, I walked toward the museum, and entered through the exit, walking past several security personnel who watched without making any effort to halt me.

I spent the next five hours wandering through the museum backwards. Obviously the man had been stabbed, probably multiple times, from the blood stains on his suit. I never told anyone about seeing him.

Without taking notes, Dr. Mya watches me as I tell her this story. She'd come to my hospital room herself to wheel me down to her office, which smelled of cinnamon again. Today she wears a black pantsuit with a sleeveless blue blouse (she has removed her jacket) and has resumed her calm, methodical demeanor—the previous session's rumpled psychologist a vanished species. I'd meant to explain about Emily, or at any rate I'd wanted to explain things to

Dr. Mya, but I told about the goat suit instead. I'm not sure why and when I finish the story, I can't think of anything else to say.

"Were you frightened that day in the alleyway?" she asks me.

"No, just surprised."

"You weren't worried about leaving the scene of a crime?"

"Who said there'd been a crime?"

"So the man stabbed himself in the chest?"

"I didn't see anything that might have helped them."

"If the same thing had happened here, say on Kalakaua Avenue, would you still have walked away?"

I move the goat suit to Kalakaua, see him falling back within sight of traffic, blood in his mouth, ruining his suit, and the hollowed look in his eyes. I shrug. Who can say?

"Would you have tried to help him," she asks, "if the crowd hadn't called for the police?"

"I don't know. It happened quickly: he stumbled in the alleyway, collapsed, and then they were calling for the cops. Fast."

I punch my cast against the rail of my chair to illustrate how quickly the incident took place. Watching him fall, it hadn't occurred to me to call anyone, not even when I understood the blood on his suit was real. I hadn't moved toward him or away from him, simply watched. Why have I told her this story?

"Listen, these scars," I say, "gesturing toward my back with my good arm. They aren't what you think."

She gazes at me, waiting. Behind her, the blinds shield us, except at the edges where light blazes through. What has Emily told her? What have they said to one another? Emily wants me to recuperate at her house, have a registered nurse live with us during my recovery. Whatever my insurance and UPS won't pay, she will. "I've already made calls," she said. "Everything's settled."

251

"I'm a masochist."

Dr. Mya's eyes don't waver behind her brown-rimmed spectacles. She has an eerie ability to see into you the way a dog does. Maybe she doesn't understand what I mean.

"Rough sex," I say, and gesture toward my back again. "That's all."

"Consensual?"

"Of course."

"Every time?"

"What?"

"Was it consensual every time?"

I stare at her, "It doesn't matter anymore."

"Jane," she draws my name out in her mouth. "Was the rough sex consensual every time?"

"I never said no."

"Did that mean it was consensual?"

"Yes."

Her pencil spins in her fingers like a pinwheel.

"Why did you stop seeing him?"

"I'd started seeing someone else."

"Why?"

"He scared me a little."

"You started seeing someone else because Nick scared you a little?"

"Well, it was more complicated than that."

"How did he scare you?"

I think of the harness, and the climbing rope, the dress belt and the way Nick dug his knee into my spine to pin me. Declensions running through my head like Psalms. Had he scared me? I can't be sure anymore. More than anything I'd felt helpless, and for some reason, finding Audrey had empowered me. Betrayal had made me feel less vulnerable.

"Things became confused. The boundaries blurred, you know? At first it was just sex, and then it was the way he talked to me, and ordered for me, his hand on my neck

252

when we were walking, expecting me to move in, to marry him. And he had these contraptions—these devices—and I didn't even feel present anymore. It's like I had no identity. I could have been anyone with my hands bound. And by the end it was so fucking horrible, I was afraid to see him. I was afraid to walk into his house because I'd made this agreement. Somehow I'd made this agreement and I didn't know how to get out of it."

I start to cry, then startle out of it when Dr. Mya's pencil, which she has managed to drop, rolls from her lap onto the carpet, and glides toward the front wheels of my chair. Betrayal has always made me feel less vulnerable: a flash of red in the slick of the pavement.

"Jane, had you practiced masochism with lovers before Nick?"

I shook my head, "Not sexually anyway."

"But emotionally?"

"Sometimes."

"You've been an emotional masochist with other partners?"

"With Emily, I think."

"You had a sexual relationship with Emily?"

"Didn't she tell you?"

She doesn't answer, only sits awaiting my response. I almost miss the freakish display of the previous session: it is unnerving how rigidly she maintains control of herself.

"Yes, I had a sexual relationship with her."

"How long did your sexual relationship last?"

"Less than a year."

"Do you consider yourself a bisexual?"

"Do we have to tag everything?"

She lets that one go, almost grinning at me.

"Why did the relationship with Emily end?"

"I'd started seeing someone else."

If she'd had her pencil, I'm sure she would have made a

note of that. She tenses in her chair. *Non-monogamous masochist seeks dysfunctional male or female for non-spiritual connection. All vices welcome.*

"Why had you started seeing someone else?"

"Emily wanted to."

"So your relationship was non-monogamous?"

"It became non-monogamous, yes. She said she wanted to see other people."

"Did you want to see other people?"

"No. It just happened."

Dr. Mya reaches behind her and picks up a pen from her desk. On the bookcase beside me in an oval frame, two gleaners bend in a golden field. They wear muted colors and weathered faces; from the painting, I know exactly how rough their clothes feel. I think of Hiromi hunkered in Emily's garden, always tending.

"How about with your lovers since Nick? Have you been sexually or emotionally masochistic with recent lovers?"

"No."

"Why haven't you practiced masochism with other lovers?"

"I fantasized instead. I didn't think they'd be into it."

"Because they weren't sadists?"

"That's too easy, isn't it? Nick was a sadist and that's why things got fucked up? I have no responsibility, no role? I didn't contribute in any way?"

"How did you contribute?"

"I let him wail on me."

"Because you're a masochist?"

"Yeah."

"Who has never practiced masochism with anyone else?"

"It's not like you need a fucking learner's permit. *Practiced masochism.* You make everything sound like you're reading from a fucking textbook."

"You contributed because you consented?"

254

"Yeah, I consented."

"Because you never said no?"

I want to crush that yellow pencil beneath the wheels of my chair. What does any of it matter anymore? Her skirt stretches across her knees, and she holds my file on her lap the way old women hold afghans.

"Are you trying to give me an out? I was part of the scene; I let it happen."

"Do you consider yourself a difficult person to love?"

Warily, I examine her, but her face gives nothing. In her hand the pen cradles, immobile. She doesn't wear rings on her fingers.

"Yes."

"What makes you difficult?"

"I'm withdrawn, secretive. I have trouble communicating what I feel."

I could have added *coward* the way Audrey did when she evicted me, but I don't need another tag line. It wasn't Tantalus who rolled a stone uphill forever. The Greeks envisioned gods and goddesses who punished by repetition, and erred that way as well. Could I have kept my mother in the kitchen longer that April morning? If it hadn't been that morning, wouldn't it have been another morning? Metal buckling against cement, blood on the windshield, dust settling in the air, and me, eating gingersnaps with milk, still explaining: she was so tired. She was just so tired.

XXXIII.

At the U.H. men's volleyball game that Friday night, Nick and I ate Red Vines while watching the terrifying blitzing power of the men's spikes. We almost pitied the poor bastards on the opposing team whose blockers sucked so badly that their outside hitters were forced to dive into the firing line repeatedly, making for a double beating as the U.H. crowd rose like fervent worshippers to chant, stomp, and cheer. Often during these games, I had to remind myself to breathe as the stadium thundered around us, silencing only for serves and slams.

Among the sport's enthusiasts, Nick looked quite formal in his clay-colored oxford shirt, black Docs, and belted khaki slacks. He'd kept his black leather jacket on to forestall the chill of the stadium. Still damp, his bangs hung in his eyes.

"So I've got news," Nick hollered at me.

"Should I guess?"

"I've got a gig in L.A. for a couple of weeks in January—celebrity torso shoot."

"How's that?"

"It's an ad campaign for cancer prevention. Twenty-two celebrity women are going to have torso shots taken, and their names will be on the back of the pamphlet or magazine or whatever and each shot will be anonymous. The viewer gets to flip through and guess whose tits are whose."

"How does this help prevent cancer?"

"Apparently, it's going to encourage men and women to look more closely at breasts."

"Ah, yes, our great failing as a society: breast neglect."

U.H. won four straight points before sending the ball out of bounds. They lost the next two points from ace serves, then recovered with a thudding block that sent the other team sprawling to the ground in a futile effort to recover the ball.

"It's the Hollywood concept: sex is the only cause that sells."

"OK, seriously, what's the shoot?"

"It really is twenty-two celebrity women mixed in with a dozen women who have had radical mastectomies. It's about solidarity and education through exposure."

"Isn't the word *radical* superfluous in that context?"

"These photos will not elucidate that question or any other, but they will certainly generate a lot of hype, and hopefully a lot of money."

"Pandering and exploitation—good thing you're in on the ground floor."

The crowd let out a collective groan when one of our hitters slammed his spike into the net. Before the other team could serve, jeers leapt from the rafters to the court and bounced around the bleachers as fans waved rainbow streamers and trumpeted air horns.

"Why would you say that?" Nick yelled over the mania. "Breast cancer prevention is a worthy cause."

"A cause worth serious attention. This is just about celebrity vanity. I mean, my god, they should at least include some medical information about how to check for lumps, how often to visit your doctor for mammograms, cancer statistics, treatment options, support centers …"

"What if these weren't celebrities? What if they were just regular women off the street? Would you still object to the concept?"

"As a statement about cancer prevention? Yes, I would. Where's the message? So they raise a lot of money for research selling these things at black-tie dinners—don't get me wrong, I see the value in raising the money—but what have they really done in terms of education? How have they helped cancer awareness?"

"Have you ever seen a photo of a mastectomy?"

I thought of the scars I knew: "No."

"So this will broaden your awareness. Anyway, to my way of thinking, money for cancer research is worth *pandering* and *exploitation*, if that's what we're doing. It may be vanity, but no one's getting paid to participate."

"Even you?"

"Air travel and hotel expenses are covered, but I'm donating my time and my work."

I watched as the U.H. setter flung the ball perfectly, holding his strange insect-like posture as the hitter drilled the ball past the opposing blockers to regain serving advantage. The crowd stomped like bulls. What difference did it make to me how celebrities approached cancer prevention? Wasn't any attention better than silent neglect?

"Two weeks in L.A.," I said. "That'll make for a nice change."

Nick smiled then, relieved finally to see me being reasonable about his project.

"Then in February I'm going to cover the NCAA fencing tournament."

"God, the beekeepers."

"Somebody discovered my hobby. I'm being paid for that one."

"And then?"

"New York for a few weeks. I've got a show there in March. We're still in talks about a show in Seattle."

I held my breath as the opposing blockers capped one of our spikes; U.H.'s setter pancaked, knocking the ball straight up with his fist, and the nearest hitter lobbed it to the backcourt on the opposing side. The visiting team returned the ball with a sloppy set/spike combination, only to have it blocked as U.H. scored again.

"So you'll be flying back and forth to the various events?" I asked.

"Probably. I've got work scheduled in the studio here as well, so we'll see how it plays out. I just wanted you to know what was coming."

"Thanks."

Two of our players collided and the crowd jumped up, craning to see the players, thirsty for some heinous injury, the knob of a protruding bone. Both men picked themselves up slowly and stretched their backs and ankles. Applauding wildly, the fans began a war cry.

Was it relief? Is that what I felt then, aware so suddenly that I'd have three months to myself? Three months without girlfriend obligations, without the roping, without Nick. No, it was joy.

On the court, the men won the third straight game to take the match, and we shrieked in the stands like schoolgirls.

XXXIV.

My classroom was cold in the afternoons—a musty draft stole inside during the winter months through the rows of windows. More often, I felt disheartened, even here in the classroom, though these students were like a haven to me: the Latin they chanted deliberately, the purity of their harried youth, their seriousness. I'd meant to show them beauty in the scope and possibility of the language; instead, I felt blind to it myself.

We'd finished a translation of Ovid's myth—an abridged version—about Philomela and Procne when Steven Hamada raised his hand. Since I was no longer the green teacher I had been, I'd anticipated apprehension about this myth; in fact, I'd come to expect disquiet about brutality in the myths at least twice a term now.

"Yes, Steven?"

"I don't understand this myth—I mean, I get that it's completely sick—but I don't understand why they're all transformed into birds."

"Yeah," said Joyce Kim, "Philomela should at least be a tree or a constellation; something more permanent."

Steven gave Joyce a disapproving look: "Why Philomela? She slit a child's throat, then helped tear him to pieces. What I don't get about this is: aren't they being rewarded, being transformed into birds? I mean, I get that sometimes a transformation is a punishment, like Arachne being turned into a spider, or Callisto being changed into a black bear;

260

but then there's Daphne, who's transformed into a laurel tree to save her from Apollo. So when Philomela and Procne and Tereus are *all* transformed into birds, are they being punished?"

"Any ideas?" I asked the class.

"Well," said Margaret Wong, "I don't think this myth is about reward or punishment, I think it's really an explanation of why these specific birds are the way they are: I mean, Procne is the nightingale—Ovid said swallow, but that's illogical—mourning, with her sad song, for her dead son; Philomela—whose tongue was cut out when she was human—is a swallow, chattering unintelligibly about her rape; and Tereus, in his aggression, becomes a bird that looks like it's wearing armor. The myth is a genesis for the birds."

"Yeah, I get that," Stephen said patiently, "but it's like all of their crimes are being equated: is killing a child and serving his body for supper as bad as raping your wife's sister, cutting out her tongue so she can't tell anyone, and holding her hostage in a fortress in the woods? Why are they *all* transformed into birds?"

"I don't think the crimes are being equated," said Martin Reid. "I think the gods just wanted to stop the cycle of revenge before it escalated. I mean, if you look at Callisto: Zeus rapes and impregnates her; Diana excommunicates her from the Virgin Huntress Club; and Hera transforms her into a black bear—all the while, the myth keeps talking about *Callisto's* guilt like it's all her own fault—but rather than allow her son to kill her while he's out hunting, Zeus transforms both of them into constellations. It's like there's a point at which even the Greeks and Romans can't take any more of the carnage."

The class mulled this over, silently. It was a pleasure to watch them consider the implications of the myth—its purpose and its method.

Then Steven looked up at me and said: "But it seems like a gift, their being changed into birds."

"Is it a gift?" I asked. "Only their physical condition, after all, is modified, not their circumstances. Did the gods transform them into birds out of a sense of compassion?"

"That's what I don't get," Steven said.

When the students, still puzzled, filed from the room at the end of class, I too was undecided. Perhaps a half-gift—a god's gift—to alter their form but not their nature: Philomela's incessant chattering; Procne's endless mourning; Tereus a bird of prey.

XXXV.

As the D.J. spun a post-punk caterwaul at the Spark late one Saturday night in January, every twenty-something on the island skin-gambled the smoky blue dark: groping their way to and from the bar, grappling on the dance floor, colliding into one another urgently with a certain studied despair. Grey had danced all evening with one honey after another, stopping by the bar to slug a shot, wipe the sweat off his face, and ask me again if I was sure I wanted to stay.

Reloading whiskey shots, I'd amused myself most of the evening rejecting dance offers—not that I felt compelled to celibacy—just to watch Red Audrey from the relative safety of my barstool. When we'd first arrived, I'd seen this familiar red-haired girl with corkscrew curls and an Audrey Hepburn neck on the fringe of the dance floor, and had staked out the bar ever since—the only immobile, rooted thing in the place. I had this vision of her drawing her phone number on my forearm: calligraphy numbers like some underground code.

The bartenders were all California boys who'd come to Oahu for the surfing and headed straight for the beach when the bar closed up at 5:00 a.m. They weren't, to be kind, my type. Emily's sometime boy, Ray, was always sunburnt—even his hair blistered white—and looked like a mutated candy cane. Emily could get him riled up for anything. Anxious for brawls and eighteen-foot swells, the guy didn't hinge properly; and given the way he'd huddled around me most of the night, I reckoned I'd been adopted as his latest crusade: "Emily says your boy's fucking you up."

"Emily would."

"So your boy's fucking you up?"

"What?"

"So your—"

"No, Ray."

"Lift up your shirt."

"Ray, don't touch my stomach. Pour me a whiskey and fuck off."

"Just show me—one quick flash."

"I swear to Christ, Ray ..."

"Alright, but I'm aware of this. I'm aware and I'm gonna wreck that guy next time I see him."

Maybe no one should be expected to keep my secrets when I couldn't keep them myself, but I wanted Ray to know like I wanted my throat cut. I hated that lanky candy cane prick and his big-brother posturing.

"Another whiskey," I called without looking round.

I didn't want Nick wrecked; we'd had wreckage enough. But his absence, his absence was a narcotic, the first clean breath I'd had after a long submersion. While Red Audrey pushed her way off the dance floor and traced a line to the bar, I shot the rest of my whiskey and contemplated my keen and raging body.

Like everything else about the bar, the people were vague. With electric lights as subtle as shadows, you never really saw anyone until closing when it was too late to matter. Red Audrey wasn't aware of me until I held my mouth against her ear, my fingertips light on her wrist.

"Kamikaze?" I asked.

She stepped back to look up at me, calculated something, and then nodded. Behind her on the dance floor, the D.J. switched records.

The aching music and this girl spinning coasters on the

bar like pinwheels, I was memorizing her skin—pale and delicate—while I ordered the glass, double vodka. She was half kneeling on the black seat of the stool, her blue skirt resting halfway down her thighs, and she wore soft blue knee socks like she'd just stepped out of a French girls' school. Her collarbones made my stomach cramp.

"You don't look old enough to be in here," I said, handing her the drink.

She pulled her I.D. from her pocket; when I took it from the shallow of her palm, she cupped her fingers around my hand like a flower closing. I grinned at her.

"Jesus, your name really is Audrey."

Her head cocked to the side as she tried to figure out what I meant. In the photograph of her driver's license, her eyes looked dilated and wild like a maniac. Eyes: blue, it read. I looked across at her to make sure. Somehow, swallowing had become difficult.

"Thirty-four? You expect me to believe you're thirty-four?"

The crowd was on a techno fix: music rumbling over every silhouette in the blue smoke. My hair was whacked: moussed straight out like a bunch of black weeds. A line of deviants mobbed the bar looking for IVs in chilled glasses, and Red Audrey still had my hand.

XXXVI.

In Audrey's lavender living room, even the lamps cast a soft purple glow over the oatmeal-flecked carpeting and the plush lilac sofas, as if I were inside a bruise, my head still light with kamikazes. It was 3:00 a.m., and Audrey had gone to the kitchen to make a pot of tea, and a couple of tomato and cheese sandwiches.

She brought the tea and sandwiches out to the coffee table, where we ate sitting on the floor. Her eyes were pale marbles, gently blue. Over the past several hours, I'd discovered she sketched and painted, and had established quite a reputation: her work had showed locally at the Dan Bishop Gallery (posh) and McGuire's (innovative) in addition to various galleries I'd never heard of throughout the Pacific Northwest. Twice a week she volunteered to teach art to genius third graders in Aliamanu. It had been ages since anyone spoke to me about teaching with such obvious delight.

"I have fourteen eight- and nine-year-olds and the classes are wild. They love watercolors and chalk—anything to make themselves and me filthy. I've worked with older kids, but so far the third graders are my favorite: old enough to have vision and intentionality for their work, not yet hyper-self-aware."

I sipped my mint tea, listening to her enthusiasm, her hands gesturing as she spoke like one of the tai chi surfers from Anna Banana's. Some crazy Cowboy Junkies song murmured in the background, and my solitude diminished as she explained about kayaking down winding rivers in Montana.

"I went sea kayaking once," she said, "along the coast of Port Townsend. Have you ever sea kayaked?"

I shook my head.

"God, it took two hours to paddle to this imperious lighthouse that looked like it was just a football field away. I was exhausted and starving and feeling kind of icky—my gloves were frozen, and my legs were trembling, and I wanted to capsize on purpose and swim for shore. Then these sleek little heads popped through the surface of the water: seals. They floated and dipped and swam around us for the longest time. Somehow their being there made it easier. Just staring at us with their enormous brown eyes."

I closed my eyes to imagine the seals appearing in the swells, the current quick and snagging as it had been on the northern coast of Ireland. I could almost feel the rocking of the kayak beneath me, could almost hear the throaty whine of gulls drifting high above the brackish water.

Audrey brewed another pot of tea while I rummaged through her CD collection, settling finally on a Soul Coughing album. The flat felt cool and dark; I refused to consult my watch. Nearly all the wall art in the living room was photographs, black and white shots of dilapidated buildings, a color print of a green bicycle leaned against an orange door, a tight shot of a black man perched on a stool in an alleyway. Above the dining table, a large vibrant painting of a rooster—his legs shimmering gold—cast a defiant gaze over the room. Sober now and still, wondrously, buzzing, I waited for the red sprite, determined to keep her talking.

During college she'd taken a bus tour of the European continent, and cycled through the south of France and Italy after graduate school. Audrey seemed to remember everything vividly—from obscure townships to her favorite delicacies—whereas for me, so many of my travel experiences were half-memories, a blur of museums and architecture that might have been any city.

"Did you ever visit Switzerland?" she asked me.

"Twice. Once I took a train up the Jungfrau, and spent the weekend in the little village in the valley there."

"Did you see the Lion's Monument in Lucerne?"

"Carved in the cliff face above a pool? Yes."

I'd thought of Aslan, C.S. Lewis's Christ-figure, when I'd seen the great brown lion prostrate in the cliff face above the still pool. It had been profoundly moving: the lion's body fallen before a Swiss shield, the mane unfurled like a flag. My recollection now, so acute, surprised me.

"That look on the lion's face," she said, "do you remember? A strange expression—a kind of peaceful anguish—and the spear broken in his side; I stared at that lion for hours, and then came back the next day to stare some more."

She filled our cups with tea, and smiled at me, "Do you know, I think anguish is the only pure emotion? I think that's why that sculpture moves me so much: the purity of anguish in the lion's expression."

"What does that mean: pure emotion?"

"Well, it's not like suffering or love. With anguish there is no subjectivity, no interpretation. Clearly, anguish is the same in every culture, every language."

"I don't see it. Anyway, you interpreted the lion's anguish with the modifier *peaceful*."

"Nevertheless."

"Well, that's a compelling argument."

We talked until the morning glowed around the curtains like a storm and our voices cracked with overuse, until I became afraid to kiss her. Afraid of how soft her ringlets would feel in my hands, afraid of the mess of another girl, the impish face grinning at me like a maddening Cheshire Cat, as if seduction were effortless.

Voices carried up to us from the sidewalk below with the wind and swept the curtain deeper into the room. She knelt in front of me, palms on the floor, silent and watchful.

Outside, a car alarm beeped twice, then a door slammed. I leaned back against the base of the sofa, trying to swallow the worry that clutched at my throat and belly.

"Butterflies are cannibals," she said.

"What?" I muttered, thinking of fanged butterflies tearing wings and antennae from their helpless mates.

She leaned forward, not touching me, her mouth a hive of butterflies, a swarm, a murder. Convulsions jerked through me, repealing resistance and doubt, suppressing Nick's existence, the scars, my costumes, squashing my analytical self and leaving only sentient response. Her mouth like lemon peel, like li hing mui, coaxed me forward until we were both kneeling in the middle of the bruised room: chaste, devout, consumed.

XXXVII.

The second Sunday in March, Grey surprised me at the studio, popping his head in the front door and calling for me as I climbed from the bath.

"I need a lost day," he said apologetically as I came out wrapped in my towel, my hands behind my back. "Are you up for it?"

I hadn't spent any time with Grey in weeks. At UPS, he'd been promoted to Hub Manager and now worked twelve-hour salaried days, sprinting from crisis to crisis. Since I'd been partnered with Chance Chang, I didn't mind Grey's absence on the ramp as much as I'd expected, but keeping time with Audrey had blunted my socializing, too, and I felt that absence so much that his arrival this morning was a particular delight.

"A lost day sounds perfect. Where will we go?"

"I thought Waimea. We can get lunch at Kua Aina."

I slipped into my surf shorts and a long-sleeved shirt, grabbed a towel, and sprinted to Grey's Honda for our drive to the North Shore. Bright and clear, the day lent itself to opened car windows and a meandering cruise through pineapple fields.

"Jesus, Janie, I'm going mad," Grey said, passing me the opened bag of Funyuns.

"Work?"

"Yeah, I never should have taken this job. I'm thinking seriously about quitting."

"And then?"

"That's where I run into trouble. More than anything, I just need a long vacation."

"I know exactly what you mean. I'm actually looking forward to a teachers' strike. A bunch of us singing vigilant songs and carrying around clever, radical signs, marching in an endless circle—I'm enamored to this notion of civilized protest—no spoiled tea or rolling heads, just a simple and disciplined revolt."

"You're serious, aren't you? Aren't classes going well?"

"I'm completely disengaged this semester—the classes have become rote: the promptly completed homework assignments; excellent test results; the same, inevitable questions; all so disciplined and boring—it's like I don't even need to be present for the students to do well."

Grey looked over at me, his face decidedly haggard—crow's feet etching his eyes—and shook his head sadly.

"OK, no more work talk," he said. "This is a lost day. Let's talk about something pleasant."

We sailed past a couple of haole guys in a smoking VW bus, as I thought of pleasant things: Audrey gently rolling my wrists in her fingers as though sifting for treasure; the slight husk of her voice; how she hadn't pried about my bruises, even when she traced the marks on my back that first night in her bed; the way she asked, "Would you like to watch me sleep?" I left her flat every morning at 4:00 a.m., her breathing quiet and steady as I slipped from the bedroom to bike home.

"You look like you've lost weight, Janie."

"Well, that's pleasant."

"I thought I'd see more of you with Nick gone, but then Emily mentioned a redhead."

I shook my head, smiling like a goof, "You bastards."

He laughed at me, pleased to have found a pleasant topic after all.

271

"I don't know why I'm surprised," I said as indignantly as I could manage: "Gossipmongers."

"Oh, come on, we're just glad you're happy. Look at you, for Christ sake, fucking glowing. Almost balances the emaciation."

"Fuck off."

Somehow, I didn't mind being kidded about Audrey; the subtle glow of the lavender flat and the 4:00 a.m. bike rides often draped an illusory shroud over my visits to her flat, whereas Grey's ribbing—a soft kick to my belly—insisted the girl was real. Proof, my mind said, he's noticed the change in you. She must be real.

"What's she like?" Grey asked.

I started to answer that she was like the dentist, which astonished me—Audrey like the dentist?—and I ended up saying: "She's an amazing artist."

Grey parked the car in the crabgrass at the edge of the main road overlooking Waimea Beach. Alongside the guardrails on our walk down to the beach we passed a long stretch of cars, confirmation that the parking lot had filled by 9:00 a.m. The surf curled in six-foot swells, and dozens of children with tangled hair sprinted in and out of the water, squealing.

I followed Grey as he walked along the rock cliffs well back from the water, gulls coasting over the beach, bickering bickering, as a couple of women the size of swamp cows adjusted the bottom halves of their bikinis. Overhead, the white clouds shifted quickly in the brilliant, breezy sky.

"What do you think?" Grey asked.

I followed his outstretched hand to the great bulk of Waimea rock, where four military guys hurled themselves one after the other from the 8-meter leap in various contortions of a cannonball.

"Insanity."

On a lower ledge, two small girls with cranelike legs

stood holding hands before they stepped off the ledge and shrieked the length of their plunge into the water.

"Have you gone before?"

"No," I said, watching Grey edge toward the rock, his arm still extended on point.

"I haven't jumped for years. Last time had to be in college. It's good fun, Janie, just what we need."

Paralysis, indefinite hospitalization, this is what he thinks we need? He reached his hand back and grabbed hold of mine, pulling me toward the rock. As I watched, several scrawny boys with distended bellies stepped effortlessly from the highest perch, jackknifing with a modest splash.

Pausing to toss our towels and slippers hastily aside, he gripped my hand again and hurried toward the stepped backside of the rock, where three sand-coated children poked a dead crab with sticks. We climbed the backside of the rock, and I resisted his urges to leap from the higher perch, waiting instead behind five Filipino girls at the lower ledge, the last of whom smiled at me and said, "It's fun after the first time." Then she dove into the blue water and popped out much closer to shore than I expected.

"Ready, Janie?" Grey held onto my hand.

I wished I hadn't watched the little girl jump. From the ledge, I could see rocks under the surface below us. *We are going to die*, typed relentlessly through my head.

"Ready?" Grey said again, and we stepped from the ledge into nothingness.

My body light as it fell, wind swirling through my shorts and against my skin, the drop going on for so long that I opened my eyes and amazingly continued falling, Grey's hand in mine until the surface of the water slapped, then swallowed us. My feet touched rock and I kicked off and swam from the deep cold quiet.

Grey kissed me in the shallows, sea water darkening his curls, a lunatic grin splayed across his face.

"Wild, Janie. Wild. Feels like you fall for centuries. Let's go again."

And I did. We jumped four times from the lower perch, and once, psychotically, from the highest. By the time we'd showered, and hiked back to the car, I could have eaten three of Kua Aina's colossal burgers.

Giggly and high, in sweatshirts rummaged from Grey's trunk, we sat at one of the outdoor tables under the wooden awning, watching trucks and minivans roll past on the two-lane road. Even the sociopath stalking women cyclists with a baseball bat—the broadcast topic at the table nearest us *(he's landed four girls in the hospital so far!)*—couldn't dampen our moods. A lost day, a lost summer, Grey's irrepressible grin, white and glaring as the afternoon, anticipated carefree, mischievous months.

After devouring our burgers and fries, we bought shave ice for the road, Grey's usual mix of coconut, blueberry, and raspberry, and mine of watermelon and lemon, each atop ice cream. On the ride home, pleasant things sprang readily to mind.

XXXVIII.

The first morning I woke at Audrey's, she brought pancakes smothered in apple sauce and organic maple syrup, orange slices, and a pot of herbal spearmint tea to wash down the stickiness, on three bamboo trays which perched precariously atop the duvet on her enormous bed like nervous birds. Her bedroom, sparsely furnished in white, let in a tremendous amount of light; I checked my watch throughout the night in my confusion. Small blue fish painted in the deliberate lines of hieroglyphics floated along the upper border of the room. A bookcase laden with modern fiction, and an ornate orange-toned secretary's desk lined the walls on either side of the small closet.

She wore cotton boxers with the waistband turned down and a white tank top. In the morning light she looked young and alarmingly jubilant.

"What do you say to a hike this morning?" she asked.

"Where are we hiking?"

"Manoa Falls."

"It's going to be filthy."

"All the better."

With my ten-pound locks I secured our bikes to the chain barrier at the trailhead and we crossed the small footbridge past the enormous green leaves of the elephant ear plants. Five minutes up the trail, winding along a stream through kukui nut trees, bamboo, mountain apple trees, and ferns under a thick rainforest canopy, mud sucked at our hiking boots. The vinegar smell of fermenting fruit—thick as humidity—swathed us. Tangled tree roots and large rocks required quick scrambles and deft ankles. Dense and moist, climbing the trail simulated a sauna experience; Audrey stripped to a bikini top and I doused myself from the water bottle incessantly.

Though we'd left her flat at 8:00 a.m., a number of hikers passed us on their descent to the trailhead, each spattered with mud in a familiar pattern.

"Mosquitoes aren't bad at all," a topless Japanese man shouted at us on his way over a crest.

Audrey's short legs powered up the trail at a pace I had to work to support. Used to surfing with locals and hapas, I laughed every time I looked at Audrey's shockingly white body. Did the girl never venture into the sun?

"Oh, it's raining!"

She started hopping around, face upturned, in a blissed dance.

"How long have you lived here?" I asked, amused.

She turned toward me, eyes dilated, mouth cocked with pleasure. I smiled in reflection.

"I grew up here. God, I love rain. Isn't it beautiful?"

Her face streaked with rain; hair mashed against her head; the top of her shorts soaked tight against her belly. I thought *beautiful* failed to capture the wonder as this girl trod on the brilliant orange cups of the African tulip tree that blanketed the ground at her feet.

By the time we reached the falls, a torrent of rainfall dashed from the pool, down the stream, and over the pathway. Though the rain had eased the discomforting humidity, we tossed off our shoes and packs and charged into the achingly cold pool until the falls pummeled down atop us, rinsing away the mud. Lichen stubble covered the dark rocks clear to the shallow bottom of the pool. After several minutes I finally caught my breath, though my body had yet to adjust to the frigid water. Audrey pulled herself from the water onto a wide round stone, shuddered compulsively, and looked down at me like a haughty cat.

"We'll never be old!" she yelled.

"The hypothermia will kill us first."

Even as we clambered from the pool, the rain ceased and the hot, oppressive damp returned. Shivering into our towels, we squeezed water from our socks and lay them out on a moss-glazed rock.

"Stunning," Audrey gasped and handed me a bottle of insect repellant.

Light glanced off the stones and the falls, filtered through the leaves of the canopy, spilled over us like redemption. I re-applied repellant as she took out one of her sketchbooks and several pens from her pack. Lying back on my pack, I shut my eyes and listened through the thunder of the falls for the insistent scratch of her pen.

"I have a sketch of the first time I saw you."

Surprised by her voice, I started, and glanced over at her.

"What are you talking about?"

"The first time I saw you, I still have the sketch."

"From the bar?"

"No, from Moanalua Gardens. You were barefoot, playing Ultimate Frisbee with a pack of beautiful boys at the park. I'd spent the afternoon there, sketching some of the kiawe trees. This was ages ago. I still have the sketch in my studio."

"When Grey was our supervisor, we'd play Saturday afternoons after shift."

"One of the guys stepped on a bee and screamed like a toddler the day I saw you. You pulled the stinger out for him."

"Yeah, I remember that. Jerome stepped on a bee: he was such a whiny little bitch; he sat out the rest of the game. I can't believe I didn't notice you, though."

Had I really overlooked this cream-skinned little redhead?

I remembered Jerome panicking about an allergic reaction he'd had once after making a fort on a yellow jackets' nest when he was six. *Twenty-nine stings*, he'd repeated over and over like an incantation. *Twenty-nine stings.*

"I have a sketch of the second time too."

"When was that?"

"At Magic Island. Barefoot again, playing volleyball with a hostile group of women."

"You mean competitive, not hostile. I play tournaments there some weekends."

"Someone grilled oysters that afternoon and you guys stopped playing to eat."

"Must have been a pick-up game. What were you sketching at Magic Island?"

"You."

I sat up to scrutinize her more closely. Concentrating on the falls, she referred to her pad fleetingly as her hand dragged across the paper. Her hair had dried in dark ringlets around her face. Before the night we'd hooked up, I'd noticed Audrey in the bar, but assumed she was straight. The idea that Audrey had noticed and possibly even pursued me kicked reason from my head.

"I don't have a sketch from the third time, but I'll bet you remember."

"At the Spark after closing. Grey, totally fucking hammered, had passed out at the bar. We were waiting for Emily to finish counting the till upstairs. I'd been watching Joe, that greasy-haired goliath bouncer, hit on these chubby Filipino chicks when I noticed you looking at me—I thought you were looking at me. It was hard to tell through the tinted windows."

"I was looking at you."

"I had this impulse to rush outside and tackle you. You looked like a pixie with your little skirt. But Emily came down and saw me staring at you like a fucking adolescent—

Jesus, she can be nasty. I humped Grey to the car and didn't even let myself look back at you."

"So you and Emily Taylor dated?"

"Ancient days."

"And you and Grey?"

"He's married."

"That doesn't necessarily—"

I grinned and shook my head.

"I'd been curious about you before, but that night you left the bar I determined I'd fuck you."

I laughed at her: such a small, dangerous creature.

"Oh yeah, a campaign?"

"And here you are."

She stopped drawing, laid her sketchpad on top of her pack, and crawled toward me. I laughed, leaned back on my elbows, and let her hover above me, her curls haphazard around her delicate face and the astonishing blue of her eyes. She smelled of rain, sweat, and mud. Petite and smooth, her hands slipped through my hair, clutched my neck, and forced me backwards until I lay flat on the rock shelf beside my pack. Still damp, both of us with chicken skin, my hand stretched up her thigh.

Could two sketches—two versions—of me actually exist in her studio? Did I already have a past with this woman?

On our descent late that afternoon through another rainstorm, dodging roots and stones, Audrey asked for a story. I thought of the pool beside the falls and her mouth on mine, how I could see the deep green of the trees through her ringlets in the heights above me. How pure her face looked, her watercolor eyes. I told her my mother's story of Eden:

"God was bored and invented a hunt. After calling the animals to him, God told them: 'I have hidden something precious and you must each hunt for it in your own way. Seek and find.'

"Turning the earth with their claws, the honey badgers dug wildly, snuffling for a scent of something precious. Through the garden the dog pack pressed their noses to the grass, searching for a trace to follow. The cats lay in the sun and slept. High up in the trees, the birds chattered with the monkeys: 'What is this thing we seek? What is precious?'

"The elephants trampled around, bossing the pigs to root and the leopards to scour, swinging their great trunks to batter down copses. Soon, the garden trees bent under the weight of too many animals; the pathways furrowed from claws and hooves; fractions of trampled flowers; the lake filled with silt from the forage and still they found nothing.

"Apart from this, a woman stood. It occurred to her that God is a trickster. So she called out: 'I have found what is precious.'

"'Yes?' answered God.

"'Nothing.'

"'Oh?' God asked.

"'The dogs search in vain for a scent; the birds spot a vacant sky; the badgers find dirt, and the fish spy the sea. Your hunt is no hunt for nothing is the prize.'

"'Your answer is imprecise,' said God.

"'Oh?'

"'Nothing is the hunt, but it is not the answer. You have used the answer to solve the hunt.'

"The rest of the animals had gathered around now and squawked and squirmed and tried to get a view of the conversation between God and the woman. Even the cats were awake, their tails snaking in the sun-soaked grass.

"'Well,' said God, 'do you know the precise answer?'

"The woman nodded and left the ramshackle garden through the tumbled-down wooden gate. She understood the precious thing was reason, and reason could not remain in the derelict garden of beasts."

XXXIX.

Even with the door thrown wide, the office reeked of marker and Delvo sat at my desk in some kind of swoon—even her hair was wired—with poster board cast onto the desktops and floor and chairs; fluorescent-colored carnage with black slogans in bold caps: **VALUE EDUCATION; FAIR PAY TODAY; YOUR CHILD'S EDUCATION IS WORTH MORE; I LIVE IN MY CAR.**

"*I live in my car?*" I asked her.

"My dear Elliot, grab a marker and help me; I've promised to have fifty of these completed by 2:00 p.m."

"What are you doing here? I thought you'd be dead drunk on the floor of some bar by now."

She continued drawing large, exact lines of text, as if she hadn't heard me: **INDENTURED SERVITUDE IS RUDE.**

"Don't you know they've settled?" I asked.

"Who?"

"Delvo, the strike is off. The governor agreed to a ten percent raise for seven extra teaching days a year. The TAs are yelping up and down the halls like fucking puppies."

"They've settled?" Delvo said dazedly.

"That's what I'm telling you."

"Elliot, you wouldn't be foolhardy enough to invent this?"

"Never in life. Who came up with these slogans? Someone would actually have carried *I live in my car?*"

"So they've settled," she said, gazing around at the poster board. "What am I going to do with all of these? Do you think I could get a refund for the unused sheets?"

"Save them for next year's strike."

Delvo regarded me, "And you call *me* the pessimist. You've been looking decidedly unwell lately, Elliot. I've been worried. Come along to the bar with me and we'll drink to the settlement."

"I'd love to Delvo, but I have classes to teach this afternoon."

"Lovely word, settlement. Of course, common usage has corrupted it, but think of its historical precedence: settlers were cultivators—they tamed the wild places. Only the most adventurous dared settle."

"Or, in this case, a negotiator without enough skill to finagle us fifteen percent and two extra teaching days."

Her eyes, weary and kind, focused on me for the first time in months: "*Are* you unwell?"

"Tired is all."

"Well, then, you'll meet up with us after class—a quick, celebratory drink. Say you will."

"I will."

"Excellent. If you don't mind, I'll just leave these signs here and cart them home on the weekend."

When she'd left, I traced the sign on my desk—*Value education*—with my fingertip and started laughing. With the strike threat resolved, we could return to interdepartmental backbiting and administrative sabotage. I'd wanted a strike; I'd wanted to be compelled into furious action into desperate, terrible motion.

Before the Greeks went into battle, they sat quietly and combed their hair, preparing for a beautiful death. Was that courage? To premeditate before inevitability and accept it, groom for it, so serenely?

On the windowsill of Audrey's flat the night before, I'd sat and listened to the traffic on the narrow street below, where compact Hondas streamed past in boring, predictable colors. With her miniature bark-a-lot, the Chinese girl from the second floor wore a bright pink visor and shuffled down the sidewalk, allowing the dog to investigate every scent. I'd been thinking of the dentist, of our road trip to Dingle, where we'd listened to the most fabulous live music I'd ever heard. The patrons squeezed into the cluttered smoky rooms of the pub, and the place shimmering with music: the thumped beat of the bodhran; the fiddle player's eyes closed tight as if in some private ecstasy and the notes soaring; around the pub, the young men sang. I'd been thinking of her mischievous face, and how ruthless she'd been at arguments, always forcing me into a contradiction. It occurred to me, sitting on the windowsill, that I would fail each of them: the dentist, Emily, Nick, Audrey, the next one and the one after that. I would fail them spectacularly with the elegant, deliberate plunge of a high-diver: a stylish failure.

When I'd come to bed, the streetlight peered through the opened window and glared off the knee Audrey had raised to prop herself against the pillows. I lay with my head on her lap and her fingers slid through my hair like water as her other arm stretched across my chest, drew me into her, shielded me. The scent of her calendula lotion as comforting as the tick of the alarm clock, the voices of passersby pitched from the sidewalk like a baseball, the weight of her arm.

XXXX.

From the sidewalk outside Anna Banana's, we could hear the rumbling percussion as the Samoan bouncer bent in half to kiss Emily once on each cheek, then waved us past without taking our money. Inside, seven drummers lined the stage, dark faces drenched in sweat, their arms battering flat-palmed against the standing drums while before them a throng of dancers spun and leapt. Occasionally a drummer would caw a sound or possibly a command and the rhythm would shift subtly while above us round, golden lights strobed through the dimness.

We launched into the anonymous tangle of arms and torsos—claustrophobic, entombed—a primal pulse waved through the room as if we'd been cast into riptide. My eyes clamped shut; drums kicked through me until my skin burned; above us, the lights whirled delirium, euphoria; we were consumed.

At midnight the drums ceased and the long-armed men sauntered to the bar for drinks. Emily and I pressed gin and tonics to our throats and the backs of our necks. Soaked in collective sweat, my shirt oppressed me.

"It kills me that you're wearing that shirt in here," Emily said, her voice arched above the house music. Her short green sarong and black sports bra were much more suitable to the club's tropical atmosphere.

I shrugged. My latest disguise—long-sleeved croptops—meant for a brutal fucking spring on an island where even the swamp cows trudged about in tube tops and spandex shorts.

"So why exactly haven't you been able to surf lately?" she asked.

"I've been seeing someone."

"Yeah? A schoolgirl in knee socks?"

I gulped my drink and flagged the waitress.

"I always wondered about her," Emily said.

"Why, because I couldn't stop staring at her?

She smirked, bit into an ice cube, and asked, "How is Little Red? Everything you'd hoped?"

"She's soft, Em."

I wanted to add that Audrey had become a compulsion. After the first night at her flat, I'd resolved to tell her everything—what could it possibly matter to this girl I'd picked up in a club? So I told her about Nick and my wrists, and about Emily, and Grey's nun-wife and Dr. Adams' bullshit and it began to feel euphoric to unravel my secret selves, to tell all my stories to this girl as if it were just another translation exercise. Audrey seemed free of judgment; she seemed free in every way. Something about the way she listened—something pure and intense to her silence—made me keen to tell her.

"She keep your bra?"

"I've given them up."

"For you, not a problem."

"Gently, please, I'm still learning."

"But you're not sensitive."

I loved what people chose to remember. The last time Emily and I had had dinner together, she'd pulled my shirt up to examine my markings. I'd told her they only looked bad, that they weren't sensitive. She said they weren't bruises but oil stains.

"Fuck off."

"And the Sadist? Has he upgraded to handcuffs and face-masks?"

"You want some water?"

"Dodge."

The waitress brought our third round, her black nail polish creeping me out as she handed back five ones. I took three sips, watching the barefooted hippies twirl like gyres on the dance floor.

"Response required, honey."

"I've got ladder rungs on my back, Em."

She set her drink on the table, swept her hair behind her ears, applied her serious expression, and stretched her hand out to me.

"Let me see."

"Here? I don't fucking think so."

"What? Nobody's looking, you paranoid."

"The guy at the next table has been staring at us for fifteen minutes."

She looked over her shoulder at the thick haole guy slouched on his stool, who appeared to be wearing some sort of soccer uniform, a cigarette slack in his mouth. He'd turned his entire body so that he faced our table as if we were a television screen.

"Can I bum a cigarette?" she asked him.

Soccer-boy fumbled a cigarette from his pack and Emily held his hand as the butt slid into her mouth. When he extended his lighter, she turned back to me, her face bright as a demon's. I leaned into her, lit the cigarette, and shook my head. The tanned flat line of her belly, toned cut of her arms, tumble of brown hair; Christ, the chick was a walking prick tease: annihilating.

"How long are you going to play this game?" she asked.

I took the cigarette from her and inhaled, no longer able to think of the roping as a game. The previous weekend, Nick had insisted on taking me to Punchbowl. A picnic, he said. At the same grave, he'd tried to pose me before the shrine like a fucking muppet; the artifice glared between us as unrepentantly as the midday sun, and I fought him, refused, walked back to the car alone.

"You know I missed you," he had said, when he caught up to me. "I used to think of my trips as free zones. If I met a woman, then no harm, right? But I don't even look anymore. You're enough for me."

Enough, I weighed the word in my mouth, thinking of Audrey's hands light on my wrists as if my skin were a Braille chart. The inside of her lavender flat like a bruise, like a shield, and if I had told him then, would he have agreed that the bruise was a free zone, the girl no harm?

He'd bought a harness and that night in his bedroom, Latin freighted through my brain—*teneo, -ere ...* to hold, to possess. *Tenuero, tenueris, tenuerit, tenuerimus, tenueritis, tenuerint.* I will have possessed. You will have possessed. He will have possessed—as PJ Harvey's "Rid of Me" blared in the background, her quirky rage an anthem in the dark. The boy was slick and he'd wigged me out.

At Anna Banana's the drummers had taken the stage again, the pummel rippling through the crowd like a desperate heartbeat. I stabbed the cigarette into the ashtray. I wanted to tell Emily, *This will all end badly,* but I smiled instead, the gin sweet in my mouth like summer.

I let her French manicured nails slide between my fingers when she led me to the bathroom. She locked the door and eased my shirt over my head as gently as a mother undressing a child. And then Mother was crying.

"It's not that bad, Em. It's just the week after. Still swollen, you know? I only notice when I lean back."

"Christ. Oh, Christ."

In the grungy bathroom, scraps of paper towel littering the base of the trashcan, pink soap filming the sink, I held her against me. The walls around us throbbed: another free zone, another harmless girl.

XXXXI.

Audrey was tired. So exhausted that she was no longer able to hold her tumbler in one hand, but had the glass clasped in both hands like the hilt of a sword. She stood in the kitchen, her lower back nudged against the sink, and stared at me. We had been fighting for decades, so long that glaciers had softened and flooded Australia, the sky had filled with birds, the entire world was shrieking, and we stood in this peri-winkle kitchen, waiting for something to give.

She was looking at me with the same look my father had given my mother whenever he came home to find the kitchen in ruins, or had been called by a distraught local merchant who claimed my mother had left without paying again, or those times my father found her bleeding. A look that I had always thought was unfathomable sadness, the sort of look my heart mimicked whenever I was with my mother: despair for her, for my father, our family. But I was wrong.

The look my father gave my mother, the same look Audrey gave me, meant simply: excepting this, we might be happy. They had named the thing between them with silence, acknowledging only what it cost—all that it cost.

So I had become my mother at last.

"We never talk about this," Audrey said again. "Why don't we ever talk about this?"

"Because it has nothing to do with us."

We were not talking about my back and wrists. We were not talking about Nick. We were not talking about Emily.

288

"You don't live in a vacuum, Jane. Just because you disassociate, doesn't mean we all do. All these compartments; all these different characters you conjure up to deal with the people in your life. I've watched you in a room with people, Jane, and you always seem like you're alone. You're so focused on yourself—this self-obsession of numbness—that you're hollowed out. Sometimes when I'm talking to you I just wait for the echo."

"My self-obsession of numbness?"

We were off track. The train derailed, crushing villagers, suburbs, an entire city. This had started with me being outraged. I was the one with the legitimate issue.

Earlier that afternoon, Dr. Adams had called me into her office to stage an intervention. It was priceless. She sat on the edge of her desk in front of the red-cushioned chair and talked to me with a practiced maternal murmur. Hands folded in her lap, legs crossed at the ankle, her blue earrings—dolphins—battered against her neck as she told me what a fine job I was doing. How my students consistently achieved high marks. How the midterm feedback from my student evaluations had been positive. My peers found me a pleasure to work with. Excepting one little issue, she added. An issue, she said again, not necessarily a problem.

She paused. I looked at the stacks of books on the floor, the crumpled heaps of paper strewn about the desk, the shelves, the other chairs, the disarray of academia, then stared back at her. Her forehead furrowed with gravity. It was tough. Whatever was coming was tough. I concentrated on her earrings.

With a tremor in her deep rich voice she asked: Was it drugs? Did I have a problem with drugs? My moodiness, my attire, my erratic behavior all spoke to a drug problem. How could she help? she asked. She wanted so much to help me. The blue dolphins bobbed importantly. My students loved

289

me. There was so much to stay clean for. I was all potential (I'm paraphrasing). I had my whole life ahead of me.

Naturally, I was outraged. Who the fuck did she think she was, accusing me of having a drug problem? I'd eaten at her house, for Christ sake. Had my students complained? No. Then what the fuck was I doing in her opium den of an office talking about a non-existent drug problem with a woman who had just finished telling me my students were doing well and even liked me?

I mean, if we wanted to start reading into things, why not read into the fact that her office was a fucking sty? How about reading into that one? What does it mean when someone is disorganized? Maybe they're on methamphetamines. Maybe they're ruining their lives with heroin. Maybe they have no integrity. Maybe they're just slovenly. Maybe, had she ever considered, people had character flaws and drugs weren't a factor. I mean, what the fuck? Here I relied on this argument a number of times, as I stood and backed toward the door, stepping carefully around the towers of books in the walkway. I mean, seriously, I intoned with as much moral dismay as possible, what the fuck?

She let me get to the door before she called out: "I've scheduled an appointment for you with the nurses' office. You take a complete drug test Tuesday morning—hair sample, blood, and urine. This is non-negotiable and I encourage you, Dr. Elliot, not to take it to the Dean. As the head of the Classics Department, much is left to my discretion, and the more quietly this is handled, the better for all of us, especially you."

I let the door close on her. My temper flared inside me like kerosene.

I'd driven straight to Audrey's and busted into the studio, where she was working on a chalk drawing of a kite or a hang-glider—something winged.

"Is it legal?" I demanded after walking her through the saga. "They can't legally make me take a drug test, can they? I mean, I took one for UPS, of course, but that was different. That was company policy. Everyone had to take one. This is just me taking one because some asshole voiced a suspicion that's completely unfounded."

Audrey had said nothing.

"I mean, there will be a certain sense of vindication when the test results are negative, but I resent being made to do this. It can't be ethical. It can't be legal. Isn't this an invasion of my privacy? Some rights are being violated. I feel really violated. Maybe I should call the ACLU."

"Maybe you should just take the test."

"You're kidding."

"I think you should take the test. Adams is right; it's in your best interest to keep this whole thing quiet. You clear your name and that's the last you'll hear of it."

"I'm not a fucking drug addict."

"I know."

"It's wrong to make me take this test."

"I know you're not a drug addict, Jane. But you can't blame them for being troubled by your behavior."

"You cannot be serious. You think they have a right to do this to me?"

"I think they're responding to—I think you're different and they're responding to that. They've noticed something's wrong and the only thing that fits with what they've observed is drug use. I think they genuinely want to help you; they've just misdiagnosed the problem."

The light was failing through the windows and the room darkened around us, blurring the chalk lines more desperately on the easel. I'd always loved the studio; it was like being inside a lantern. The large windows made everything brighter and the smell in the place was crisp and tangy with paint. Sometimes when I couldn't sleep I'd come down to the studio and look at the works in progress, trying to decipher the strokes of Audrey's vision—to glimpse her imagination taking shape.

Something inside me was rotten. I felt ill, even in this room of light. I left and walked the three blocks to her flat. Audrey would have to clean up before she followed me, and I tried to settle myself, to mute the festering inside my belly. I thought I could taste bile.

It was dusk when Audrey climbed the stairs to the flat. On the landing, I heard her shoes drop in tired thuds. The door sighed closed and then she was in the kitchen, pouring a whiskey. Wasn't I betrayed? Wasn't I wronged?

I sat on one of the barstools and waited for her to comfort me. Now that she'd had time to think about the ludicrous proposition of an employer forcing me to take a drug test—surely once she'd considered from a rational perspective she would see that I had no alternative but to call the ACLU. No one turned on the kitchen light as night crept in.

"The drug test is not the issue, Jane. This is about you. This is about hiding in your clothes and smarting when you lean back in a chair. You don't see it, but everyone around you senses the change in you. I move my hand sometimes and you flinch. You claim you're numb, but I think you feel too much. Bruises and scars, cuts down your back, you're so pale now that you look anemic. I don't understand why you let this happen. I don't understand why you let him do this to you."

She waited but I wasn't speaking.

"You with Nick affects you with me. You with Nick affects you at work, and you with Emily and you with Grey. We're all related to this sick shit. And I don't understand where your impulse comes from. You're a brilliant, cocky woman and you keep going back to this sadist as though you want to be punished for something. I don't understand it. We never talk about this. Why don't we ever talk about this?"

Her look then was my father's: excepting this we might be happy. Oh the triumph.

"My self-obsession of numbness."

And then I hear it. It echoes right through me.

XXXXII.

I didn't want to tell this part. I'd like to say the Saturday evening I came to the photography studio with takeout from the Thai restaurant down the street, Nick admitted that he'd wanted to quit as well, he was frightened too, we'd agreed. I'd like to say no hard feelings. Didn't we both deserve that much?

In the studio, the air conditioner droned through the ceiling vent, the air felt cold and unnatural, and most of the lights had been turned off since the staff went home at 6:00 p.m. I set the boxes of Thai on a couple of stools and called out to Nick. All that day, I'd debated writing a letter instead of coming to the studio to see him, but I knew he'd argue, he'd want the personal debate, and I'd regretted following my coward's instinct before. In the end I had to say *over* so he believed over, so I believed over.

He came out and smiled at me, unrolling the sleeves of his clay-colored oxford, buttoning the wrists, his eyes a deep beautiful green. I thought of Audrey's painting of a woman in a wooden chair with an egg balanced in her palm. The woman's hair dark and shorn, her dress hiked to her knees, legs bare—the collapsed elegance of her posture and the egg and the pristine chair. I was never gentle. When Nick tried to kiss me—his unmarked wrists at my hipbones— I pulled away, turned my face, thought *traitor, traitor;* meaning myself, naming him and the practiced humiliation we'd inflicted on one another in the dark, our habit of carelessness.

And I felt it then, the purity of it burning through me: rage. The myths—the scaffold of myths—that constructed me, I doused in turpentine and lighted. I'd thought pain would be another path to love, the long way round. If my grief were etched on my skin—the vulnerability of the girl on the kitchen floor unaware that a car engine has turned over in the garage—then my grief would be a real and visible wound, a wound that could heal. But it hadn't worked that way: now my body was scarred too. Even from this distance I have no adequate explanations. That evening in Nick's photography studio, I set a fire, and expected a glorious consumption of the room and its contents, I expected cinders as I showed him my wrists.

"Look at me. Look what you've done. Look at me. You fucking sadist. You fucking demon. It's over. It's all over, you mother-fucking psycho."

The shock of his face, the horrible stillness of the room, the sickness pitching through my belly and singeing my throat, my mouth, my nose; I trembled with the taste and the hum of it. I rushed forward and punched him in the throat; our bodies hurtling backwards into the stools scattered curried pork, green beans, pad thai noodles across the tiled floor.

Camera tripods collapsed into an arbor of light stands. The floor slick and stinking of coconut, an overturned stool rammed into my back; clay in my vision field, I tried to kneel: blood in my mouth, on our hands, from his nose. I dropped my arms, taking shots to my jawbone as though knuckles could change anything.

Maybe they could. Maybe it should've taken more to move me. Maybe less.

I I I

All weekend under the banyans, I slept, fevered dreams, my face covered with a bag of frozen peaches. I kept the lights off in my studio, moved little, avoided the bathroom mirror. Monday morning, I biked to Longs Drugstore and phoned Dr. Adams to say I'd been hit by a car while cycling downtown Sunday afternoon. She told me to take as much time off as I needed, that she'd find someone to cover for me. Her worried voice, "Take care of yourself."

Then I phoned Human Resources at UPS and fed them the same story, said I'd be out for the week recovering, as if come next Tuesday, I would be a new and better girl, a girl without a finger-painted face. I bought more frozen peaches, milk, frozen apple juice concentrate, bananas, and vanilla extract, planning to live off milkshakes the entire week.

Tuesday afternoon, I woke to voices outside the studio, Grey demanding the keys and jostling them into the lock, and then Emily's face peeking around the doorway: "Honey?"

"Janie, you inside?" Grey called.

I'd sat up on the futon, the sleeping bag swaddling me in the cold, shadowed room.

"Oh my god," Emily said, half extending her arm as she walked toward me, her hand suspended awkwardly in midair. "Your face."

"Janie, are you alright? Why didn't you call us? I have to hear from some chick in HR that you got hit by a car?"

Emily sat beside me on the futon while Grey knelt at my knee, peering into my face as though he meant to read my fortune.

"Have you seen a doctor?" Grey asked anxiously.

"Jesus," Emily said, taking one of my hands in hers. "Look at your fucking knuckles. Where the hell did this happen?"

All the lies. The years of lies. I looked from one pair of brown eyes to the other, wanting so much not to disappoint either of them anymore.

Emily looked at Grey, anxiety a dialect between them, as she whispered, "Maybe she has a concussion."

"It wasn't a car. Nick and I had a fight Saturday night."

Grey stood up, yanked his hands through his curls, "He did this to you?"

"I hit him first."

"Janie, he's got eighty pounds on you, it doesn't fucking matter if you hit him first."

I shook my head, incapable of explaining properly, "It's over now."

"What do you mean it's over?"

"I gave him the sentence, he added the punctuation."

"Oh, I see, those bruises are just a grammar lesson."

"Stop it, Ryan."

He looked at Emily, his body posture a question mark.

"You're going to let this go?" she asked me.

"You're going to let this go? You're going to let this go?" Grey repeated, his voice strained, incredulous, like feedback reverberating off the hardwood floors.

I leaned back on the futon, too tired for more, "It's over."

I woke in the night with Grey asleep next to me on the futon, his hand clasping mine so tightly that some of the cuts on my knuckles bled. Emily dozed in the chair beside us, she smelled of cigarettes. When I touched her thigh, her eyes opened immediately.

"How did you get that scar on your eye?"

She leaned forward in the dark, her fingertips light against my eyebrows, her voice soft, "I fell down an escalator when I was five."

"You were right," I told her.

"About what, honey?"

"You can't keep it in the bedroom."

"Shhhh," she said. Her hair brushed lightly against my face, and I struggled with sleep while she traced each eye, down my nose, around my lips with her fingertips. Outside, a dog barked. The traitor is free, I thought. The traitor is free.

Eleven days. I hadn't seen her for eleven days. The bruises a ghastly yellow, but less painful, Audrey's blue eyes scanned my face as she stood at the threshold of her studio, before moving back from the doorway to let me enter. Inside the cool white room, four large windows high on the walls invoked the muted reverence of a church despite the strong smell of paint, tarps thrown on the ground, and the ugly, speckled smock Audrey wore. Wooden shelves stretched to the ceiling on my right, for paint, pencils, chalk, drawing pads, brushes, pails, and razor blades. Behind her easel, several rows of canvases lined the floor.

She'd disappeared into the back, and I propped my bicycle against the door, wandered over to her easel to examine a charcoal sketch of some strange creature—a large, vague bird. Around the studio Audrey had tacked various pictures from newspapers and magazines, poems ripped from *The New Yorker*, maps of every conceivable place.

She returned with a cup of tea for each of us, handed one to me, then pulled the stepladder away from the shelves, perched lightly, and watched me take a sip. Jeff Buckley's *Grace* played on the stereo in the farthest corner of the room. The tea tasted of ginger and chamomile. Her gray, paint-flecked smock rested midway down her thighs, and her hair looked especially wild as though she'd been shaken fiercely. She still hadn't spoken.

"I thought once I got here I'd think of the perfect thing

to say and then I'd be able to convince you that—that I'm bringing you my best intentions. But somehow I'm not even convinced. I'm sorry I met you like this. I wish I were braver—"

I faltered then, shook my head, stared at her small brown clogs. *I'm afraid to love you,* I wanted to say. That horrible way. *I'm afraid to love you fiercely.*

The light changed in the studio while she sat there, slanting through the window sudden and bright over her shoulder. Her hair orange, brown, red—the light shifted across us. My tea went cold. I crossed to her and crouched so that our heads were level; her knees parted, the cup at rest on the step above her.

"A man woke on the floor of a room he did not know. Beside him were the bodies of his two children, his wife. A knife lay next to his wife's hand. His family dead, the man took up the knife and stabbed his chest, but the skin did not break; the knife made no mark.

"The man ran from the house, down to the cliffs below his village and threw himself onto the sharp rocks below. His body remained untouched; he lived. He stood in the market square, offering money to anyone who would challenge him in mortal combat. Many tried, but no one could so much as bruise him. The man joined armies, fought as a mercenary without armor, returned unscathed from every battle. His body never wearied, never aged.

"Years passed and the man journeyed to the throne of the gods. He called out to them, 'You gods, I curse you. Cowards! Schemers! I defy you.' But the gods only smiled, nodding.

"'You are weak,' he told the gods. 'You are afraid of me.' One of the gods came forward, and said: 'She killed the children that you might live unchanged. She killed herself that you might be immortal. You are protected. You are free.' The god returned to his throne. 'Free?' the man said and began to laugh. 'Free with no choice, no death, no companion?' But the gods only smiled, nodding."

A worrying, inscrutable expression stared back at me from Audrey's face. She didn't move. Forgive, Audrey, forgive. I wanted to suspend myself from the ceiling like a potted plant or a tired spider. To be sketched into a different animal and rested on the floor of this cluttered white church. In the end, all I had to offer her were stories.

"After my mother died, I used to walk every afternoon to the mango grove and tell myself stories. It was like love, returning every day to that loneliness, to our ghosts, trying to remember the precise words my mother had used, the way her voice had shaped the telling. Audrey, I'm better than this. Let me prove it."

A single fat tear slipped down her face. I realized then the chalked sketch on the easel was a dragon, not a bird.

Sessions with Dr. Mya: Day 6

My mother told me that birds were really dislodged spirits looking for another body. I used to run shrieking from them among the orchard trees. The way they hovered in the trade winds, it seemed as if they were scouring the ground for me in particular. Whenever a flock flew overhead, my mother shouted: Spirit hunting. It lent an entirely new meaning to a murder of crows.

My last night in hospital, my insomnia will return and the athletic Indian nurse—the one who removed my breathing tube, the one I thought I'd invented during my post-coma delusions—will appear on rounds, wearing her mauve scrubs, her clogs, her confidence. Bustling around my bed soundlessly in her clogs, she will give me a light sedative: "Just to reduce the anxiety of being awake." With her hand on my forehead, I am a small child, closing my eyes on the image of her silver earrings, aching for mobility, for my insomniac walks through the city: the streets glowing as though painted in oil; my senses heightened by the move-ment of trees, a shift of color in my peripheral vision, the curious bulk of shadows. Somewhere beyond me, a voice, or maybe a couple passes on their way between places. And what sticks with me each time is how separate I am from the couple, the oil painting, the indistinct mound of a house in the dark and the way whichever animal might pass me continues its creeping as if I do not exist.

When Grey arrived at hospital—skin bronzed and hair

scruffy—he grinned at me in the old way, slipped a jumbo bag of iso peanuts onto my bedside table, threaded his fingers through mine, and said: "Fuck you, Janie, goddam drama queen."

I let him and Emily arrange my release, meet with my recovery team, formulate a timeline of rehabilitation. None of it matters to me: Audrey hasn't arrived.

The night before the accident, I stood in the courtyard below Audrey's flat for hours, trying to decide if I should walk the two flights of steps back to her red-wooden door and barter, or if I should catch my breath and go as she had calmly suggested while rinsing her hands at the kitchen sink. Catch my breath and go. In the courtyard, I shivered as a light rain came down against the thin red petals of a hibiscus. Above me, in the chalked outline of the building, someone pushed a window open and I waited as though something important might happen, the way a child anticipates her father calling her home to dinner in that gray time before night. Anticipates so clearly the sound of the screen door and has already turned for home when he calls her name. During my hospital stay, I return to that moment of the window being raised, the faint sound of the wood sticking, and then the clumsy rise of the sash sliding into its niche. I return to that moment because something important did happen: no one called me home.

Later that same night, I got lost in the University District following the course of student lamps in the most remote section of Manoa to a dead-end corner where well back among the kukui nut trees stood a pale wooden house with a black light above the screen door. A keg was buried in the grassless front yard. From the street, I waited for someone to come outside, for some clue as to the revelers housed in such a desolate corner. It had been raining for hours, the street glazed with the trees, the blue of the house, and suddenly a thin line of red. She had watched me from the doorway, her dress straining against her. Cigarette smoke loped above her into the doorframe.

"Are you a stalker?"

She stepped forward with her right hand above her brow as if to protect herself from sun glare. I walked toward her deliberately, pushing my hair back to alleviate suspicion. *I'm one of those harmless people walking the drenched, abandoned world at three in the morning.* She offered a cigarette and leaned against me to light it. She was slender and small, with a cockeyed smile that crept across her face and stayed.

"How far have you walked?"

My shirt was soaked through to my nipples and my khaki shorts clung tightly to my thighs. I had an impulse to reach out and cup one of her tiny ears in my palm. To cradle her.

"Don't say anything, you'll spoil the mystery."

"Whose party is this?" I asked.

"Mine a few hours ago. Now it's for sale, cheap."

"Past your bedtime?"

"I could go for hours if it were worth staying awake."

I sat on the stoop beside her and sucked at the Camel Light. It was easy to walk away from Audrey. Wasn't there always another girl? Audrey had followed Emily and then there would be another and more after her. There would be boys as well. There always had been, and sooner or later another Nick with his bag of tools and rhetoric to convince me of anything. Behind us in the house, an early Cure album played. Cigarette smoke escaped into the night, merged with the rain; her leg brushed against mine, insisting anyone can redeem me.

The Montana dykes are to blame for everything. I know I said that and I understand now that it isn't true. But I suffered from the comparison: their forthright, deliberate living as opposed to my arbitrary, dead reckoning meander. "Don't you see," Audrey had said, "it takes courage to settle; it takes courage and resilience to make a life with someone. I can't do it for both of us. I can't be another thing that happens to you; you have to choose how you live, how you love."

But what if I choose badly? What if in ten years, or worse yet five years, she turns to me one morning over a tofu scramble and says: "This isn't the life I want. This isn't the life I want." Suppose our relationship becomes, essentially, like Latin: an admirable, purposeful language diluted to derivatives. Then the utility of the language no longer matters—a tool of scientists and scholars; a root for linguists; an incantation during traditional Catholic services—since ultimately the fact of Latin's extinction belies its legitimacy and merit.

"Jane?" Dr. Mya says, watching closely as my mind wanders back to her office, her interrogation, her serious hairstyle. "How did you get to work the morning of the accident?"

My first impulse is to say that I biked. I used to catch a ride with Chance Chang until he quit to go on some crazy-assed backpacking odyssey through India. After Chance left, I biked to work, but I was late the morning of the accident; again I saw the peanut butter alone on the cupboard shelf. It was after six, and I didn't know where I was; I had been lost when I first wandered upon this house, I had been walking.

"I took a taxi because I was late."

Where had I picked up the taxi? I remembered grabbing the peanut butter on my way out the door and sprinting from the cul-de-sac, my clothes still wet from the previous night's rain. I hadn't had time to shower. Had it been raining that morning? Yes, the street had shallow pools of water along its surface, and I'd been leaping to avoid the worst puddles but was drenched anyway by the time I'd arrived at the 7-11.

"Why were you late?"

"I'd had trouble sleeping the night before. I'd been walking through Manoa until three or four in the morning."

"So you took a taxi to work. Then what do you remember?"

"I don't remember arriving at work. But I remember the taxi. The driver had a nasty scar on his cheek, under his eye."

The evening before the accident, I'd cooked pasta with zucchini, mushrooms, and roasted red peppers. Audrey came up from the studio late and said she wasn't hungry. I'd just poured gin into a tumbler when she said she wanted me to leave—the liquid swirled over the edge of the glass and soaked into the placemat.

"What are you talking about?"

"I want you to go."

I stood up, dazed, as if I'd been kicked in the chest. Had something happened? Why didn't I know that something had happened? I walked toward the sink, still not believing. I'd just made pasta. I'd just poured gin. All the pots washed, dried, and put away in the cupboard.

"What's happened?"

She rinsed her hands at the sink, turned the faucet off, and looked at me, her face paler even than usual. Her eyes more black than blue.

"This morning after you left, I lay in bed for hours. I couldn't make myself get up. All morning, all I could think was that I'll never be able to convince you. I'll never convince you not to panic. I'll never convince you that I love you. I'll never convince you that it's easier to leave than to stay. I'll never convince you to settle."

She kept one hand on the faucet, as if she needed to hold onto something. Her body, flexed and tense as a jaguar, warned me not to take another step forward. I wished I had my gin as a buffer, but to return to the table might be seen as a concession.

"Jane, you haven't even left a toothbrush here. You bring everything back and forth in your pack. I don't want to be the next chick you leave a *Best Regards* letter."

I stepped backwards, the sense that I'd been kicked again in the chest so convincing that I actually leaned on the counter as I retreated. What kind of fucking ragtime trip was this? I sank into the chair at the table and stared at the tumbler of gin. She sounded like she despised me, like she had despised me for a long time. I thought my struggle to stay had been a private one—a conflict between my character and my desire—but Audrey forced me to consider that we had been in silent contention all along: each needing assurance from the other that this train went to a different and better city. I downed the gin to keep from vomiting. Not a single assurance occurred to me as my esophagus caught fire. Then she called me a coward.

Dr. Mya touches my hand and my mind trudges back into her office again. I hate the squeaky hallways, the fluorescent lights, the murmuring relay of shifts and rounds, the discomfort of this wheelchair in this spice-scented office with this severe professional, the fact that my right arm still won't respond properly to my neurosurgeon's tests. Audrey won't come. Nick came, but Audrey won't. The whole fucking scene is inconceivable.

I feel itchy. Dr. Mya seems to need assurances too. She needs to be convinced that I will recover, that somehow my dislodged spirit will find a body. As she stoops beside my chair, her mascara masterfully applied to her probing eyes, she reaches her hand up to my forehead in a reassuring gesture I have come to crave in this hospital, and I feel my headache diminish as clearly as someone walking backwards from a room.

With her hand on my forehead, she says, "You hear the screen door slam."

I hear the screen door thwack behind me. A fog over the airport, rain on the tarmac, and my leg starts to burn.

"You hear the screen door slam."

I do. I hear it.

306

"My leg—"

"Jane, look at me. Look at me. You hear the door."

I look at her and I hear the door slam and I'm standing in the cul-de-sac. Rain punches everything in sight and I am drenched long before I find a familiar street. Petals smeared along the pavement, the smell of cigarettes washed clean.

"It was raining."

"Yes."

"I left the house and it was raining."

I remember shivering in my clothes in the backseat, the yeasty taxi smell, my head sore with wakefulness. At the airport, the tarmac was slick. I'd climbed up the ramp to the underside of the airplane. I can see the cargo door now, the hatch lock in my hands.

"The lock was stuck—the latch wouldn't turn."

"The latch?"

"The latch on the cargo door was stuck. I couldn't get it to turn."

"The door wouldn't open?"

But it did open. The door opened partway, but the netting was stuck.

"I got the door to open, but there was something wrong with the netting. It was tangled around a large package. I was trying to tug it loose—the netting, the package— whichever would give. It was raining and everything was slippery: the ramp, the tarmac, the cargo door. I remember something was wrong with the netting."

"It was stuck on a package," she said.

"And I couldn't untangle it. I took off my gloves and started heaving on the straps, that latch, the netting, but they wouldn't give, so I leaned back, and heaved with my whole body, dangling from the netting like some goddam bat. When the straps broke or released or untangled, and I fell. I remember falling. I fell and fell and then my leg—"

"Your leg?"

"My leg hurt so bad I thought it had been torn off. I remember being sick. That's it, though. I remember white and being sick."

"White?"

A shroud of white, I want to say, a halo.

"A glow of it. A glow of white when my leg felt like it was being torn off."

I want to leave this place. I want to be well. A flash of red in the pavement, as red as Audrey's jeep; a glow of white in my head like a halo; "Catch your breath and go," she said. "Go," she said. A window sliding upwards, a path through an orchard, a sprawling fall: Audrey.

Dr. Mya squeezes my good hand; she's still kneeling beside me. That long plunge from the ramp, reminiscent of the leap off Waimea Rock with Grey on our lost day, had not ended in a kiss. When the netting seized up around me, a wincing—a searing—a radiant pain flashed through my body. I don't remember hitting the tarmac, only a sort of muttering, obscure muttering like the tide in the dark.

Afterward

While I stayed at Emily's, the live-in nurse (who came, sadly, from the school of Crumb rather than athletic Indian nurses) tortured me with constant exercise despite my casts and headaches, in addition to a battery of cognitive tests more thorough than anything I'd used conducting research experiments at the Linguistics Institute. By the time my casts were removed and I officially began physical therapy at St. Luke's Rehabilitation Clinic, the therapist assured me of a complete recovery. So I left for the orchard with Grey and Emily.

Grey assigned himself as the Maui Field Officer and worked three days a week for Mako Surf Company. The rest of the week, he assisted my father with orchard projects. He and Emily bought a truck for Emily's commute to the airport, and Grey's various marketing meetings at surf shops around the island. On the evenings when Emily had gone back to Oahu to tend bar or supervise production of her latest documentary, *The Extinction of Indigenous Species in Hawaii*, Grey read to me as we rocked in the wooden swing we'd built among the new-growth trees. We read Didion essays, Perez-Reverte mysteries, short stories by Poe, Welty, Carver; whatever my father and Therese kept in their library, we read. Later, Grey and I would call this time our sabbatical, pretending our days were as carefree as some child's summer holiday, though for us it was already fall. The only boycotted subject was love—except for Grey's

309

observation as we washed dishes one evening that from his perspective love meant never having to initiate.

I knew Emily had tried to call Audrey a number of times after my release from hospital. I'd overheard Grey and Emily bickering about it. Grey told Emily calling only made things worse.

"It'd be less complicated if you weren't involved. That's all I'm saying."

"Jane asked me to call the little bitch. How is it possible she wouldn't come to see her? What kind of fucked up shit is that? I mean if your ex were in a car wreck or something, you'd go, right?"

"No, I wouldn't."

"Bullshit, Ryan. You know you'd go. You're a responsible person, and that's what responsible people do."

"What if this had happened when you and Jane weren't speaking? Would you have visited?"

"Yes. But I wouldn't have said anything."

While living in Emily's house, obviously, I had access to a phone and might have rung Audrey myself, but I didn't have the nerve. I thought of writing her a letter, but I didn't want to dictate it to anyone, so I waited until Maui when I could navigate the rutted paths alone, and then I scrawled:

Come to the orchard.
Best regards,

Jane

I didn't post the letter until January, hoping futilely that I'd think of something better to send instead. Ultimately, I enclosed a plane ticket, and posted the letter from town during one of my trips to the physical therapist.

Three mornings a week, Therese drove me to my appointments; the cab of her truck had become my confessional. As

310

she drove—foot jammed into the clutch, right arm dragging the shifter as the truck groaned, eyes focused forward—I told her all that I could bear to tell, giving an accurate sketch of events, and feeling, in spite of my embarrassment, the necessity of opening all the cages.

My physical therapist, a retired professional dancer who currently competed on the triathlon circuit, promised me I'd be mountain biking by June. She said physical therapy, like running marathons, required a great deal of pain.

"There's a moment every race when you've hit the wall. Your body has given everything: you taste blood; your muscles knot and cramp; your legs wobble; you gasp like a horse. You're going to break and you know what you do? You know what you do? You run through it. You run through it and then a feeling of euphoria rolls over you and you're running faster than you ran before."

Therese always stayed in the truck and read the paper while I chased euphoria, and one afternoon when I came out, she reached across to me and turned my head towards her. Her sharp little eyes examined me and she held onto my head, her grip so assured she could have snapped my neck.

"You want to be well, Jane, you know what you do? You forgive yourself. It's that simple. OK? Forgive yourself."

Then she let go, turned the engine over, and we drove home listening to a Tracy Chapman CD.

The old shepherd, Toby, had died the previous summer, and my father and I went to a neighbor's to pick a chocolate lab pup from a litter of eight-week-olds. We named the pup, Hazel, and let her tear around the orchard paths like the hellion she was. For my right arm, I carried a tennis ball, squeezing it to strengthen my muscles, and Hazel's favorite game involved stealing my tennis ball and playing keep away around the lowest branches of the new-growth trees. We were out there one chilled afternoon in February, Hazel gnawing on my tennis ball beneath a mango tree while I lounged on the swing reading Steinbeck's *Cannery Row*.

I didn't hear the truck, though we expected Emily that evening, but Hazel dropped the ball in the grass and cocked her ears. In a moment, she bounded down the trail and began snuffling and leaping her dance of joy. From the swing I saw copper-colored hair. By the time I got to them, Audrey, squealing delightedly, had dropped to the ground as Hazel butted heads, licked indiscriminately, and wriggled her body like a fat brown fish. (Hazel's theory of existence required thoroughness in all things.) And I watched them until Audrey finally looked up, her eyes narrowed to protect herself against the small ramming body, her long throat exposed in the afternoon light, and I knew I would go blind with her, that we were beyond all walking, that we were winged.

Jill Malone is the daughter of an Evangelical minister who traveled widely. Her parents both taught English and read aloud to their children every evening. She went to a German kindergarten, grade school in the rural Southern United States, middle school in the affluent east, high school and college in Hawaii, and graduate school in Washington State. Jill manages an independent bookstore and digs books about seeking. She holds an M.F.A. from a state school, and lives in Washington with her partner and son, their three dogs, and a lot of outdoor gear. This is her first novel.

www.jillmalone.com

For more information about Bywater Books
and the annual Bywater Prize for Fiction,
please visit our website at
www.bywaterbooks.com